THE KERNOW CHRONICLES
MERLIN'S LEGACY

J.D. Roberts

Copyright © 2017 by J.D. Roberts

Cover Illustration and Design by Danika Lindsell

Second Version: April 2018

All rights reserved.

ISBN: 9781973451891

DEDICATION

To my dearest husband, and most frustrating editor, Sam.

CONTENTS

Prologue	1
Chapter One	3
Chapter Two	15
Chapter Three	29
Chapter Four	48
Chapter Five	70
Chapter Six	91
Chapter Seven	115
Chapter Eight	140
Chapter Nine	155
Chapter Ten	184
Chapter Eleven	203
Chapter Twelve	219

PROLOGUE

She had no idea that he was there. How could she? He had made *every* effort to ensure that she would not. She could not catch even a glimpse of him. Such a mistake would never be tolerated. His body was overtaken by an involuntary shudder as unwanted images of the ruthless punishment that would be meted out to him whipped through his mind. He pulled his thoughts roughly back to focus on the scene before him. It would not do to lose his concentration now.

He had started watching her early, ready in place to see her awake. Then he'd caught glimpses of her progress through her home; the lighting of rooms leading his way. Her days were unfamiliarly indulgent to him, with no strict schedule and undreamt of hours of leisure. He'd got his first job at twelve years of age, and had often worked for weeks with no break. And now here she was, clearly visible through the huge window of the peculiar building that she often went to near her home. She was chatting with carefree smiles to the tiny, old lady perched atop a high stool that he was sure she could not get down from unaided.

She was coming out now. He stared. There was something about her that intrigued him. She strode around purposively; with none of the crippling shyness he had suffered from. Unlike him, she knew she was worthy of a place in her world.

He inhaled sharply. She'd stopped and her gaze had fallen directly on the spot where he was hidden. He had chosen carefully; he was *sure* she could not see him, but why then was she staring so intently? His whole body stiffened as he strained not to make the slightest movement. Time appeared to brake to a halt and continue in a painful, slow motion, as her eyes remained trained upon his hiding spot. The first small tentacles of panic began to creep upon him. Then, abruptly she shook her head, and turned away.

He exhaled loudly in relief, his body releasing like a deflating balloon. He could *not* get caught.

Soon it would be time to make his move. But not yet. First he had to make sure, to make absolutely certain that she really was the one they were looking for.

CHAPTER ONE

Caja woke up for the first time in her life wanting desperately to talk to her parents. She sat up to run downstairs and ask them the questions burning their way up from the pit of her stomach. But then she remembered, she didn't have any parents, had never known them or even met them. The wave of confusion would have knocked her flat if she hadn't still been in bed.

And then it all came back to her. Who was he? That was what she had to ask them. Who was the man in her dream? They alone in this world could tell her. She had to find out who he was.

His face was stained on her mind. Such a forceful face, thin but bursting with strength, the eyes scorching into her, a mocking sneer traced on the lips. And with the face had come such a powerful feeling of foreboding that she now felt sick. Something was going to happen. Something bad. Her breathing quickened and in spite of the cold, a sweat broke out on her brow.

Slowly sitting up, she glanced to the left catching sight of the clashing hodgepodge of clothes that she had tossed onto her chair the night before. They brought a pinch of normalcy back into the moment, and her breathing began to slow.

Of course, today was her first day back at school. It was

her second year at Penrow High, and she had close friends she was eager to catch up with. She shook her head, trying to free herself from the unwelcome vision of the man's face and replace it with the day ahead. She sluggishly scrambled out of bed. A shower would do it. Would wash away the lurking fear that was scheming to pull her down into a place she didn't want to go.

She felt much better after the bracingly chill downpour, and the image in her mind faded to a dusky sketch. Dressed in her uniform, she jogged down the cramped stairs into the tiny kitchen.

Seeing Caja, her Aunt took a quick step backwards, a look of alarm on her face.

'Goodness, I don't think I can ever get used to that uniform!' she exclaimed with a feigned look of horror, 'you should be careful who you creep up on in that. You don't want to give some poor old dear a heart attack.'

'I know, it's revolting,' said Caja laughing, grateful for the distraction, 'thank god everyone else has to wear it too. I think it's an attempt to make sure we all look as hideous as possible, especially now that we're teenagers.'

Her Aunt, Flora Dingle, always made her laugh. She had brought her up since she was a tiny, newborn baby and was therefore in all ways but one, her mother. It had been just the two of them for as long as she could remember although there had been a few male figures that had come into their lives for brief periods of time as her Aunt's suitors.

It was surprising there were not more, Caja mused. She was old enough to recognise that her Aunt was a very attractive middle-aged lady who had grown older with grace. She had plum hair that was cut in a stylish bob and clever blue eyes that contrasted brilliantly with her dark hair. She was eccentric in her ways, with a love of life that left little room for worry, and that revealed itself in her unapologetically bright and often kooky clothes.

Caja herself did not look much like her Auntie, although many remarked on the similarity of their raucous laugh that often exploded from out of nowhere. Caja's hair was a wild, deep red that tumbled down her back in long, untidy waves, her unusual blue eyes were ringed with black, and her skin was a mass of freckles.

'Here love, I have something for your first day back at school,' said her Aunt as Caja munched on some slightly burnt toast, sitting at the kitchen table. Caja looked up as her Aunt handed her an intricately woven scarf, the colour of the sea on a cloudless summer's day. 'It's already getting quite cold and it reminded me of your beautiful eyes, just like your father's,' she carried on.

Caja standing up gave her Aunt a big sideways hug squeezing her tightly around her waist, 'thank you, thank you, I love it!'

'You're welcome darling. Now let me down,' replied Flora, her arms swatting away at Caja, 'before you squeeze the life out of me'.

Caja smilingly released her, playing with the scarf between her fingers, 'it's so soft. And a gorgeous colour.'

'Yes, I picked it for the particular shade of blue it is. It will help keep away any piskies. For some reason they are absolutely terrified of it,' added her Aunt breezily.

Caja looked at her and smiled, not having a clue what she was talking about, something that happened quite a lot.

After breakfast Caja picked up her schoolbag and ambled over to the bus stop that was just on the other side of the road from their little cottage. It was a small but gorgeously quaint cottage made from light stone and located in the tiny Cornish village of Trethewyn. It had once been the gatehouse of Kilmar Castle almost half a mile away but the castle had burnt down and the estate had been left derelict for years now. As her gaze fell on the overgrown garden a blurred version of the man's face bounded once again across her vision. She sighed uneasily, the fear beginning to rise again but at that moment the bus appeared from around the corner and slammed on its brakes to slide to a standstill beside her.

The door clanged open and Boris, the old bus conductor yelled, 'back to Penrow High School then are we Caja?' He was partially deaf, some said from the din of the rattily old bus, and always shouted.

'Yep Boris, I am, going into Year Nine now,' she answered, clambering into the old bus with one last, anxious look at the garden behind her.

'Well I'll get you there on time. Don't you worry young Miss.'

'Thanks Boris,' she mumbled making her way to a seat at the back where she could watch the heath and gorse of the rolling Cornish countryside go by, although frighteningly fast. With the bus tearing along the tiny, narrow lanes, Caja was soon distracted by the necessity to hold on tightly if she wanted to stay in her seat. Every now and then she would catch glances of the rugged coastline of high cliffs, small bays and wheeling gulls that so characterised the area. It was a beautifully sunny early autumn day and the sea was sparkling under the lavish attention of the sun. She settled in for the long ride to school.

*

'Caja Delaney,' she replied, when asked her name at registration at the front desk. 'Caja with a j… but pronounced with a soft y…like yoghurt,' she added. Everyone said her name wrong.

Delaney was her parents' surname and she had kept it even though her mother and father had died only a month after her birth. Tarlia and Ben Delaney had both been killed in an airplane crash flying back to Cornwall. Her father had been flying the plane at the time as he was a keen pilot, and her mother had been beside him. There had been a particularly violent storm the night of their trip and the burnt out wreck of their plane had been found in moorland in Devon the next day.

Caja, a little new-born baby, had been left with her Aunt

Flora Dingle in Trethewyn, and had lived with her ever since. Her childhood had been a happy time with Aunt Flora, but she still thought often of her parents conjuring up different idyllic fantasies of what it would be like if they were still alive.

'Que pasa amiga!' came a cry from nearby as a small petite figure launched itself at her.

'Aggie, Aggie, Aggie. It's good to see you. How was France?'

'Totes gross bogs. Nice and sunny though. Although I'm soooooo over baguettes,' replied Aggie, her short tufty, sun-bleached hair tickling Caja's face as they hugged.

They walked down the hall chatting excitedly and entered into their new room heading over to some desks where a girl and boy were sitting conversing earnestly.

'No, no, no Luke,' the girl was saying emphatically, 'she is definitely, definitely a woman.'

'But my dear girl, have you seen those arm muscles, and those quite tremendous calves?' he replied, indicating with his hands their impressive size.

The girl was tall and slender, with sharp cheekbones, and a self-assured air. The boy stood at least a hand shorter than her and had very short brown hair, which looked like it had a tendency to curl if left uncut. He had blue eyes with extremely long eyelashes. They both looked up as Aggie let out a loud 'Ahem'.

'Why Agatha Jones and my darling Caja Delaney. What a pleasure!' said the boy grandly leaping up to give Aggie and Caja big dramatic hugs which they responded to with grins.

Luke stepped back indicating the girl he had been chatting to, 'and may I introduce my friend Jennifer. Her parents are old friends of my parents, and they've recently returned to Penrow. Jennifer will be in our class.'

Caja and Aggie greeted her warmly. Any friend of Luke's was a friend of theirs.

'So I hope you haven't been scared off too much already by little Lukey here,' said Aggie to Jennifer, 'he's an odd one but we love him all the same. Anyone would think he was born a century too late. He would've fitted in much better in some stuffy Victorian era.'

'No, no, it'd take more than that to scare me off! I knew Luke when he was little, and even then he was quite strange. I'm used to him,' said Jennifer laughing.

Luke frowned at them all, 'well I think that's enough discussion on how terribly odd I am. What's going on this year? Have you seen the new arrivals?' Luke nodded his head in the direction of a group of three girls, sitting at the front of the classroom, heads held high, gazing around with a haughty brashness unusual for new students.

'They look like peacocks, a bit up themselves,' said Aggie loudly.

Luke made a frantic quiet down gesture. 'Shhhh Aggie. I've heard they're a bunch of bullies. Rather aggressive. From that local school that shut down. They've already laid into poor Leila for looking at them the wrong way.'

'Well, I'm not going to let a bunch of new girls push me around,' replied Aggie, although a little quieter.

Caja nodded vigorously. 'Yeah Aggie. We don't have any bullies at Penrow High and…' she lowered her voice to a whisper as all three of the girls turned round to stare straight at her, 'and we aren't going to put up with any now.' She turned quiet as the girls continued to stare at her menacingly. 'Um. Do you think they're staring at me?'

At this, one of the girls with lifeless dyed-blonde hair, lifted up her arm and made a dismissive gesture with her hand at Caja, before turning away with a shake of her head. Her two friends shook their heads in imitation before continuing to whisper together, glaring over occasionally at Caja's table.

'Freaks,' muttered Aggie.

'Just ignore them,' said Jennifer with Luke nodding seriously in agreement.

They turned around so that they were no longer facing them, and talk quickly focused back on what they had been up to in their holidays.

The morning raced by until they found themselves at lunch in the great canteen hall, sitting at one of the long tables by the huge windows that looked out onto the sports fields.

Luke began to amuse them with stories of his generally gallant deeds in the holidays as Caja gazed out of the window, her attention caught by a man walking carefully in the shadows of the trees. As she continued to watch, the figure looked all around him, before fumbling with one of the doors to the side entrances of the school, and swiftly disappearing. Her anxiety returned like a train slamming into her, making her breathing harsh and uneven, and she felt the first globules of sweat begin to trickle down her face. She was absolutely convinced now; something was going to happen, something awful.

'Are you ok Caja?' asked Luke, disturbing her from her panicked thoughts.

She focused on controlling her breathing. 'Yes, well, yes kind of….I just keep getting this feeling. Like something's going to happen. Something really bad. And I can't seem to shake it. I'm not sure of course but it's just…really….well,' Caja replied mumbling off into silence as she saw the slightly baffled looks of her friends.

'Ah, what kind of feeling? As in a premonition? Have you foreseen my heroic and greatly mourned death?' enquired Luke questioningly with a shade of a smile.

'No silly, I haven't seen anyone's death or anything,' Caja replied punching Luke playfully on the arm, ' it's just…oh it's probably just my imagination or something,' she continued, trying to brush the subject aside. 'Are you still up for coming over to mine after school?' she enquired brightly.

Although Aggie and Luke had known Caja since the beginning of secondary school, they had never yet been to her house, preferring the bigger town of Penrow to the tiny village of Trethewyn. They had finally promised to come and visit, and Caja was excited that they would be visiting her home at last.

'Of course we are Caja. We promised. Back of beyond here we come,' replied Aggie unenthusiastically.

'Well I for one, think it will be fun Caja,' said Luke, 'I'm looking forward to seeing your home and the great ruins of Kilmar Castle. I've read quite a bit about them.'

'Thanks Lukey. Jennifer, would you like to come too?' asked Caja politely. Although she had spent the entire morning with Jennifer, she had not yet really had a chance to speak to her. Jennifer seemed almost wary of Aggie and Caja, and had spent most of the time talking only to Luke.

'Oh no, no thank you. I must get home. My parents will be expecting me,' replied Jennifer quickly. Caja breathed a small sigh of relief.

*

Before they knew it, the first day back at school was over and Caja, Luke and Aggie were packing up their things. Jennifer had left already, apparently eager to get home.

Caja suddenly slumped back down in her seat, horror springing up on her face. 'Oh....no,' she moaned.

'What is it Caja?' asked Aggie turning around quickly.

'My scarf, the one my Aunt only gave me this morning. It's gone! I swear I had it here before. How could it have gone?'

'Well, it's got to be around here somewhere,' said Luke sensibly. 'C'mon we'll all look. I remember it. It was that sublime cerulean creation no?'

'No, no it was blue,' answered Caja shortly. 'Oh, she's going to kill me!'

Luke shook his head in resignation, 'I'm sure we'll find it. It can't have gone far.'

Aggie had stopped her searching and was just staring.

'Are you going to help Aggie?' asked Caja frantically throwing things out of her locker.

Aggie shook her head, 'I don't think we need to look any further. I think I might know where it's gone.'

Luke and Caja stopped to see what she was looking at. Standing by the door of the classroom were the three new girls from the local school who were all watching their frantic searching with interest. There was a gloating look of contentment on all their faces and the one who had pointed at Caja earlier was swirling her hand teasingly around her neck.

'They wouldn't would they?' gasped Caja.

'I really don't think we should underestimate them. I'd say they definitely have something to do with it,' replied Luke, as the leader of the group continued to fling and stroke an invisible scarf around her neck.

'The question is, what are we going to do about it?' asked Aggie quietly. But before they could do anything, the three girls who had clearly had enough fun, turned on their heels and heads preened high stalked out the classroom.

'Orghhhhh...' groaned Caja in frustration. 'I can't believe it. Goddamn it! Bloody, thieving slugs! It's too late to do anything now though. We've got to catch the bus otherwise we're gonna miss it! We'll have to think of something tomorrow.'

Luckily, they just managed to make the bus. There was only one every hour, and Caja knew that if they missed it they would have to change Aggie and Luke's visit to another day and then it might never happen. Soon she had forgotten the scarf incident in her excitement at the visit, and they were rumbling along chattering. Boris was up to his usual tactics, speeding along the dangerously narrow roads with much slamming on of brakes, and near misses with other shocked road users.

'Wow, you do this twice a day!' Luke exclaimed to Caja at one particularly dicey point as Boris almost drove up the back of a slow-moving tractor just skidding to a halt centimetres behind it. 'I'm astonished you're still with us!'

Clinging bravely on to the seats in front, Luke and Aggie stared out the windows around them. The ancient, high hedges blocked out most of the views but now and again a gap revealed a farmer's tidy field, or in stark contrast a glimpse of the wild coastline of grey cliffs and pounding waves. It was early autumn and the days were beginning to grow colder and the winds that wracked the Cornish coast were increasing in strength as the winter approached. Due to its exposed position surrounded on three sides by sea, Cornwall was subject to great storms from across the Atlantic and prone to sudden changes in weather, with the dense Cornish sea mist apt to appear unexpectedly at any time. They had all known days that started out fantastically clear and sunny but had abruptly changed as the dank mist crept in silently from the sea.

'Oh crikey!' Luke yelled as they came to a sudden stop with such abruptness that he shot out of his seat and ended up on his bottom in the foot well.
'Here we are!' said Caja happily, giving her hand to Luke to help haul him up. 'Follow me'.
Aggie and Luke followed Caja out of the bus, with Luke rubbing his behind ruefully, and crossing the road arrived at her home. 'Welcome friends, to The Gatehouse Cottage, residence of myself and my wonderful Aunt Flora Dingle.'
'Flora what?' said Aggie grinning.
'Flora Dingle,' said Caja, giving Aggie a friendly push, 'Dingle was the maiden name of my mother too; they were sisters.' Luke and Aggie glanced at each other behind Caja's back, and followed her through the little wooden gate of The Gatehouse. Caja rarely spoke about her parents.
Aunt Flora greeted them at the door gaily decked out in her long flowing emerald green dress and her happy boots, so called because of their eye-watering mix of colours.
'Darlings, friends of my dear Caja. You are most welcome. Come in, come in.'
They traipsed in after her into the welcoming warmth of the kitchen where Aunt Flora set the kettle on the stove. Aggie settled into an old chair by the hearth whilst Luke stayed standing, staring enraptured at Aunt Flora. Caja looked

at him perplexed and pushed him into a chair next to Aggie.

'So what are your plans this afternoon children?' Flora asked.

'Children! Auntie I'm 14 next birthday you know,' retorted Caja offended.

'Sorry, so what are your plans today semi-grown up children?' said Flora with a smile.

'We're going to explore the ruined castle and grounds', said Aggie quickly before Caja could say anything else, 'Caja has told us all about them.'

'Well, you'll have to be careful looking around Kilmar Castle. It's too dangerous to go inside. But you can explore the outer ruins and the grounds. It was owned by the Kilmar family until they died out, and then there was a dispute over who it would pass onto which was never resolved. It's been in ruins for almost a hundred years now. We're in the old Kilmar Gatehouse,' Flora explained as she busied herself with the tea-making.

'Fascinating,' said Luke staring dreamily at Aunt Flora.

'Right, we're out of here' said Caja loudly, throwing her bag at Luke. It hit him squarely in the face but did not appear to pull him out of his trance in any way.

'But what about your tea?' exclaimed Flora.

'We'll have some when we come back. We'll be home in time for dinner,' yelled Caja as she disappeared out the kitchen door and into the back-garden with Aggie following. Luke remained sitting in his seat staring happily at Aunt Flora. After a few moments of silence with Flora looking at him quizzically, Aggie returned yanking Luke up by the arm and dragging him outside.

'Luke Rainer, what is wrong with you, said Caja laughing.

'She's amazing your Aunt. Amazing. So vibrant and…and beautiful,' he replied happily.

'Ok, whatever, Romeo. Please don't embarrass me. Now let's get out of here'.

They set off exploring, spending the rest of the afternoon

in a drizzly rain clambering over moss-covered stones of the old ruins and making their way through brambles and bush in the ancient walled gardens. The main structure of the castle and one old tower were still standing but the wings and the grounds had fallen into complete ruin.

As an only child, Caja had a great time showing them all the things that she had only ever explored alone; a hidden lake with an old dilapidated jetty; an ancient maze with overgrown hedges and a miniature castle in the middle; and a garden with crumbling sculptures arranged in a circle with a giant unicorn fountain in the centre. On their way back to The Gatehouse they came across a strange, stately archway standing all alone in the midst of an overgrown garden.

The archway still enclosed an old heavy wooden door that looked like it had not been opened for centuries. It was covered in ivy, with late-flowering, violet wisteria winding its way all over it.

'How strange, to have a door like this, just standing by itself,' said Aggie peering up at it.

'It's always been here. I've never thought much about it,' replied Caja.

Luke walked over to it and gave it a push. Nothing happened. 'Let's try and open it,' he said.

Aggie and Caja looked at each other and shrugged their shoulders in consent. Why not? They all leant their shoulders against the ancient door and pushed with all their might.

'Yuk, I think a beetle just climbed down my t-shirt,' moaned Aggie still pushing.

Caja started to giggle.

'I think I just felt it budge. Keep pushing,' encouraged Luke. Suddenly with an almighty groan the door gave, falling open and taking all three of them with it.

'Ow, my face! Geroff me!' yelled Aggie.

Luke was lying on top of her laughing his head off. She heaved him off and they looked around to see how Caja was, but to their shock found that she had completed disappeared.

CHAPTER TWO

In the instant the ancient door fell open, everything went black and Caja felt herself falling and falling, as though through space. Her eyes wide with shock and fear she pedalled her arms and legs desperately, yelling in terror. Where were Luke and Aggie? Where was she? What had happened to her home and the garden? All around her she could see what looked like glittering stars shining out from the yawning blackness. She had no time to study them however as she landed abruptly with a great thud, and everything around her went black as she lost consciousness.

*

The first things Caja could see when she awoke were green leaves hanging above her. They were so fresh and bright that they didn't seem real. Gradually her gaze came into focus and she could see the tree attached to the leaves, an enormous oak, bigger than any tree she had ever seen before, standing tall above her. She seemed to be nestled in a corner of the tree trunk, its roots wrapped around her protectively.

She stretched up her arms and lifted her head to look around. She was at the edge of a wood, the trees behind her and sweeping moors in front of her. Just beyond the moors, at the end of her vision, she could see the shimmering reflection of the silver sea. All around her was colour; the verdant green of the trees, the staggering blue of the sky above. There was a vividness and breathless clarity to everything that stunned her although at the same time the landscape was familiar. She could not see any sign of human life however. Slowly her senses came back to her. She felt great, overwhelming confusion. Where was she, how did she get here and where were Aggie and Luke?

A noise behind startled her and she jumped up in fear.

A skinny boy, a few years older than her was standing there, looking at her with a puzzled gaze. 'By Taranis you startled me. Who are you? I rarely see people around these parts and by the look of you, you're a long way from home.' He took in her rather bedraggled appearance and her sea-blue eyes etched with bewilderment.

'I...I think I'm a long way from home,' replied Caja hesitantly, 'I don't know where I am.'

The puzzlement on Jory's face increased, 'you don't know where you are?'

'Well, I remember being with my friends in a garden, and then suddenly it went all black and now I'm here and I don't even know where here is. Can you help me?' It came out in a rush, desperation in her voice.

He took in her beseeching look slowly. 'Well, I guess I can try. I'm Jory Hobart by the way. And I'll help you as best I can...Maybe we should start from the beginning. Now, can you tell me where you're from?'

'Well yes, of course. I'm from Trethewyn, in Cornwall. My name is Caja....Caja Delaney'.

'Caja. A Kernewek name. And I know Trethewyn well; I live just outside the village. But I've never heard of this Cornwale. Trethewyn is not far from here at all, in Kernow...which is where we are now,' he added uncertainly.

'Kernow? I know that word,' replied Caja looking confused, 'isn't Kernow the Cornish word for Cornwall.'

He looked at her unsettled, 'Aye....So you're saying

Cornwale is Kernow or Kernow is Cornwale?'

'CornWALL,' said Caja frustrated, her apprehension making her sound harsh, 'yes, Kernow is Cornwall and Cornwall is Kernow, at the bottom of England yes?'

'Ingland? No, I haven't heard of Ingland. Albion is upcountry of Kernow,' added Jory cautiously.

Oh boy, thought Caja, realization dawning, Albion was the old word for England, he was probably living in some made-up fantasy world, and spent most his time in fancy dress. Or he might be from the local mental health institution. One had opened up recently quite nearby, despite the resistance of the locals, and she had heard that some of their more settled patients were allowed to leave and walk the nearby countryside unaccompanied.

'Well,... if you could show me the way back to Trethewyn... I would be most grateful,' asked Caja slowly as if talking to an idiot, 'is that something you can do?'

Jory looked at her slightly confused, then after a moment's thought nodded curtly and indicated that she was to follow him. 'Aye. It shouldn't take long. It's only 2 miles or so from here and it's close to my home' he added rather sharply.

As Caja trundled along beside him she studied Jory and his abnormal clothes. He was wearing sturdy looking boots, with walnut-brown trousers that were too big, tied tight at the ankles, and what looked like an old grey woollen shirt, open at the neck. His light, brunette hair was cut short and he was a little taller than her, although thin enough to be considered gaunt, and probably two or three years older. He was deeply tanned with dark brown eyes in deep sockets, assorted freckles and a generous mouth. There was a stern look to his face however, and she also noticed the remaining traces of what must have been a corker of a black-eye, as well as bruises reaching around his neck.

'What are you gawking at?' Jory suddenly demanded turning around and forcing her out of her careful observations.

'Nothing,' said Caja tartly, pulling a face behind his back.

Blimey, he was a bit of a grump and did he have eyes in the back of his head?

'Well, stop staring like a complete gubbins then.' He obviously hadn't taken too kindly to the way she had spoken to him before.

'Don't worry, I'll be out of your hair in no time,' Caja mumbled.

Jory didn't respond although his shoulders tensed and his head stiffened.

As they traipsed on, the landscape became more and more familiar; the wildness of the grey moors dotted with granite rocks and a multitude of gorse, heather, and stunted trees bent in submission to the prevailing south-westerly winds. The vividness of the countryside must be due to the clear sunny day thought Caja, trying to justify the strangeness of everything around her. She didn't even want to contemplate why the weather might have changed so suddenly from the soggy grey afternoon she had just left. There were too many things to think about that might throw her completely off balance, and for now she just wanted to focus on getting home.

The more they walked, the more confused Caja became however. At times, she was sure she knew where she was; there was Carnkie Tor with its two distinctive shaped boulders clearly outlined on the top. But the next minute upon rounding the Tor, the scenery would become unfamiliar, and Caja would have to admit that once again she did not have the faintest clue where she was.

'Not far now Caja,' said Jory. He seemed to have softened somewhat during their walk.

'Are you sure this is the way?' she responded beginning to doubt this boy's capabilities. 'I can't even hear the A39.'

'The A what? What's that? Someone's house?'

Caja shook her head in bemusement. He really was a strange one. He probably shouldn't even be wandering around on his own she thought, although he seemed confident enough in where he was going.

Glancing around her she became even more baffled, as she realised she clearly recognised a nearby copse with a gurgling stream running through it. They should be only minutes from her house.

'Maybe you know someone who can help us?' Caja said again slowly as if to a child.

Jory studiously ignored her, 'and just around this corner...yep..there it is...You can see Kilmar Castle. You must know of Kilmar Castle. It's the biggest building around and it's right next to the village of Trethewyn, where you live.' This was said with a slightly dubious note, as if maybe she didn't know where she lived. 'You know it right?' There was no response. Jory looked around and saw Caja standing there open-mouthed, clearly shocked at the sight of the castle.

'Who...when...who on earth rebuilt it?' she stammered staring at the magnificent and intact castle in the near distance that she had only ever known in a state of ruin.

'Why I don't think it's ever been rebuilt,' replied Jory confused, 'it was only built around 50 years ago and it's stood proudly since then. Are you alright? You look very pale.'

Caja did not respond but just stood there, her face wan, her mouth still wide open.

'Caja, Caja, hello?' Still no response. With a worried look, Jory took her hand and sat her down on a boulder nearby. 'Caja, what's wrong? Why've you stopped talking? What is it?' he asked loudly, but in a concerned voice.

'I don't understand... I...I don't understand. How could this possibly be here? What is happening? Why is everything so different? I don't even know where I am anymore or even what day it is!' she blurted out tears beginning to pour down her cheeks.

'Well, I can tell you that, we're in Kernow. In the Hundred of Trigg. It's 298 years after the death of Merlin. This is-'

'I'm sorry' stammered Caja abruptly, interrupting Jory's explanation, 'did you just say Merlin? Merlin as in a Wizard with a pointy hat Merlin?'

'Uh yes. Merlin as in the Wizard Merlin. Greatest Wizard of the last few centuries. Possibly of all time. He was around during King Arthur's time when all of Kernow was united. That's all changed now.' He looked at her sadly, 'since Arthur's death and Merlin's disappearance there have been so many disputes. The Hundreds are all run separately by the different Nobles with no unity, some…'

He was distracted from his explanation by Caja laughing, somewhat hysterically, which caused her to fall off the boulder where she collapsed into a heap on the leave-strewn floor. 'M..M…Merlin..', she was saying in between her tears, 'M…Merlin a Wizard…and Arthur!' Which set her off even more, and she lay there, her chest heaving and tears streaming out of her eyes. At times she would let out a great roar but for the most part she was engaged in silent laughter characterised by a lot of fist pounding and leg shaking.

Jory looked at her in worry. Good god, how had he managed to pick up such a mad one? She looked like she had completely lost the plot. He couldn't leave her though, much as he wanted to, he could not just abandon her. He waited for her hysterics to subside, patiently watching her, lips pursed and brow furrowed in perplexity. Gradually she quietened down, and eventually she just lay there on her back in the dirt, staring up at the sky.

'I'm sorry Jory, I believe I owe you an apology,' she finally said faintly, not looking at him. However crazy the situation sounded, it appeared she was somehow in a different place to the Cornwall she knew. Where or when, she was not sure. The castle in front of her was most certainly a complete version of the Kilmar Castle she knew in ruins. All around her was evidence that she was in Trethewyn, just a different Trethewyn to the one she lived in.

'I thought you were mad. But now I realise as nuts as it sounds, that I appear to have been transported…,' she felt the urge to giggle at the word but carried on, 'somehow to another land, or even to another time.' God, it sounded even crazier when she said it out loud.

Jory, however did not look at her as if she was completely insane, as she had expected him to. In fact a growing comprehension was dawning on his face. 'I've heard talk of this kind of thing before,' he said thoughtfully, 'can you tell me more about what happened?' adding in a mumble, 'it might even explain your bad manners and odd attire.'

Caja explained further; where she lived with her Aunt in The Gatehouse in Trethewyn, and the afternoon she had just spent with her two friends, culminating in the opening of the gate, and her sudden appearance here.

'Now, I don't know how all this works but I've heard talk of a different land that can be accessed through gates or portals. I always thought it was just a myth. Unfortunately I don't know much more than that. However, I do know where we can go for help,' declared Jory confidently, 'we're going to go and see my Great Uncle Ennor and Great Aunt Talwin.'

At this he stood up also pulling Caja up in one swift heave to her feet. 'But first we must stop at my house. I live with my Uncle Cardew and Aunt Ursula.' Upon mentioning his Aunt and Uncles' names Jory's mouth turned grim and his eyes lost some of their warmth. 'They'll be angry enough with me as it is for not bringing back the firewood that I was sent out for. And I've been gone quite some time.'

'O..k..,' sighed Caja, 'I guess I don't really have any other option… And it would be most kind of you,' she added quickly seeing Jory's stern face.

He turned without another word, and they set off once again, with Jory striding off assuredly towards the east and Caja following dispiritedly behind.

*

'I think I may have found it! Finally!' crowed Talwin in triumph. Ennor hurried over to her, a look of intense interest upon his face, 'let me see. Let me see. What is it? Have you found where it is? Truly?'

'Yes, here. See, see,' said Talwin pointing eagerly to a piece of paper in front of her, 'you know how I found that article about old Bentley Blake being in such a state over the near sale of that staff?' She did not wait for a response. 'Well, I decided to delve a little further into it and request these private papers from Helena. Look what I found in Bentley's Last Will and Testament.'

Ennor gazed earnestly at where she was pointing, mouthing the words *Unknown Oak Staff* as he read the handwritten lines added next to the entry.

At last he straightened up slowly, his face unreadable, 'Talwin…I believe you may have solved it. Oh Talwin, at last! You are the most wonderful Wizard wife a man could ask for!' His face dissolved into a wide grin of joy, 'we must leave for Blake Manor now. We can send Helena a message straight away so she's expecting us.'

They rose quickly and began immediately to start their preparations. They had a long journey ahead of them. As Talwin was busying herself outside the cottage sending the message via the solemn menhir, she stopped unexpectedly with a start, 'Ennor!' she exclaimed forcibly her face falling, 'she is here!'

Ennor who had hurried outside at her first call stopped as well, a look of immense gravity spreading across his face.

'You are sure?'

Talwin nodded her head with absolute certainty.

'Well that changes everything,' Ennor replied.

*

They had stopped in quickly at Jory's Uncle and Aunt's ramshackle farm, and Caja could see why he did not talk of them with much warmth. Aunt Ursula was not there, having gone out for a gossip with some neighbours, but unfortunately Uncle Cardew was. Cardew was a bony, tall man with sallow skin and a wracking cough that sent him into paroxysms every few minutes or so, scaring off anyone that happened to venture too close. He did not notice Caja for a full ten minutes when they first arrived, as he was too busy yelling angrily at Jory for the lack of firewood. Jory just stood there with his head down saying nothing. In the midst of a tirade about Jory's extraordinary ungratefulness and spiteful ways, he noticed Caja and stopped mid-rant.

'And who might this be?' he asked, his face suddenly taking on a look of curiosity and something akin to greed.

'This is my friend from school,' explained Jory, 'She-'

'What's your name?' interrupted Cardew advancing towards Caja, 'and where are you from? I've not seen you around here before. You are not one of these irksome magical types are you?'

'Caja,' she replied, 'I have only recently moved here…uh… with my family from… En…uh Albion…And no I'm certainly not magical?" she added questioningly looking for reassurance from Jory.

He nodded in agreement adding, 'yes, Caja is from Albion, and you know I would never be friends with one of those people Uncle.'

'Well that might explain the strange accent,' said Cardew looking at her suspiciously, 'although I don't know if anything could explain your bizarre attire. Your clothes certainly do look expensive,' he added peering at her and stepping closer, 'in fact, they're really quite…quite…' At this Cardew dissolved once again into a fit of coughing, saliva and spit spraying everywhere. Caja, realising she was in his target range made a hasty retreat backwards.

'Time to go I think. I must be getting Caja off to where her folks will be meeting her. I'll make sure I'm back later tonight so I'm ready for farm duties as usual in the morning,' said Jory hastily before his Uncle could take any more interest in Caja. 'Follow me Caja,' he added in an upbeat tone backing out of the door.

'Well, you just make sure you are back in time for your duties boy…. You shirk them too often…. And after all we've done for you…' started Cardew again in between splutters. He begrudgingly let them leave, his coughs following them as they hastened out.

Jory led Caja out of the unkempt farmyard at almost a run, and across the open moors making towards a looming wood visible in the distance. Jory let out a sigh of relief once they had got out of earshot of his uncle's barking cough, and mumbled something that sounded like 'bleddy old tosspot.'

'Is that your real Uncle?' asked Caja, 'he doesn't look like you one bit. And what is it with all this magical talk? Is there really magic here?'

'Aye, there is Caja. But I really don't know much about it. There's not many that can use it nowadays and most are with the Nobles or at the Academy. Cardew is my mother's brother. My parents… well…disappeared and I was left with them. I've been living with them since I was about four I think. They resent my presence and make me work hard for my keep,' replied Jory with an inscrutable look on his face.

Magic, thought Caja in delight. Could she really be in a world where magic existed? Suddenly this odd world was a lot more fascinating. She glanced at Jory wanting to know more. He was marching firmly ahead though, his face set in a grave expression. She looked at him in sympathy. So they had both lost their parents when they were young. It seemed they had more in common than she thought. She realised how lucky she was to have an Aunt who loved her though.

'My parents died,' she said simply, 'and my Aunt took me in like your Uncle and Aunt. But she is different to them in every other way.'

Jory swivelled around briefly with a softened look at this admission, but then turned away again adding resolutely, 'they provide me with somewhere to sleep and food, and that's enough. I don't like to talk about them much. Now, we must make haste as we've a way to go before the sun sets'.

At this Jory quickened his stride and they pushed on across the open moors following a barely worn track through the thick meadow grass. Caja recognised the landscape around her although she was now aware of the many differences, including most noticeably the scarcity of roads and built-up areas.

There was also an extraordinary tranquility to the evening which would have been quite spellbinding, if she didn't have to concentrate all her efforts on trying to keep up with Jory without falling over. He was striding along now at an incredible pace, especially for such a skinny boy.

'Could you slow down just a little?' she eventually pleaded.

'I'm sorry Caja. But we really must get through the woods before darkness falls. Once we're on the other side we can take refuge in a small hut I know for the night. Then we can set off again in the morning. If we set off early enough I believe we can reach their dwelling by mid-morning.'

'What do you mean 'believe'?' Caja panted struggling still to keep up, 'you've been there before right?'

'Um, actually… no,' replied Jory, 'my Aunt Ursula won't let them come round, and I've never had the chance to visit them although I did meet them once, when I was a young tacker.'

'But didn't you say to your Uncle that you would be back ready for tomorrow morning?' Caja carried on.

'Aye, well I couldn't tell him the truth could I? They would never 'ave let us go. They're no friends of Talwin and Ennor. I'll have some explaining to do when I get back.'

After a tiring hour of marching across the grassy moors, they entered the woods around dusk. Caja gazed upwards in wonder. The great oaks that greeted them were enormous, towering so far above them that it was difficult to make out the tops of their canopies in the failing light. The path carried on into the woods, and they finally slowed down as it became harder to pick their way through the shady interior of the forest.

Caja glanced yearningly behind her at the disappearing light of the open moors. As she reluctantly turned to face the dark forest, she glimpsed one of the huge trees appearing to turn to follow them, its solid craggy trunk twisting slowly with a deep creak. But when she spun fully back around it was just the immobile tree it had been before. She stared in wonder behind her, and then promptly fell over a tree root and into the back of Jory who yelped in surprise.

'Sorry Jory,' she mumbled, 'just …just um…struggling to keep up.'

They followed a narrow trail overgrown at times with thorny undergrowth which Jory easily pushed aside with his bare hands. The further they ventured into the wood, the darker it became and the more the trees closed in upon them. There was not a breath of wind, and the rustling sounds of small animals and birds could be heard all around them. Caja, although in general quite brave, began to feel the first prickles of fear. All she could see were the shadowy outlines of the gloomy trees and bushes around her. She followed Jory closely, virtually touching his back, grateful that he seemed to know exactly where he was going.

'I'm sorry Caja. I reckoned we would've been out of these woods by now. It's not quite safe here after nightfall,' he eventually muttered quietly.

This did not help Caja's nerves.

'What d'you mean by "not quite safe"?' she whispered back.

'Well, you know, there may be animals around, such as boars, wild dogs and possibly even…' He was interrupted by the distinctive sound of a wolf's howl far off in the distance. 'Um…wolves. That's what I was afraid of,' he added unhelpfully.

'Wolves!' whispered Caja loudly, 'you never said anything about wolves before you dragged me into a spooky, weird forest in the dark.'

'Well, there've not been wolves in these parts for over a century although I'd heard rumours they'd come back, and that howl seems to have settled it,' whispered Jory with too much composure for Caja's liking. 'Keep your head now and your wits about you, and we'll be all right. It's not much further.'

Caja continued to follow Jory, peering around anxiously

for any signs of prowling wolves. Again they heard a haunting howl, this time answered by another much closer than the first. Caja started in terror, and felt all the hairs stand up on her body in fearful attention.

'Don't worry now. We're almost there,' said Jory quietly, although a little of his confidence had dissipated.

Again a mournful howl, quickly followed by another, and another. They were coming from different directions, a couple to the left, and one behind. Caja's heart was in her mouth, and they were now walking so fast again that she was beginning to stumble every few steps over roots and forest debris. After what seemed another interminable few minutes, she could see some light ahead of her, as the trees began to thin out.

'Almost there,' said Jory with palpable relief. They were virtually jogging now as the path widened and the light from a half moon began to filter through the increasingly sparse trees. As Caja's breathing began to calm somewhat, she caught a glimpse out of the corner of her eye of a large shape moving to the left of her. She stopped and turned abruptly pulling Jory by the back of his shirt as she did so.

'What the-,' Jory whispered loudly, stopping as he turned and saw the reason why Caja had alerted him.

In the thick of a gorse bush there were two piercing orange eyes staring out at them. As they watched, a large grey wolf materialized stepping out of the bush whilst keeping its fiery gaze focused upon them. Caja stopped breathing. She had never felt such fear. Another noise startled them and looking around they saw another even larger wolf emerging onto the path behind them. Both the wolves' lips were bared revealing their teeth dripping with pale, dirty-yellow saliva.

'Quick, we must keep going,' Jory said urgently bending to pick up a heavy branch as he did so. They turned to carry on along the path, and were brought up short by yet another wolf who had slunk onto the path in front of them.

'Don't worry Caja,' whispered Jory rather shakily, 'I have this under control.'

Caja snorted faintly hysterically in response, and then grabbed hold of his arm panic-stricken, as the grey wolf took a step even closer, eyeing them menacingly. At this Jory closed his eyes and started mumbling under his breath quietly. Caja looked at him in disbelief. Was he praying?

Jory ended the mumbling with a loud sort of grunt, and at this the branch he was holding burst into flames. Caja stepped back in surprise forgetting her fear for a moment. The wolves were brought to an abrupt halt, staring warily at the flaming branch, which Jory was now swinging vigorously from side to side. The leaner, grey wolf in front of them hesitated, then looking at the other two, emitted a deep, peculiarly human growl. At this seeming encouragement from their leader they all turned again towards Jory and Caja, and carried on advancing towards them.

'What's going on?' whispered Jory in panic, 'they're showing no fear...' At this, the leader of the wolves made a huge leap at Jory, front legs extended forward, sharp teeth gleaming in the light of the flames aiming directly for his throat.

CHAPTER THREE

Caja screamed as the large grey wolf launched itself at Jory. Jory fell back thrusting the lit branch at the wolf but the wolf just brushed the branch aside, landing with its front claws ripping into Jory's bony shoulders, a fierce growl arising from deep inside its chest. It whipped its head sideways to go in for the kill, but instead of finding the soft skin of Jory's throat, it was thrown backwards by a tremendous force tumbling backwards into the other wolves that had crept up behind. All three wolves fell into a jumble in a bush and then leapt up onto their feet whining in fright.

Caja looked around and gasped. Standing behind her was an imposing man wielding a staff from which a powerful force of silvery gleaming light was emanating. The man was tall, and of some age, but stood with a pronounced strength and great command. His white hair reflected the dazzling silver light and his stern face was regarding the wolves with quiet fury. Jory was gazing at the tall man in amazement. Caja could see he was bleeding extensively from where the grey wolf had torn into his shoulders.

'Ennor!' Jory exclaimed.

The man looked at him in surprise followed by evident relief. He lowered his staff, and the silver beam faded away. 'Why is that Jory? And I see you have Caja with you thank goodness.'

The grey wolf seeing Ennor's attention diverted for a moment took the opportunity to leap again this time for Ennor, hackles raised and claws drawn-out, aiming for the man's exposed neck. Ennor did not even glance around this time but swung his staff with whirlwind speed towards the wolf's head, landing with a great thwack and knocking it out cold. The other two wolves looked at each other calculatingly, and clearly deciding this was too much for them, turned tail and fled.

Ennor turned to them both. 'Thank heavens I've found you. I've been searching far and wide this day for you Caja. Although I did not imagine that you would be with my errant great-nephew here.'

'Me,' said Caja in astonishment, 'you've been searching for me?'

Ennor just smiled softly at her and turned to Jory. 'It's been a long time Jory,' he said holding out his arm to help Jory. 'I'm sorry to see you've already had an encounter with Menadue's pets. It's lucky I was able to find you in time. We must get you back to Talwin to look at those wounds,' he added looking at Jory's shoulders in concern.

'Me,' Caja repeated mouth gaping like a stunned fish, 'how do you even know my name?'

'There is much to explain but little time to do so,' replied Ennor. 'We must hurry home before the wolves have time to return with even more of their companions. Let me see to those wounds quickly first.' With this he pulled out some rags from his cloak, which he used to expertly bandage Jory's shoulders.

'That's the best I can do for now. We must get back to Talwin. These wolves possess dark magic, and their wounds will eventually kill unless attended to. Follow me. I've my horses on the outskirts of the wood.'

They followed him out of the now completely dark wood emerging once again onto the wild moors where they saw two horses standing tied to a tree. Jory was beginning to stumble and it was obvious that he was in great pain although he still managed a smile every now and again upon hearing Caja muttering 'me?' in perplexity behind him.

'Jory, you'll ride with me on Elderson. Caja, you will ride Parsley,' instructed Ennor pointing to the smaller, dappled pony.

Caja's face dissolved into panic. 'Whoa...slow right down there Mr...um...Mr. Me ride a horse? I've only ridden once before and even then I fell off, and that was just a little pony. Really, me and horses just don't go together. Maybe I could just walk ...'

'Parsley will follow Elderson and me. You will not need to do anything and there's certainly nothing to fear. Now hop up, we don't have much time,' replied Ennor brusquely picking Caja up by the waist and depositing her on Parsley's back as if she weighed nothing.

A sudden piercing howl close behind them stopped Caja from climbing straight back down, and instead she adjusted herself uncomfortably in the saddle looking anxiously around her. Ennor tilted his head to listen carefully for a moment and then leapt onto Elderson, lifting Jory cautiously to sit in front of him, trying not to further agitate his wounds. Yet again, the baying of another wolf rent the silence.

'We must be off, and quickly. Follow me Caja and do not look behind you,' Ennor said urgently, and immediately set off swiftly moving into a fast canter.

Parsley followed with a lurch obediently behind with Caja gripping on clumsily, her face screwed up in concentration.

As they raced across the moors, skirting thick gorse and bounding over small hillocks, the sound of the wolves' shrieks could be heard coming from all directions. Many more were joining the three who had attacked and they could be heard gathering together to form packs. Ennor urged the horses on faster as the howling intensified. Up over a tussocked-hill they flew, and down the other side dodging granite boulders, their horses jumping to clear a deep ditch as they neared the bottom. Caja grasped on for dear life, her muscles straining, aware of the sound of their hunters gaining ground behind. Across the silent moors again, the horses breaking into a full gallop now.

Ennor turned to yell over the noise of the thundering hooves, 'hold on Caja. Have strength now. But remember, do not look behind you. I fear a vorgon has joined the chase,' he urged her again through gritted teeth as he skillfully directed Elderson on.

A vorgon, thought Caja. What on earth is a vorgon?

She could see they were heading straight towards the aluminium sea now reflecting starkly in the moonlight. Where could Ennor be leading them?

Jory appeared half-comatose in front of Ennor, his head lolling from side to side in time with the rapid gait of Elderson. The sound of the wolves pounding feet could clearly be heard now. They must be close Caja thought in panic. She felt the irresistible urge to turn her head. With all her strength she resisted, heeding Ennor's warning. She must not look. But there was also a much louder more distinctive thudding now, the sound of something much bigger than a wolf pursuing them. A terrifying, drawn-out screech confirmed this paralysing Caja with fear. What creature could have made that sound? Was it the vorgon? Again she resisted the impulse to turn around.

A vicious growl and a sharp crack, and Parsley stumbled as if something had snapped at his heels. He gallantly continued racing on, his chest heaving and the sweat beginning to pour off him, exuding the pungent smell of fear. Another yap and a triumphant howl, and at the corner of her vision Caja glimpsed the wolves now right beside them. A dark shape darted in front of her and made for Elderson.

Ennor turned and standing in his stirrups bellowed, 'enough!' lifting his staff and throwing out the same blinding silvery light in a vast arc that stopped the wolf mid-lunge tossing him back with tremendous force into his fellow pursuers in the darkness behind them.

There was the noise of yapping and floundering

confusion.

'We're almost there. Be strong Caja!' yelled Ennor gripping onto Jory with one arm, whilst urging Elderson onwards.

Almost where? thought Caja, but emboldened by his confidence she encouraged Parsley on.

The cliff edge rushed closer and closer to them, and just as Caja thought they must stop or fall to their deaths, Ennor veered sharply to the left pushing easily through a dense bush and descending steeply into a hidden hollow encircled by trees. To Caja's intense relief, they were forced to slow down as the horses picked their way carefully down the rocky slope.

'I must talk briefly to the giants and then we can move on,' Ennor whispered to her.

'Giants?' Caja spluttered, unable to say anything else.

Parsley, stumbling from exhaustion, brushed against one of the dark boulders beside them. It slowly unfurled revealing itself to be the figure of a gigantic man, who had been crouched in a peculiar foetal position beside them. Caja gazed riveted, he must be at least ten feet tall.

Another blood-lusty roar filled the air, and Caja could hear the wolf pack at the entrance that led down into the hollow. All around her, shapes were unfolding and emerging from their slumbers. The giants were all enormous, with abnormally large heads, even for giants, tousled dirty hair, and stumpy, hands and bare feet. They wore long grubby tunics, over roughhewn trousers and filthy shirts. Ennor was leaning from his horse talking rapidly in a strange guttural language to one of the larger giants who was still sitting on the ground yawning. He looked around listening to the yapping and scampering sounds of the wolves running down towards them and then slowly nodding to Ennor he stood up quickly, causing the ground around him to shake.

'Come Caja, we must be out of here,' whispered Ennor urgently to Caja who had been sitting on Parsley staring with awe at the giants.

It was not a moment too soon. As they pushed their horses into a canter again, the wolves entered the hollow and the vorgon upon seeing his prey, shrieked in triumph. Without thinking, Caja turned her head to look around, and immediately her blood ran cold. In the midst of the wolf pack was a creature unlike anything she had ever seen before. It was truly terrifying. Dressed strangely in a long, feathered cloak with a paler scruff around its neck, its head was that of a giant vulture with extended neck, whilst its body appeared to be that of a large scrawny human, with bended bony wings for arms. But it was its unique eyes on its bald, beaked head that really stood out. They were glistening white and mesmerising, a luminescent swirl of whirlpool patterns that seemed to suck her in. She could not keep from looking at them. In fact, she was beginning to feel peaceful now, not as scared as before. It was a inexplicably pleasant feeling. Her own eyes began to close and her hands began to slip from Parsley's reins.

Ennor, sensing something was wrong, turned his head. 'Caja!' he yelled, 'Caja, look at me! Look at me,' he commanded. Caja heard his voice as if from a great distance. She tried to turn away but the eyes were too engrossing.

'Caja, you must look at me!' Ennor yelled again at the same time flicking his wrist gently as if batting away a fly. A pale turquoise flame leapt out of his fingers and raced towards Caja, shuddering to a halt a millimetre in front of her cheek before tapping her lightly on the face. Caja jerked as if she had been slapped, and a violent shiver ran through her as she felt a renewed strength emerging from within. With a grunt, she tore her gaze away from the vorgon.

'Caja, keep looking ahead. Do not look around again. You will not be able to look away a second time. The giants will take care of our hunters. Now hold on, we must ride like the wind!'

The giants were now advancing towards the wolf packs, grunting in glee and swinging colossal clubs around their heads. As Caja and Ennor raced up the other side of the hollow they heard a fantastic racket behind them of yelping and crashes as the giants set upon their enemies. Emerging onto the cliff tops again, Ennor spurred the horses into a gallop and the sounds of the great fight gradually dissipated as they made their way further and further from the hollow.

'We must continue on now, and reach Talwin as soon as we can for Jory's sake,' shouted Ennor not looking around. With this he made another sharp left, and turning away from the cliffs they headed inland, their horses straining under them.

*

The rest of the journey took many hours and it was deep into the night when they finally arrived at their destination. Caja had clung tiredly onto Parsley for the entire journey, at one stage slipping around until she was sideways on, clasping his shaggy mane for all her life. She had managed to noiselessly right herself with some difficulty, but without attracting the attention of Ennor.

The moors had raced past her and although drowsy with exhaustion, she had looked around her with increasing wonder. The windless night had been clear, and the mass of stars and constellations above her had seemed dazzlingly bright with multi-coloured galaxies clearly arrayed. They dashed past a circle of giant stones shining grandly in the luminous moonlight, and a long tapering river where Caja had caught glimpses of young girls with what looked suspiciously like fishtails playing upon the rocky banks. Shortly before they arrived, Caja heard a distinct keening sound and looking overhead had seen three giant birds sailing high above them displaying bright green plumage with flowing yellow and orange tails that reflected like streaming fire behind them in the starlight.

At last the horses had slowed down, and come to a halt in the midst of a cosy glade in a tightly packed forest. A towering, pale menhir was standing silently alone at the edge of the glade, as if on guard, whilst tucked in amongst the trees next to it shone the welcoming glow from the window of a tiny stone cottage leaning haphazardly against one of the giant oaks that surrounded them.

Caja almost fell from Parsley, so depleted was she from the ride and worn down by the overwhelming events of the day. She noted with concern that Jory was now unconscious. Ennor carrying him, led the bedraggled Caja through the small oak door into the cheery room inside. The room functioned as both a living room and kitchen and most of the light and warmth was coming from a roaring fire, although melting candles perched on wooden mantles around the room also cast their light into the nooks and crannies.

In one of the snug armchairs dozing in front of the flickering fire was a small, elderly lady with beautiful white hair elaborately coiled upon her head. She started as they walked in and jumped up with surprising agility and grace.

'Thank goodness you are back. And you have found Caja!' she said in a musical voice, 'but someone is hurt', she added in consternation noticing the prone figure in Ennor's arms. 'Who is it? He looks badly hurt. Although, I do believe it is….yes….Jory!' At the mention of his name a look of unease flittered rapidly across her face but was quickly replaced with concern. Advancing towards them she helped Ennor lay Jory down upon the table.

'They were attacked by Menadue's followers in Trigg Woods. He must know that Caja has entered Kernow. Although how he found out so soon confounds me,' Ennor said quietly to Talwin shaking his head with a puckered brow, 'Jory's shoulders took the worst of it. The wounds will need healing before the wolves' darkness sets in and takes hold. He is a strong lad though, although he could do with some feeding up.'

Talwin immediately started tending to Jory, carefully cleaning and dressing his wounds, laying on a gloopy yellow ointment with a strong smelling odour that smelt like camphor. When she had finished she glided towards Caja and embraced her saying, 'I am Talwin, wife of Ennor'. Caja, who had been standing exhausted almost in a daze, gladly accepted a soothing hug.

Ennor sat down at the table wearily, 'Caja had a brief run in with a vorgon.'

Talwin looked startled for a moment and then gazed at Caja in keen interest, 'well, it appears you came out of that encounter unharmed. Which is very lucky. I do not know of many who can escape the gaze of the vorgon.'

'What…what do they do?' asked Caja hesitantly.

Talwin sighed, 'they take away your humanity. They turn you into a beast, and a vicious one at that.' Noticing Caja's exhaustion she added quickly, 'but we can talk more of that later Caja. Take a seat there, you look utterly worn out.' She indicated one of the armchairs in front of the hearth.

Caja gratefully sank down into the ancient but inviting chair leaning towards the fire to warm her frozen hands.

Caja felt immeasurably overwhelmed by all that had happened to her in the last few hours, and leaned back in the chair completely drained. At least she now felt safe here, with Talwin and Ennor. Ensconced in the wonderfully yielding armchair, Caja's eyes began to close and before she knew it she had fallen into a fitful sleep, her dreams crowding her mind with star-filled archways, pounding hooves, and vicious, snatching teeth.

*

Caja awoke blissfully unaware of where she was and feeling exceptionally relaxed. Slowly her senses returned and she realised she must be in a bedroom at Ennor and Talwin's house. The odd-shaped room was small with a tiny circular window set into the thick wall revealing a small patch of the surrounding wood. The room was upstairs although she had no memory of there being an upstairs in the tiny cottage. It was daylight but not much light penetrated into the dense forest and the trees were outlined in shadow. Sitting up carefully, aware now of her aching muscles from their perilous ride, Caja immediately noticed a very unusual fact about the room. There was no door.

Hastily, she slipped out from under the enormous enveloping duvet, and jumped out of bed, noting that she was now dressed in a very long, very old-fashioned nightdress.

Ah, but she could hear voices. Soft voices coming from beneath her.

Disconcerted, she searched around her and then noticed the trapdoor with a curved, wooden handle in the corner of the room from where a muted light was emanating. Walking quietly on tiptoe she knelt down beside it and put her ear to the slight crack.

'I certainly wasn't expecting him to be involved in this. It does complicate matters somewhat,' Ennor was saying softly.

'I know. The poor boy. Do you think we need to worry about him though? Can we trust him?' replied Talwin.

'We cannot allow him to interfere with our plans, that's for sure. He does bring some added risk to our task. It'll be hard enough as it is. But he may actually be able to help us.'

Talwin glanced keenly at him, 'yes, I believe you may be right,' she mused, 'perhaps he even has a part to play in the Prophecy. I've kept an eye on him over the years and he has shown no sign of Cynthia's traits. And he has had to live with those terrible Villants. He's shown some character in doing that!'

Caja realised they were talking about Jory. Why could they not trust Jory? He couldn't possibly be dangerous could he? There was a sudden silence from below and then a quiet knocking on the trapdoor making Caja flinch in surprise.

'Caja, are you awake?' came Talwin's voice.

'Y…yes,' replied Caja nervously.

'Your clothes have been washed and dried, and are on the side by the window, and there is a warmer jumper for you to put on too. Then come downstairs. Ennor and I wish to talk to you.'

She did as she was told finding her clothes all folded on the side, and a chunky, green jumper that fitted her perfectly. It had the added bonus of covering her long-sleeved, grey top and short-sleeved t-shirt with psychedelic patterns that had so intrigued Cardew. This way she'd fit in better, although she was pretty sure no one would be wearing jeans. She heaved up the trapdoor and ventured down the small steps that twisted round and round sharply until she entered another oddly circular room set out as a dining room. She was definitely not in the cottage she had been in last night.

'Where are we?' she asked Ennor and Talwin who were seated at the round table, steaming mugs in hand.

'Good morning Caja,' said Talwin with a smile, 'we're in Gwydhenn, our home. The room you were in last night was only the cottage section. The rest of our home is set within Gwydhenn, the great tree you may have seen on your way in. He is one of the many oakens of the Falkelly Forest. He's been kind enough to give us protection for many years. Come sit down, I have some Rosentea for you.'

Caja sat down marvelling at the thought that they were now sitting inside a tree. It did explain the shape of the rooms. Although Talwin had talked as if the tree was alive. After all the events of yesterday this was something Caja could well believe. She could almost feel the living presence of the tree, its trunk wrapped protectively around them. Caja recoiled as there was a sudden groaning and creaking sound and the whole room noticeably moved slowly up just an inch and then quickly back down, as if the tree had just …well … shrugged.

'He likes to do that with new people,' said Ennor chuckling, 'he has a great sense of humour, dear Gwydhenn.'

There was a clattering and Jory appeared from another trapdoor hidden in the corner of the room. Running through the middle of the stairs however there was a pole, which he slid down in a triumphant whoosh.

'This..place..is..just….great,' he said grinning happily. 'I swear Gwydhenn did a massive hiccup just then and I clean fell over.'

Caja was looking at Jory in amazement, 'Jory, you look so well! How did you recover so quickly? Isn't your shoulder hurting anymore?'

'Aye, I feel fantastic. That ointment Talwin gave me has almost completely healed my cuts. She works wonders! But then again she is a Wizard,' replied Jory with reverence.

'A Wizard? Someone is going to have to start explaining things to me around here!' exclaimed Caja thumping her small fists on the table in front of her. 'Wizards, trees that hiccup, giants, wolves. What *is* going on?'

'Here, have some Rosentea and breakfast, and we will explain as much as we can Caja,' said Talwin laying some bread, butter, multi-coloured jams and bright fruits that Caja had never seen before on the table. 'I understand that it must all be very bewildering'.

She handed Caja a mug of hot, milky-pink liquid that smelled of roses. Caja breathed in the heavenly aroma and then took a tentative sip. An explosion of taste made her close her eyes in pleasure. Sweet and wonderfully comforting, like nothing she had ever tasted before.

Talwin smiled at her. 'Ah, the wonders of Rosentea. It's made from spriggan roses found in hidden glades in the forest. It restores a sense of wellbeing. Those spriggans might be mischievous creatures but this is one thing they do better than anyone else,' she explained. Caja relaxed as she felt a sense of peace sweep over her.

Jory plonked himself down in one of the chairs and started gulping down the Rosentea that Ennor handed him. 'De..li.cious,' he said in between slurps, 'never had anything like this before. Aunt Ursula usually gives me cold weedtea,' he shivered in disgust at the thought, 'I'm starving though.' And he began to grab some of the bread and slather it with a luminous, purple jam.

Caja, realising she was ravenous too, followed Jory's lead. She was not sure if it was because she was so hungry but the food tasted mouth-wateringly good.

'Caja, we realise this must all be very unsettling for you. We ourselves didn't realise you would be quite so young,' started Talwin, 'we'll try and explain as best as we can, but even we don't have all the facts.' She turned to Ennor expectantly.

'Our land and yours have always been closely connected,' he carried on, 'we believe at one point there was much interaction between the two worlds, but this stopped many centuries ago. They were initially very similar; we think there is in fact a chance that they were one world that broke into two, many millennia ago…Over…'

'Ah,' Caja interrupted, 'so I'm not in the past then. I haven't gone back in time?' With these words she made a melodramatic swooping gesture with her hands.

Ennor looked at her amused, 'no Caja, this world is not the past of your world. Over the last few hundred years there's been only the briefest contact and only a handful of people have known the secret of the two worlds' existence. Connections or gates between the worlds are linked to people called GateKeepers. Only the GateKeepers can open the gates that are located at various points around the country. We know where quite a few of them are, but not all of them. The ability to be a GateKeeper is passed down through generations and they exist in both worlds. Caja your family, the Dingles are GateKeepers and you yourself are a GateKeeper.'

Caja gawped at him, her mouth stuffed with bread, not moving. 'Aooo', she gasped through her crammed mouth accompanied by flutterings of bread crumbs.

Ennor brushed his sleeve off and smiling at her carried on, 'there were once GateKeepers across the land. One in Kernow, or as you know it Cornwall; Kembra, known as Wales in your land; Alba – your Scotland; Albion - England, and Iwerdhon – your Ireland. As far as I know there is only one left now in Kembra in our world, and one in Cornwall in your world. Our GateKeeper in Kernow was a great friend, Tomas Goodwill, but he died a few months ago with no children. He was the one who predicted your entry into our world Caja. Upon his deathbed, he revealed to Talwin and I, that the one who entered Kernow from Cornwall after his death would be the GateKeeper from the Prophecy. She would help us in our battle against Menadue. We've been waiting for you to come.'

'Menawho?' asked Caja, 'and anyway I don't think I'll be much help here. A Prophecy? I don't have any idea what you're talking about. Besides, wouldn't you be better at doing all this with your magic stick thingy and your silver light stuff?'

'It's a staff Caja. And yes, it does seem on the outside that you may not be of great service to our cause. But having someone from your world will be very useful,' replied Ennor, although with a slightly dubious note. 'The Prophecy has been passed down from Wizard to Wizard for centuries and comes from Merlin himself. Unfortunately they don't all believe in it anymore, but Tomas was a great believer as are Talwin and I. It clearly states that it will be a GateKeeper from your world who will help us find Merlin's Legacy. An otherwordly GateKeeper.' Retrieving a piece of paper carefully folded in his pocketbook he read aloud:

Merlin's Prophecy

This, a portent for those who must risk all to save even the unworthy,
Take note of my word and do not falter or hesitate.
Thrice a century will past, years lost to dissension and strife,
The moors ever steady, the masses ever changing.
The threat from the descended Dark will rise at its greatest of any epoch,
Intent on destroying the sacred bond and the magic that dwells within it.
With the Sun and Loer Delks in hand,
At the most powerful zenith the Dark will strike.
Aided by my Legacy, released and protected by the otherworldly gatekeeper,

The Twofold Power, strengthened by the moes is the sole hope.
Or all light will be subdued by the Dark's ultimate dominion over
land and sea,
And the souls of the earths will be lost.

Caja looked at Ennor puzzled, clearly not impressed, 'waffles on a bit doesn't he?'

Ennor nodded benignly with a note of amusement, 'well, if there was one thing Merlin was not, it was concise.'

'Did he actually mention my name though? That's the question. Maybe he meant someone else and they're here somewhere already!' Caja continued whilst still busily eating. The idea that she might be able to help in any way in this strange world was sheer crazy talk in her eyes.

'Tomas said it would be a GateKeeper from your world, from Cornwall. And we already knew that the only GateKeeper surviving was you,' explained Talwin gently, 'your mother would have been a GateKeeper before you but she may never have realised as there was no one to explain it to her, and there was never any need for the Gate to be opened. The Dingles have been GateKeepers for many generations.'

'Does that mean my Auntie Flora is one too?' asked Caja excitedly.

'No, it's passed down from parent to child, and I think you have proven you are a GateKeeper by your presence here,' answered Ennor.

'Oh,' answered Caja in disappointment. 'But how did you know I'd entered Kernow?' she continued, 'and what's with all this magic, and who is Menapoo?' She let out a machine-gun burst of laughter before continuing to snicker into her tea.

Ennor smiled again, 'Talwin is able to tell when a gate has been opened and someone from your world has arrived. It's one of her many powers. So we knew that you must have entered. No one from your world has been here for many, many years. We don't yet know how Menadue found out so quickly though. We believed we had an advantage over him in this.

As to magic, well it does exist in this world. It used to exist in yours too but has all but been forgotten. We call it Telluric Magic. Telluric Magic is connected to the earth and that connection has virtually disappeared in your world. Magical abilities are passed down through families. It's becoming less and less common here as certain families die out, and new ones are just not appearing. All of the Noble families used to be able to practise Telluric Magic but only the Penwiths, Templetons and Salisburys can now. There are barely a handful of children born a year within the whole of Briton who have a connection with the Telluric. But the Telluric connection does not reveal itself until the children reach puberty so there could be even less in the next few years. Before puberty they are just like everyone else.'

Jory, who had been cramming food into his mouth whilst looking from one to the other in fascination, started at this. 'I never knew that. I know a little about magic and we've a Healing Zard in the town nearby and I saw a Druid ritual once, but I didn't realise you weren't magical from birth,' he said staring thoughtfully into his plate.

'Yes. We've never been able to predict whether a child will become magical or not. Once their Telluric connection is revealed the child is sent to Ambrosius Academy in Truro where they're trained in their powers. They start as an Initiate, and leave as a Junior Zard, Senior Zard or Wizard, depending on their abilities. Talwin and I are both Wizards, and met at Ambrosius Academy,' he added smiling at Talwin.

'Now Caja, Menadue is also a Wizard and is the evil force revealed in the Prophecy. Menadue and his followers, such as the wolves, use a different, foul magic that has no relation to the earth, called Ereburic Magic'.

Jory uttered a sigh of understanding, 'Aye, so that's why the wolves weren't afraid of the fire.'

'That's correct Jory. Evidence of Menadue's presence and intentions have been growing for some time now with more sightings of wolves, hobgoblins and piskies. Unfortunately the Nobles of Kernow are in a shambles, and not united enough to face this threat.'

'Nobles? So who are the Nobles, and what about Merlin? Is he a real person then? And King Arthur? And Lancelot? And Maid Marian? And where are your wands?' Caja babbled, her eyes gleaming.

'It appears we have similar events happening in our worlds and various interconnections in our history. However, they will never be exactly the same although there will be many parallels. Yes, there was a King Arthur in our world who united all of Kernow, and Merlin was his main adviser and tutor. Lancelot was one of his Knights of the Round Table. King Arthur died almost three hundred years ago though, and Merlin disappeared almost immediately afterwards. It was Merlin who set up Ambrosius Academy and helped King Arthur rule this kingdom. And I believe Maid Marian is a myth from the Robin Hood tales, nothing to do with our history Caja. And we don't need wands in our world to use magic, although our magic can be enhanced through powerful objects such as my staff.'

'Hee hee wands. They're what children play with,' chortled Jory quietly.

Caja scrunched up her face and stuck her tongue out at him.

'It's important you know a little more about our world though Caja. There's a Noble in charge of all the different Hundreds of Kernow,' carried on Talwin, 'although they were once united under King Arthur, they now try to run Kernow together through the Kernow Assembly. Although there are so many disagreements. And we're afraid that some may even have formed an alliance with Menadue.'

'So what's a Hundred?' interjected Caja.

'You have the 9 Hundreds of Kernow each ruled by a different noble; Penwith, Kerrier, Pyder, Powder, Trigg, East Wivel, West Wivel, Lesnewth, and Stratton.'

'Excuse me, was that in English?' Caja asked with a cheeky

grin. The tea had certainly made her more relaxed. Catching Jory's eye she giggled and he smirked back at her.

Talwin gave them a serene look and continued, 'well interestingly we're not actually speaking English as you do in your world but Kernewek, the language of Kernow. You're able to understand everything and speak back to us because of the unique bond, the Nexus Bond as it is called, that exists between the worlds which allows us to understand each other.'

'No way! I'm speaking another language right now. That's so cool,' exclaimed Caja, putting her hand out to pour some more Rosentea.

Jory looked similarly impressed.

'That's probably enough Rosentea for you now, Caja,' said Ennor gently, 'and you too Jory,' he added as Jory also went to fill his cup. 'Too much, can make you feel, a little, well light-headed and silly'

They both frowned in disappointment.

'Well, I've always been terrible at learning new languages,' said Caja, 'this is much easier! Auntie Flora would be most impressed!' At the mention of her Aunt, Caja's face suddenly fell. 'But she'll be worried sick about me. I must get home! Ennor, Talwin you must help me. I've been gone a whole night. She'll be in an absolute panic. And what will Luke and Aggie be thinking?'

Ennor gave her an understanding look, 'we'll do all we can to help you Caja. Time does move at a different pace here so you may find that very little time has passed when you return. We'll need a GateKeeper from our world to open a gate for you to return but since Tomas' death we know of no others. The only way a GateKeeper can open doors in other worlds is by using a roaming key. This brings us back to the Prophecy. Talwin and I have been researching this Prophecy for many years and believe we may have unravelled the mystery behind Merlin's Legacy mentioned in it. And if we're right, Merlin's Legacy is also a roaming key. We believe you, Caja have a vital role in finding this Legacy and protecting it from Menadue and we believe it'll also help you return home.'

Caja's face was a mass of confusion. She opened her mouth to protest but Ennor carried on louder, 'we can all set off together to find this roaming key,' and adding to Jory's obvious surprise, 'and since we'll be going to Truro, Jory you should come with us too, as you can visit Ambrosius Academy, which you will undoubtedly be attending next year.'

Jory's face turned quite ashen, 'What?' he stammered taken aback, 'm...me...but I...well....how did you know? About the magic?'

CHAPTER FOUR

'It was how I found you in the forest. I was close by when I felt the use of magic. But Talwin and I had guessed already, as your Mother and Father were both gifted with magic and therefore you were likely to be. We were just waiting to see if it would appear,' replied Ennor calmly to Jory's disconcerted question.

Well that makes sense, thought Caja; it explained how Jory had set the branch on fire when faced with Menadue's wolves. She gazed at him in admiration; this certainly made him more exciting in her eyes.

'Well, why didn't anyone tell me!' Jory exploded, crimson-faced and furious. 'What have you been waiting for? I've spent the last few months thinking I've been going mad. Things moving around me...Fires lighting before I've lit them. I never even thought about magic to begin with. Maybe I would've if somebody had bothered to tell me about my parents!'

Talwin's eyes were filled with sympathy, 'you're right Jory. It was wrong of us not to tell you. We didn't want to tell your Aunt and Uncle, as you know what they think of magic. And they'd never let us near the farm or you.'

'But couldn't you've found a way to tell me!' he grumbled resentfully, 'my Aunt and Uncle hate magic. More and more people are turning against magic you know, and it was hard to always cover it up. I couldn't understand why I was suddenly able to do it. I never realised it didn't appear until you were older. Nobody talks about magic in Trigg. And I had no control. But…' he added softening, 'at least now you know… Maybe you can even help me?' he asked entreatingly, a glimmer of hope appearing upon his angry features.

'Why yes Jory, of course we can help you and we're going to,' replied Talwin firmly.

'But what about this Legacy, this roaming key though?' interrupted Caja, 'it's great about Jory and his magic and helping him. But I really need to get home. And what's all this about me having something to do in the fight against Menadue? Do you even know where this key thing is?' she demanded gazing from Ennor to Talwin in consternation.

Talwin turned to face Caja, 'yes, we do, we found out only yesterday where Merlin's Legacy is. We've been searching for a number of years but we believe we now know its exact location. We were about to set off to recover it when I felt your arrival Caja. And then we knew; we must be on the right path, as your arrival upon the day of our discovery could not just be coincidence.

You're meant to help us find it Caja and release it, as the Prophecy states, and protect it from Menadue, so that he can never lay his hands on it.'

Caja unleashed a frustrated sigh, 'Ok ok, I have to protect it or whatever. But what is it, this Legacy, this roaming key? Is it like a big, ginormous key? And will it really help me get home?'

'No, a roaming key does not generally look like a key. It can be any object. We've traced this one to the Hundred of Pydar, which our friend Noblewoman Helena Blake rules. We found it mentioned in some old manuscripts from the Blake Manor where the family have lived for centuries. It seems the Legacy is in fact Merlin's staff.'

Jory gasped in wonder, 'Merlin's own staff! Wow, that's just incredible. It must be one of the most powerful magical objects ever made. I thought it disappeared with him though?'

'Yes, we thought so too. However, it appears the staff was handed over to the Blakes for safekeeping. The family were once great allies of Merlin.'

Caja frowned, 'right so let me get this straight, it's a staff I am looking for? And this staff will help me return home?'

Ennor nodded, 'it's well known that Merlin's staff was also a potent roaming key. And yes you're right Jory, it was and is one of the greatest magical objects ever created. A roaming key can be used to open the gates between the worlds, although only by a GateKeeper.'

'Ok, but what's this about me protecting this staff?' asked Caja still disconcerted.

Ennor smiled, 'Ah, that's the best bit. All you have to do is take the staff with you once you've opened the gate, and hide it in your world. Even Menadue with his enormous strength cannot open the gates between the worlds.'

Caja let out a whistly, weary sigh, 'if it's the only way I can get home…and if it'll help in your fight against this Menadue I guess I'll have to. So where do we need to go again?'

Talwin replied this time. 'It's at the Blake Manor in the Hundred of Pydar, Caja, just outside Truro. We'll all go together. Noblewoman Helena will help us find it. But we cannot leave for two days as…'

'Two days!' interrupted Caja loudly.

'Yes, Caja,' said Ennor sternly, 'we've heard from Noblewoman Blake, and she's away in the South visiting the Penwiths to discuss Menadue. We cannot search her home until she returns. It'll also allow us some time to train Jory to control his magic. Telluric Magic can be very dangerous without training. And Caja, we can teach you more in the meantime about Kernow and our world, so that your journey to Truro will not bring about quite so many surprises. We understand it's hard when you know your family will be worrying, but it is necessary, so do try and be patient.'

'Caja trust us. We will do all that we can to help you return home,' added Talwin. 'Now come let us prepare for the day ahead.'

*

Despite her frustration with the delay in returning home, Caja found the rest of the day full of enchantment. Talwin and Ennor took it in turns to teach Jory how to harness his magic, pouring over books together in Gwydhenn, or instructing him outside the cottage in the glade on various ways to connect to the Telluric's four strands of magic. Caja sat watching in fascination as bushes exploded into bright green and orange miniature stars; and winds appeared from nowhere bringing with them beautifully intricate snowflakes that transformed into white petals as soon as they landed.

When not engaged with Jory, Ennor or Talwin sat with Caja and told her more of Kernow and its varied inhabitants. Seated on two carved stumps near Gwydhenn, Caja listened captivated as Ennor told her about the magic of the land. He explained that Telluric magic was intimately connected with the earth they lived upon, and based around the four strands of earth, water, wind, and fire. Those with magical abilities were deemed to have a special bond that allowed them to tap into the natural magic of the land. All spells involved manipulating one or a number of these elements and combining them with their own human emotions and desires. Magical abilities tended to be unique to each person.

'You see Talwin is a great healer. This reflects the caring side of her personality. And she tends to use water in her magic which comes from the calm flow within her. I myself am not such a great healer. And I tend to use fire more, which comes from my more forceful nature.'

Ennor then solemnly told her about the dark magic, Ereburic Magic, that existed in their world, 'this does not originate from the land at all,' he explained, 'but solely from the person themselves. The power of Ereburic is derived from the depths of dark emotions; jealousy, greed, anger, the desire for revenge, among many others. Its force depends upon the strength of these emotions. It can be extremely powerful and destructive when originating from something as strong as the intensity of human rage.'

Caja listened uneasily, her eyes wide. 'But what of Menadue? Why does he use this Ereba…this dark magic? And why does he use it against Kernow? What does he want to do? And…and where did he come from?' she asked earnestly.

'Menadue was born here in Kernow, but he disappeared for many, many years and we believed him gone forever. It's clear now he spent that time training in the Ereburic Magic, and his return has brought along with it the reappearance of wolves, vorgons hobgoblins and other creatures of the Dark. His rage feeds his dark power and appears to have no limits. We believe he is a great threat to Kernow and possibly all of Briton. We don't know where he's currently hiding though. He appears and disappears at will.'

Ennor let out a long sigh before continuing. 'Talwin and I've been trying to unite the Nobles against the threat. We hope there'll be a vote in the Kernow Assembly soon on the matter. But many won't believe he is a threat as he was certainly not evil when he left, and he's been gone for almost forty years. And they certainly don't believe that he's the Dark force named in the Prophecy. Many of them don't even believe in the Prophecy!'

'But why?' asked Caja, 'why does he want to do all this, take over Kernow?'

Ennor looked at her with profound sadness in his eyes, 'it's a long story Caja and not one I can share with you now. And besides I'm probably the wrong person to answer such questions,' he added wearily, 'come now it's time for lunch.'

*

In the afternoon, it was Talwin's turn to beguile Caja with stories of the many magical creatures that still lived in

Kernow. She talked of the spriggans, a mischievous imp that lived in the Falkelly Forest around Gwydhenn. They could only be found when they wanted to be, and loved to play tricks on humans, scaring lone travellers by ambushing them and forcing them blindfolded into the depths of the forest, and then usually leaving them with no idea where they were. Then there were the naiads, elusive creatures, half woman-half fish who lived in the rivers and oceans around Kernow. Talwin explained that they were self-centred beings who spent most of their time preening themselves although the river-naiads were generally friendlier than the wilder sea-naiads.

'Sounds just like some girls I know,' muttered Caja. She learnt more about the giants that she had encountered with Ennor; that they were dying out with only a few hidden tribes left in the whole of Briton. Menadue and his followers had been hunting them down, and burning them out of their camps. Ennor had been trying to assist them by putting up protective wards around their camps, which explained why they had been so obliging to help in their time of need. Then there were the faeries and giant firebirds that were once quite common but rarely seen nowadays, although Caja realised with delight that she had seen three of the fiery birds in the night-sky on her flight with Ennor and Jory. In the midst of Talwin's description of the Druids who worshipped the gods and goddesses of nature, Jory burst into the dining room where they were sitting with a broad grin on his face.

'Caja, we need you. I need a guinea pig to practise some spells on,' he blurted out.

'A guinea pig?' said Caja dubiously, 'I'm not sure whether I've ever aspired to be a guinea pig. You might turn me into a toad or something!'

'Don't be silly. I can't do anything that advanced. It's just a small spell, you'll see and I promise there'll be no lasting damage,' pleaded Jory.

Caja unwilling agreed, although the mention of 'lasting damage' did not allay her fears, and was led outside by an eager Jory. Ennor was standing in the middle of the glade, his face stern although Caja was sure she could detect a whisper of amusement in his eyes, 'Today, we've been practising weaving air to induce levitation Caja. Jory tells me you are most keen to help.'

'Help? Yes, well of course. Anything I can do to assist Jory in his training,' she said with more than a hint of sarcasm in her voice. Looking at Jory's enthusiastic face she mumbled to him, 'but if I leave here with a tail, you Jory Hobart are going to leave here with a black eye.'

'Stand there Caja, near that bush,' instructed Ennor, 'it will provide a softer landing if needed,' he muttered to Jory quietly.

'What was that? Did you say something about a landing?' asked Caja nervously.

But Jory had closed his eyes and was talking under his breath concentrating hard and with this Caja began to feel herself float off the ground a couple of inches.

Ennor let out an exasperated sigh whispering to Jory, 'as I keep telling you, you don't need to close your eyes. It really is important that you see what you're doing.'

Jory stopped momentarily to shush him, which led to Caja falling abruptly a few inches.

'Watch out!' she yelled and then continued to float upwards again. She was now hovering a few feet off the ground looking around her in awe and some trepidation. Jory carried on mumbling as Caja rose higher and higher. Slightly worried, she started flapping her arms to try and swim herself back down, but instead rose even higher.

'Whoa, hey there, that's enough. You've done it. Good work Jory. Now let me back down!' she exclaimed, now almost as high as the top of the cottage roof.

Jory frowned, a look of concentration on his face, 'how do I get her back down?' he whispered to Ennor.

Caja could see Ennor gesticulating and talking earnestly to Jory but could no longer hear what they were saying as she floated higher up and up into the trees. From up here, Jory appeared to be waving his arms around quite frantically. For some reason she began to feel a warmly-enticing sense of calm, although it was clear that Jory did not have complete control over the situation. Abruptly there was a shout, and she felt a surge of panic, as she dropped suddenly, like a stone, tumbling through the branches towards the ground. She heard the deep rumblings of Ennor's voice, and before she knew it she found herself caught lightly in the branched arms of Gwydhenn. Then Ennor brought her gently back to the ground to stand shakily beside them.

'I think you need to practise a bit more Jory!' she snapped.

Jory looked abashed, 'aye, you're right. Sorry Caja.'

'Don't worry Caja, you were never in any danger. Gwydhenn will always protect you, as will I. I'm quite astonished at your capabilities though Jory. I've never seen anyone able to levitate someone quite so high so quickly. Even if you aren't quite so good at bringing them back down,' said Ennor.

Jory grinned at the compliment, looking tremendously proud of himself.

'Particularly good with wind it seems,' added Ennor thoughtfully.

'Makes sense,' said Caja, her spirits returning with a cheeky grin. Jory beamed back at her.

*

The evening was spent in easy companionship with Ennor and Talwin, who laid on an intriguing feast for Caja and Jory, consisting of many of the delicacies of the land, some of which she devoured with relish, others which she had trouble even sniffing. She slept peacefully that night exhausted from the day's activities and lulled to slumber by the gentle swaying of Gwydhenn. The treehouse was a wonderful place to stay, the living presence of the giant oaken creating a feeling of safe and soothing sanctuary.

The next morning they were once again up early, with Jory

hard at work in his training, and Caja receiving tutoring in the ways of Kernow. Later on in the afternoon as the sun sunk towards the uppermost boughs of the giant trees, Caja and Jory were given some time off to explore the surrounding forest and visit the Hidden Lake. Ennor and Talwin wanted some time to send messages to various Nobles via the menhir, the giant stone standing guard in the glade, through which they were able to communicate with other Tellurics.

'Now, do not venture too far. We leave at first light tomorrow and you must be back for an early night to prepare yourself for the journey ahead. Follow the path from Gwydhenn and you'll reach the hidden lake eventually. A talk with the lake-naiads there may come of some use, as they are talented prophesiers. Be wary though, they're contrary creatures,' warned Talwin as they set off.

Caja was excited by the prospect of finding naiads and spending some time with Jory. She was intrigued by what she had heard about Jory's parents and was keen to find out more. As they marched along the narrow path though, Caja found herself struggling once again to keep up with Jory's longer strides.

'So Jory... When did your parents disappear... and have you never heard from them?' she enquired panting behind him.

Jory turned with a pained look. 'They left me when I was very young, three years old I think,' he said abruptly, 'and I've not heard a word from them since.'

Caja felt sorry for Jory's obvious discomfort, but could not stop herself from trying to find out more. Her Aunt Flora had always said she was too inquisitive for her own good. 'But surely you must have some idea where they might've gone?' She took a deep breath trying to keep up and talk. 'D..did they not say anything to you before they left?'

'No, they did not,' he replied brusquely, 'surprisingly, they didn't think it worth their time to inform me where they were going before they abandoned me.'

'A..and you've never... heard anything about them all this

time?' she persisted panting.

There was a moment of silence from Jory. He seemed to be trying to overcome a great conflict within himself and would not turn to look at Caja. 'I've heard rumours Caja,' he said at last wearily, 'when I was growing up. People talking when they did not know I was around. That my parents had gone evil. That they'd given everything up to dedicate themselves to the Dark side...I...I've no desire to talk of this anymore,' he added bitterly quickening his stride so Caja could not actually walk and carry on asking any more questions, even if she had wanted to.

The distance between them began to grow as Jory continued at his determined pace. Caja felt herself growing nervous as she saw him disappearing around a corner and out of sight. 'Jory!' she called, 'Jo...!' She stopped abruptly, sure she had heard Jory replying. But it could not have been Jory, for the voice was coming from behind her, in a gentle, whispered tone.

'Ca...jaaa....' ? It was so soft she strained her ears to hear, searching around intently. Where had it come from? She stood stock still in the middle of the path. Again she heard the whispering, almost like the rustling wind calling her name, 'Cajaaaa....Cajaaaa.'

Jory appeared again from around the corner. 'Stopped for a reason Caja?' There was no answer.

'Caja, what are you doing? Have you forgotten how to walk?'

Caja turned slowly to him, 'Jory, I believe the trees are talking to me.'

Jory scoffed, 'don't be daft Caja. I've never heard of the oakens talking to people. It's probably just the wind. Listen.'

The wind obediently whistled through the trees around them making a whooshing and whispering sound.

Caja frowned, 'perhaps you're right. B...but....I was sure it was my name.'

Jory cupped his hands to his ears in an exaggerated gesture of listening. All they could hear was the sound of the breeze winding its way around the pillar-like trees.

'Sorry, I can't hear anything Caja. Let's get on.'

'Ok,' sighed Caja, 'I'm looking forward to seeing the lake-naiads... I guess it could have been anything in this weird land!'

Jory nodded patiently to her as if to a small child, and set off once again leading them through the forest.

Caja responded by poking her tongue out and waggling it at his rapidly disappearing back.

'I can see that Caja,' he added as they trundled on forwards.

The overgrown path wound around the great oakens that gently, almost imperceptibly bent towards them as they passed, and eventually led out to a bright clearing which contained the Hidden Lake. The water was a glassy green, fed by numerous streams and surrounded on all sides by dense forest. It remained clear and brimming with life, a watery refuge for many creatures. As Caja and Jory approached they heard a number of its inhabitants slithering back into the safety of the lake, although they could only catch glimpses of the life beneath.

'It's beautiful,' gasped Caja.

They positioned themselves quietly on one of the smooth obliging boulders and waited. Talwin had told them that in this way the lake-naiads would eventually come to see them, but that they should remain silent as the naiads could not tolerate noise or raucous behaviour. After quite some time with Caja sighing every now and again in impatience, shimmering ripples started appearing on the lake in front of them. Gradually the ripples increased until there was a swirling eddy directly below them. Caja found she was holding her breath in anticipation.

Finally the top of a head emerged, followed closely by another and another. The lake-naiads slowly arose, revealing their scraggly, algae-green hair, large, soulful eyes and luminescent skin. They bobbed gracefully up and down gazing at Caja and Jory with expressions of curiosity and faint amusement, two in front and one shyly hiding behind.

'Caja and Jory. We've been looking forward to meeting you. Greetings,' trilled one of the naiads with emerald-green eyes in a voice that sounded like the tinkling of water, 'although you are much less impressive than we imagined.'

Caja raised an eyebrow at Jory with laughter in her eyes and whispered, 'I think that's you they're talking about.'

'Probably,' Jory whispered back.

The naiads continued to stare at them with expectant gazes.

'Um…and greetings to you,' stuttered Caja uncertainly

'Greetings, we come to ask whether you can do us the great favour of revealing our futures,' asked Jory in a firm voice.

The three lake-naiads smiled in merriment at this with the coy one putting her slender hands to her face to giggle behind her graceful fingers.

The emerald-eyed one who appeared to be the leader nodded. 'Certainly Jory Hobart, your future lies open as a book to us, although…..although there is also much uncertainty there. You do recognise that everything can change, you control fate as much as it controls you?'

The one beside her with enormous, turquoise eyes heaved a tremendous sigh. 'You both have so much ahead of you. It's too exhausting to think about it. Thankfully we don't have your future… But no fate would deal us your hand. Our beauty is too great for us to partake in such calamities!' she exclaimed with a rippling laugh.

The leader gazed at Caja now looking vaguely disconcerted. 'But so much has changed since you last came to see us Caja, there have been powerful and dark powers influencing your path.'

Caja looked at them confused. 'Huh, me? I haven't been to see you before! In fact this is my first time in your land.'

The timid one who had not yet spoken again giggled.

'And I can vouch for that,' added Jory.

The turquoise-eyed one smiled mischievously at them. 'The fate of so many rests with you both. Are you sure you are up to the task? ... Although there is no point in answering that question...,' she tittered, 'as you have no choice.' This she found even funnier than before dissolving into flowing laughter with the one behind joining in. Caja grimaced at Jory who was starting to look unsettled. This was not turning out to be quite as much fun as they had anticipated.

The leader glanced at her two companions with a tinge of exasperation, 'I can tell you only so much. Be wary of those you trust. I see impending betrayal in your future.'

Jory's face took on a warning hue of crimson. 'From who? Tell us more about this betrayal?'

'You cannot trust anyone. This is an era of great portent where nothing is clear. Do not believe what they say.'

Jory shook his head in frustration. 'What who say? What do you mean?'

Caja glanced at him anxiously.

Again the mysterious smile. 'We will not disturb the future and its reckonings. It is all we can divulge.'

'Well, what's the use in telling us then!' blurted Jory abruptly his temper flaring. 'Who aren't we meant to trust? Everyone? Is that all you can tell us? You're pretty bloody useless.'

Caja screwed up her eyes in frustration. This was not good.

The emerald eyes of the leader darkened, as did her silvery skin to a dull stormy bronze. All the naiad's laughter stopped instantaneously, and everything around them, including the sparkle of the water, seemed to fade. Anger gleamed in the eyes of all three, changing colour dramatically to a glinting obsidian. Without warning they rose, and grabbing hold of Jory's feet pulled him swiftly into the water, before diving under and dragging him down with them. Caja did not have time to think let alone object; before she knew it there was no one there, and she was left alone on her boulder. The water had turned almost immediately still and serene. She sat completely stationary, momentarily stunned, mouth open.

And then she began to yell. 'Jory, Jory! Hey naiads! Bring him back! Where've you taken him? Jory, come back!'

What could she do? She swiftly clambered off the boulder, slipping in her hurry to reach the ground. Taking off her shoes she tentatively dipped her feet into the cool water. But what was she thinking? What could she do in the lake? She stood paralysed by indecision. Should she race back to Ennor and Talwin's or would it be too late by then? Should she try to rescue Jory herself? But how? She groaned in desperation and without a plan started to wade into the water.

'Jory! Jory. Please bring him back. Please. He didn't mean anything. He's just got a temper. Please, please…,' she cried as she waded deeper and deeper. She did not notice the tears that began to fall and trickle down her cheeks. Eventually one rolled off the end of her chin and faintly plopped into the clear, jade waters of the lake. At this the waters rippled again, and the naiad in charge silently appeared.

'What is it Caja? Why the tears?' she purred softly.

'Oh thank goodness…You're back. Please bring Jory back. I know he's a pain and rude but please bring him back. He's my friend. I'll do anything.'

'Anything Caja?'

'Yes, anything. Tell me what I must do to bring him back.'

The naiad stared intently at her, considering for a moment. 'Very well. There will be a time in the future when we'll need you. You must promise to help us when we call for you.'

'Yes, yes. I promise-'

But the end of Caja's sentence was cut short as the naiad rose out of the water and snatched hold of Caja's hand with her own. The naiad's slim hand was cold and damp, like that of a lizard. 'You understand you will have no choice. You must come to us when we call,' she murmured a glint of darkness in her eyes.

'Yes, yes. Anything. Of course. I'll come.'

The naiad smiled enigmatically, and raising her other hand out of the water placed something soft and completely dry in

Caja's hand. 'For you, to help on your journey. We're not all so unkind. You will find it of some use in the not too distant future.'

Caja looked down, and gasped in surprise. It was the turquoise scarf that her Aunt had given her on her first day back at school.

'But how-? Where?' she stuttered. But looking up she found that the naiad had gone and the lake was quite still again. She glanced around uncertainly before wading back out of the water to dry land, hastily stuffing the scarf back into her trouser pocket. Perhaps they'd send Jory straight back to Gwydhenn? She soon found out that this was not the case however, as a gasping, bedraggled Jory was catapulted out of the water chest first, landing on the ground next to her with a loud thud accompanied by copious amounts of moaning and panting.

'Bloody naiads….Could've drowned,' he panted.

'Well why do you have to be so bloody quick-tempered all the time!' yelled Caja, her distress quickly turning to anger. Crouching down next to him she picked up a small stick, 'What… did… you… think….shouting at…them….would…achieve?' she bawled striking him on his back and legs with every word.

'Ow, get off. I almost drowned you know. You're going to finish me off! Get off me Caja!'

Caja stopped hitting him and sighing in disgust stood up. 'Is this why you're covered in bruises? Are you always letting your temper get the better of you?' she demanded.

'Could be…' muttered Jory quietly standing up slowly with a look of shame on his face. 'Come on, let's get out of here before they change their minds.' Before she could say any more he was making his way quickly back along the path, drenched and shivering, with much stumbling and laboured breath.

They completed their trip back in total silence, Caja as usual barely able to keep up with Jory marching ahead. Eventually, they turned a corner and entered once again into

Gwydhenn's glade, relieved to be home again. They were both unsettled to see two horses outside the cottage, evidently worn out from an arduous ride, their coats shining with sweat. Two men were standing beside the horses talking with great agitation to Ennor and Talwin. It was clear that something was going on.

'Gorran! Why I didn't expect to see you here!' cried Jory, yelling out to one of the men who turned at the call of his name.

Now Caja could see he was younger than he had first appeared, in fact only a few years older than Jory. Gorran looked startled for a moment before quickly recovering and walking towards Jory with a welcoming grin of recognition. As he strode towards them he stared at Caja with keen interest.

Caja could see she was probably going to have to get used to a lot of attention in this strange land; she knew she looked quite different to the locals of Kernow. But she did not mind so much getting attention from him.

'My friend Jory. I am surprised to find you here,' he said shaking Jory's hand vigorously, 'those Villants usually keep you on a tighter leash. What are you doing here? And why are you so wet?' He spoke with the tilting lilt of a Welshman.

'Ah, just been bathing, having a dip in the um...lake. Ennor and Talwin are my Great Uncle and Aunt,' replied Jory proudly, 'but what brings you here Gorran?'

Gorran looked appraisingly at Jory at this evidently new information, 'ho, you never did tell me that! That is even more of a surprise. I've come with Natan Palina of West Wivel, son of Noblewoman Amarisa and Ryol. He has grave news from the North. We've heard rumours that Nobleman Kilmar has joined Menadue, and now he's trying to persuade Bramby of Stratton to join them too. And there's been another incident of wolves attacking a village. Although this time they were joined by hobgoblins. They wreaked havoc. Seven dead I believe…' Gorran looked sadly away and then turned brightening, 'but Jory you're being uncivilised. Who is your lovely, new friend?'

Caja's face reddened at this unexpected flattery.

'Gorran, this is Caja, my friend from, um... Albion. Caja, this is Gorran, my good friend from Kembra. He's been in Kernow for over a year now working in our village. Gorran is an excellent silversmith. He's been in quite high demand from the druids.'

'It's an honour to make your acquaintance Caja,' said Gorran bowing elegantly to her.

'And yours,' said Caja frowning in slight bewilderment, and attempting an awkward curtsey that turned into something more akin to a ballet pose. She hurriedly straightened up as Jory let out a bark of laughter, which turned into a spluttering cough under Caja's glare.

'Come my friends. We must discuss the situation further with Ennor and Talwin,' said Gorran patting Jory on his back. 'Although I much regret that there's not time for more talk,' he said directing this last comment at Caja.

He was certainly most attractive, Caja reflected as they both followed him to where the others were standing. Gorran was tall with lavishly thick hair, unusually full lips and a copper-hinted skin tone that Caja would have killed for. He was dressed casually in an open-necked shirt revealing a cord around his neck dangling some sort of cross. He held himself with confidence and evident self-assurance reminding Caja of a film star from her own world.

'Caja, Jory. Our plans have changed,' said Talwin bluntly as they approached, staring at Jory's wet clothes inquiringly for a moment before continuing on. 'You must leave tonight, as soon as possible. Ennor and I can no longer come with you. We must ride to North Kernow. It seems almost certain that Nobleman John Kilmar has taken sides with Menadue and may now be attempting to turn Nobleman Bramby. We must try and talk to Bramby before he gets to him. Helena will meet you at Blake Manor. She'll be riding back from the South and will arrive tomorrow.'

Ennor turned from talking to the stranger, 'Jory, we didn't

want to put you under such pressure so early on, but we hope you'll be able to guide Caja to Truro. Do you know your way?'

Jory agreed eagerly. 'Yes, yes, I've been many times before to help Uncle Cardew take the stock to market. I know the way. I'm happy to be of help Ennor.'

'That is good Jory,' he replied adding in a lower tone, 'there may be cause for you to use your magic, but we hope not. We don't believe you'll encounter any dangers on your way.'

Jory looked solemn. 'Yes. I understand Ennor. I'll do all I can.'

Ennor, looking comforted by his earnestness, clapped him on his sodden back, glancing at his damp hand for a second before motioning towards the stranger. 'Caja, Jory this is Natan Palina, son of Noblewoman Palina. Natan this is Jory Hobart and Caja Delaney.'

The tall bald man with a stern face gave them a grimace which Caja assumed was meant to be a smile, 'I am pleased to make your acquaintance. Jory…Hobart,' he mused, 'are you not the son of those two Tellurics of questionable repute, Cynthia and Pedrog?'

Jory's face darkened and before anyone could do anything he had launched himself at Natan with his fist bunched and ready to punch. Ennor's reaction was quicker than the eye could see. His arm shot out, and before he knew it, Jory flew backwards and was thrown headfirst into a particularly prickly bush.

'Jory!' bellowed Ennor in anger, 'Can't you control yourself?'

Caja heaved in frustration; here we go again she thought.

Natan, looking shocked at the outburst, muttered some words of consternation to Talwin who made some conciliatory efforts to calm him down. Gorran was shaking his head in evident disquiet although with a trace of amusement.

Jory was labouring to free himself from the spiky bush,

pulling himself bit by bit carefully free of the thorns. His anger had abated as quickly as it had arisen and his whole body was submissive.

'Jory, you should not let such small things have so much power and control over you.' said Talwin softly.

Jory paused in his efforts to untangle himself, his shoulders drooping, 'yes, you're right Talwin,' he said quietly, 'Natan Palina, I must offer my sincere apologies. My actions were quite unacceptable.'

Natan blustering somewhat accepted the apology, 'hmfff…well…yes. You should try to control yourself you know young lad. Your behaviour will certainly not be tolerated at Ambrosius Academy.'

In an attempt to further diffuse the situation Talwin led Jory and Caja inside dismissing Gorran's attempt to join them, 'we must talk of their trip to Blake Manor, Gorran. They've an important task. You stay outside and tell Ennor as much as you can about what you know of John Kilmar and his actions.'

Once they were safely inside out of earshot, she motioned urgently to them, 'now Caja, Jory. We must prepare you for your journey ahead. You'll be staying with Noblewoman Ivy in Templeton Castle tonight in Powder. If you leave soon you will be there before nightfall and then you can reach Truro tomorrow morning. We don't want you travelling at night.' As she talked she busied herself preparing food for their journey.

She stopped for a moment looking at them steadily. 'Now, it's vital that you don't tell anyone else about the staff. Helena is the only one who knows what you're searching for. You can trust her. But do not tell anyone else. Do you understand?'

Caja and Jory nodded readily, earnest looks upon their faces.

'Once our work is completed in North Kernow, Ennor and I will come and join you at Blake Manor. We can help you use the staff to open a gate that's quite near to the

Manor. Caja, we believe you may be the only one who is able to actually retrieve the staff. As the Prophecy says. You can do this but do not try to use it! It has great, immense power, and the potential to cause incredible harm. Do you understand?'

Again Jory and Caja nodded their heads meekly.

'Now take this,' said Talwin handing some crumpled looking pieces of paper. 'This is all the information we have on the staff. Helena will be able to tell you more.'

'Thank you,' said Jory taking the papers and putting them carefully inside his shirt. 'Talwin, can I ask one thing?' he enquired submissively.

'Yes Jory, what is it?'

'If the threat is so great and there's now all this evidence of Menadue's existence, why does the Order of Avalon or Kernow Assembly not do anything?'

Talwin shrugged her shoulders in a defeated gesture, 'the Order of Avalon and Kernow Assembly are being their usual stubborn and argumentative selves and still refuse to believe that Menadue could be a threat. Some of them knew him before he went away, and can't believe he is this evil force that we keep talking of. There is just so much infighting amongst the Nobles, they don't have much time for anything else. We've decided to move ahead without them for now, as the threat is too great. Although we hope to get a vote in the Assembly soon to get the Nobles on our side and their knights at least readied for action.'

Knights! thought Caja in wonder. All this talk of Nobles, and magic staffs, and now knights. There was so much to take in. And now they would be off again on another trip to goodness knows where.

'...and Caja right away' she heard Jory saying as he moved towards the front door.

'Yes, yes,' she agreed hurriedly following Jory as he hastened outside, 'of course, right away.' She tried to look as if she knew what they were doing.

'What we doing?' she whispered to Jory as they emerged

into the glade where Ennor, Natan and Gorran were deep in discussion. Jory looked at her with a raised eyebrow, 'we're getting the horses ready to ride to Truro. I'm to take Saraid, you're to take Parsley again. Right?'

'Yep, of course. Let's get the horses ready. Oh god, do we have to ride horses again?'

'Naturally, how else would we get there? It would take us days on foot,' he replied.

'I don't know. Maybe there's a train station nearby? Or a quick ride by car down the nearest motorway would be good. It'd be a lot quicker and way more comfortable. I'd even settle for Boris in favour of a horse' muttered Caja.

Jory looked at her in incomprehension, and shaking his head entered the small stable.

As they were preparing the horses, Gorran hastened into the stable eager to talk to them before their departure. 'So you're off to Truro hey?'

Jory answered whilst bent kneeling fixing Saraid's saddle, 'yes, we should be there tomorrow. And you're off to East Wivel?'

'Yes, Natan and I leave for East Wivel straight away to try and see where Salisbury stands. It should not be a long ride though, and after I must go to Blake Manor to report to Noblewoman Blake. I hope to see you both again there.'

'Oh yes, that'd be great,' replied Caja quickly. Jory nodded in agreement.

Before they knew it they were saddled up and astride their horses ready for their journey ahead.

'Now take these letters for Noblewoman Templeton, to verify your identity. And be warned about Noblewoman Helena Blake. Do not stare at her, she does not like it,' cautioned Talwin as they said their goodbyes.

'Why, what's wrong with her?' asked Caja curiously as she attempted to make Parsley stand still.

'You'll find out,' replied Ennor shortly, 'now you must go, do not tarry. You have far to go this afternoon if you are to reach the Templetons of Powder before nightfall.'

'And try not to anger Noblewoman Templeton, Jory Hobart. She is easily riled,' yelled Talwin after them as they cantered away out of the peaceful glade. and westwards towards the setting sun.

CHAPTER FIVE

Menadue Enfer raised his hand to drink from the burnished bronze tumbler, dripping the remnants of the dark, cherry-red liquid into his mouth with exaggerated care. His unusually pointed tongue flicked out to lick the last remaining droplets from his thin, pallid lips. Sitting back slowly, he frowned faintly, staring out of the small aperture hacked into the bulky castle walls.

Despite being remarkably pale and thin to the point of emaciation he was an exceptionally striking man with shrewd piercing eyes, clear though waxen skin and a powerful jawline. Bruised shadows ringed his cobalt eyes, highlighting the stormy hues that flittered across his irises. Only a slight twitch of his upper lip, known by only a few, gave any indication of the mounting rage he was feeling. The GateKeeper's entrance into Kernow had taken him unawares and he did not like to be surprised. This, followed by the failure to stop her early on had turned the situation problematic, and certain issues were beginning to threaten his carefully laid plans.

He sat up abruptly, 'Rizno!' he yelled in a coarse voice. There was a scurrying from the adjoining room and within moments a diminutive and gnarled creature had entered and began bowing in front of Menadue.

'Yes, Master, what is it you wish of me?'

'I wish you to bring those distasteful cousins of yours to me. I require them to carry out an errand.'

'Of course Master,' replied Rizno obsequiously, lowering his bald, wrinkled head once again to the dusty ground and backing out of the room.

Menadue continued to stare with keen concentration out of the narrow window that gave him a glimpse of the rugged Northern coastline. His mind was entirely focused upon his plans. Over the years, he had achieved the invaluable skill of being able to concentrate resolutely upon a single thought, and with this a certain mastery over his mind. This had led him to scorn the meanderings of most men's minds, and their habit of weaving their lives in a randomly chaotic manner, with barely any control over the paths their existence took.

His eyes narrowed almost indiscernibly as he heard the sounds of footsteps signaling the arrival of visitors downstairs. They had arrived. Compared to mortal men his senses were remarkably keen; from their distant footsteps he could hear how many had entered the hall, and fathom the state of their minds. A wry smile played across his face; they were more agitated and nervous than he expected. They doubtless believed he had found out about their plans to wrestle power from the hobgoblins, which of course he had, but he had no intention of discussing that now. There was a curt knock at the door.

Menadue managed to respond in a voice both quiet and intensely commanding, 'enter.'

Rizno carefully opened the door and crossed the threshold with three of his cousins, their black eyes peering around furtively. Menadue did not look around.

'I have brought my worthless cousins Master,' croaked Rizno.

Menadue leisurely spun his chair around, wrinkling his nose in disgust. 'Bring them closer. Although not too close. Their rank smell irritates me. Who is their leader?'

One of the slightly larger cousins stepped forward, a strained look upon his face, 'I, Master. What is it that you wish of us?' There was an unsteady tremor in his voice.

Menadue gave a half-smile. 'I wish you to take care of a little problem for me.'

There was a pause as the leader continued to stare at a spot just besides Menadue's feet, 'y...yes, of course Master. We would be honoured to help. What is this problem?'

Menadue eyed the leader thoughtfully, 'I want you to find two humans who are causing me some minor trouble. A girl and a boy. You must bring the girl to me. The boy you can do what you like with. But the girl you must bring to me, alive and relatively unharmed.'

'Yes Master. We will do as you bid. Where might we find these two children?'

'They will be making their way from West Wivel to Templeton Castle, then on to Truro. You must be quick. They're already on their way.'

'We'll leave straight away. You are most kind Master, giving us the boy.'

Menadue's eyes darkened in disgust, 'I don't want to know what you do with him. Just bring me the girl.'

'Of course Master, we'll bring the girl...we will bring her.' His slavering words faded as the three of them turned and hurried out of the hall, clearly anxious to leave Menadue's presence as soon as possible.

Rizno remained, waiting patiently until, after several moments, his Master spoke again. 'They're quite loathsome creatures. But vicious I will give them that. Although their taste in food leaves much to be desired.'

Rizno bowed slightly as he spoke, 'I believe they'll be able to bring back the girl to you Master. They're quite formidable trackers. They'll have caught up with the children in no time.'

Menadue nodded his head measuredly without looking at Rizno, 'hmmm....we shall see. We shall see. In the meantime....' His hand spun out as he spoke and a stark light radiated out from it. At almost the same time an enormous spasm shuddered through his body, his hand plummeted as if pulled to the ground by some unseen force, and he toppled out of his chair, his body wracked with invisible convulsions, as the jug on the table opposite fell with a crash to the floor.

Rizno approached hurriedly although somewhat warily, a look of apprehension upon his face. 'Master?'

Menadue lay rigid upon the harsh stone floor, violent judders running up and down the entire length of his stiff body, his breath held, and his glazed eyes focused straight above. He did not respond. Rizno stood waiting. With a huge breath, Menadue expelled an enormous gasp and the whole of his body released, sinking gratefully into the floor. The vicious spasms stopped.

He turned to look at Rizno, 'well help me up then you fool!' he commanded, his voice still authoritative although weak.

Rizno rushed to his side, pulling up his Master by the arm and assisting him into his chair. Menadue sat still for several moments breathing heavily.

Rizno approached tentatively, 'they seem to be getting more frequent Master.'

Menadue closed his eyes, 'yes I have noticed Rizno.'

'It's important that we find the girl quickly.'

'Yes Rizno it is. She will help us with our plans. And it seems that I do not have as much time as I thought.'

*

Jory and Caja found themselves once again crossing over the plateau of moors that made up the backbone of Kernow, running the entire length of the land. They cantered along, Jory confident and stable on Talwin's piebald Saraid, Caja awkward and flustered on the plodding Parsley.

With some difficulty Caja managed to keep abreast of Jory. 'So, how d'you know Gorran?' she asked nonchalantly.

Jory gave her a sideways glance accompanied by a faint, knowing grin, 'Gorran arrived in Trethewyn a few summers back. He has managed to obtain plenty of silversmith work here, especially with the druids. He visits the farm quite often, and we have taken to hunting together as well as spending an odd night here and there in the tavern. I'm not surprised to find him caught up in the alliance against Menadue, although he's never mentioned anything to me. I knew he was doing some work for Noblewoman Palina so she must have got him involved in it all. He often talks of his hatred of all dark magic. I think he has had some run in with it.'

'Does he live near you in Trethewyn?'

'He does live nearby, in a small cottage he's rented out. Anyway why are you so interested in Gorran?' asked Jory.

Caja shrugged her shoulders indifferently, 'oh no reason. No, no. Not at all. So who's this Ivy Templeton we're going to be staying with tonight. And why would Talwin warn you not to annoy her?' she said hurriedly changing topics.

'Ivy Templeton's a well-respected Noblewoman. Her Hundred is the largest in the land. She married Tristan Templeton when she was very young and still famed for her beauty. After the death of her son however, and then only a few years later the death of her husband Tristan, she became somewhat of a recluse and better known for her irritable nature. It's told that she will only tolerate a couple of helpers in her castle and that many do not last a week. Reportedly, she once chased a helper all the way out of the castle with a broom and through the streets of the village. Just because the helper had forgotten to place her slippers by her bed. I've heard that she's been seen wandering the moors at night calling for her son, although it's over a decade since he died.'

Caja gazed ahead absent-mindedly, 'that's quite sad isn't it?' she sighed, 'so why are we staying with her?'

'Templeton Castle is almost exactly half-way on our journey to Truro. And Talwin believes we'll be safe there. Although she's a little barmy, Noblewoman Ivy will never join Menadue's forces. Unlike some other Nobles she totally believes he's evil. Anyway I'm quite intrigued to meet her, she has such a reputation and I've only glimpsed her once when she passed through my village with an escort of knights.'

They made haste across the countryside, keen not to

spend the night in the wilderness again, vulnerable to the dark creatures that often emerged under the blanket of night. The scenery around Caja was once again so familiar but at the same time so different.

Low slung clouds grazed the tops of the rugged moor peaks as they passed broadleaf oaks, willows and silver birches with leaves that fluttered in the wind like the rippling of a multitude of silver coins, reminding her of home. This was a much more untamed landscape than Cornwall however; there was a wilderness and rawness to Kernow that she could almost taste in the air, accompanied by a disquieting feeling that anything could happen here.

Occasionally, they would pass by other travellers, dressed in a similar fashion to Jory, but they would always avert their eyes and hurry away.

'Everyone's so unfriendly these days,' sighed Jory, 'there is so much suspicion and fear brewing.'

At last, just as the sun was setting and a cold wind was beginning to blow in determinedly from the sea, they came to the grand, wrought iron gates of Templeton Castle, where the family had resided for many centuries. The imposing entrance was closed and securely locked preventing access to the castle grounds which were surrounded by a high wall made from the distinctive Cornish stone.

'Not very welcoming is it? How are visitors meant to get in or let anyone know they are here?' grumbled Caja as they began searching along the wall looking for a way in. Trotting along was difficult work as the area around the walls was neglected and their path was often blocked by thorny brambles and impenetrable bush. After some searching Jory was able to find a section of the wall that had caved in leaving a tight gap which they could squeeze through, although they had to leave their horses behind, tied to a tree.

Caja pulled a face of disgust as she wedged herself through the wall, tangling herself in plant stems and roots, and covering herself in clammy cobwebs.

'I'm stuck,' she moaned to Jory, 'really I can't move.

There's a huge spider web in the way.'

'Come on Caja. Just pull yourself through. You're almost there,' replied Jory who had already gone through with an ease that mystified her, especially as he was bigger than her despite his skinniness.

There was a rustling noise behind her, and glancing back she saw a dense bush moving and then heard what sounded almost like muted sniggering. She hurriedly pulled the rest of her body through gaining some scrapes in the process, coming to stand next to Jory who was staring up at Templeton Castle in wonder. Caja certainly did not want to spend the night outside these walls.

'Wow, that is one spooky looking castle,' she said staring with Jory up at Templeton Castle. It was a majestic, turreted castle set out in a classic square formation with lofty towers situated at each of the four corners and tattered, decaying flags fluttering in the breeze. Although still intact, the castle looked completely uncared-for and dilapidated with a supremely gloomy air. The narrow windows were all darkened, and the walls were completely covered in snaking weeds and some sort of fungal growth that hid the colour of the castle completely.

They started trudging up the lengthy, pot-holed driveway. The grounds around them were also unkempt, full of tumbling weeds, and overgrown plants. Finally they arrived at the castle, and found themselves in front of a gigantic, iron studded door.

'Does anyone actually live here?' asked Jory in mystification.

'We shall soon find out,' said Caja grabbing hold of the deformed creature's head that served as a knocker, and lifting it up high she banged it exceptionally hard against the door three times. It made a huge din scaring some squawking crows out of a nearby willow tree.

'Sure you did that loud enough?' Jory chuckled, 'that should have woken them up!'

Caja raised her eyebrows at him with a grin scrunching up

her nose in amusement. After a few minutes of silence they heard slow footsteps accompanied by muttering, and then a scratching as the door was unlocked, followed by a long-drawn out creaking as the thick door shuffled hesitantly open.

'Wasup?' said Caja at the ancient, stooped lady with close-cut, grey hair who stood glaring at them. She appeared absolutely tiny, framed as she was in the entrance of the giant doorway backlit by the dim light beyond.

Jory glanced at Caja with a bemused look before turning to the old woman. 'Good evening. We are here to speak with Noblewoman Templeton and request her hospitality for the night. We have a letter for her from mutual friends.'

The old lady stared at them suspiciously for a few uncomfortable moments, 'well…hand it over then,' she croaked in a voice entirely befitting her aged and wrinkled appearance.

Jory handed over the letter from his pack whilst continuing to smile in an increasingly strained manner. There was a silence as the old woman stared at them some more, distrust written all over her face.

Finally she rasped with exasperation, 'well what are your names?'

'Ah of course. Jory Hobart and this is Caja Delaney.'

Before he had even finished the old crone had turned and headed back inside, slamming the door shut behind her with surprising strength from a flick of one of her emaciated wrists. Jory and Caja hurriedly stepped back.

'I think she liked us,' said Caja raising her eyebrow sarcastically.

'This should be an interesting night,' responded Jory regarding the bleak stonewalls.

They waited again for some time before they heard the shaky footsteps of the lady slowly approaching on the other side of the door. Again the heavy creaking as the door groaned open.

'My name is Reena. Follow me,' she whispered hoarsely.

The entrance hallway to the castle was dimly lit by

flickering candles set in rickety candelabra. Inside, the castle was as forbidding and bleak as it was on the outside. A once magnificent staircase swept up from the hallway splitting into two. They followed Reena up the mouldy, crimson carpet that coated the stairs taking the staircase to the left. Moth-nibbled tapestries lined the walls depicting scenes from a violent past; knights engaged in tremendous clashes and blood-soaked battle scenes involving creatures that Caja had never before imagined, including what looked suspiciously like a dragon.

They passed numerous closed doorways until they reached one that was slightly ajar, a faint light beckoning from within. Reena reached out one trembling hand to push the door further open revealing a small sitting room, and another elderly woman sitting upright at a writing desk, a weak fire spluttering beside her in a fireplace. Besides the desk and a rather ragged looking armchair, there was no other furniture in the room. The lady turned in her chair as they entered peering at them in the lacklustre light warily. She was younger than Reena but life had certainly not been kind to her. She was tall with deep crevices etched in her face that painted a permanent frown, and shrewd dark eyes that contrasted brilliantly against her snow-white hair.

'Come closer children so that I may see you. My eyesight is not what it used to be,' said Noblewoman Ivy Templeton in a vigorous though somewhat drained voice. At this, her hand swayed carefully upwards, and the fire immediately grew stronger lighting up the room.

Jory and Caja edged closer towards her, the fire casting flickering light onto their faces.

Noblewoman Ivy suddenly started, 'you girl, who are you? I didn't catch your last name.'

'Caja Delaney, Noblewoman Templeton,' whispered Caja, her confidence waning under the scrutiny of this rather stern and regal woman.

At the mention of her name Ivy scowled, 'but it can't be. Who are your parents?'

'Uh Ben and Tarlia Delaney. But they are no longer alive,' muttered a subdued Caja.

Ivy stared at her with a look of deep shock tinged with sadness. Then she looked away in mistrust, evidently immersed in thought.

Turning back after some minutes she muttered, 'so you're on your way to Truro to help my friends Ennor and Talwin Quintrall I gather?'

'Yes, Noblewoman Ivy. We're going to Truro to stay with Noblewoman Blake,' answered Jory.

Ivy stared at him aggressively, 'and why d'you go there? Ennor and Talwin tell me it's to help in the fight against this abominable Menadue. But why the Blake's Manor? What do you plan to do there?'

Jory regarded her nervously, 'uh….we…well….we cannot say Noblewoman Templeton. Talwin swore us to secrecy.'

Templeton's frown deepened, 'Talwin is my friend. She would not mind you telling me,' she demanded.

Jory did not look at her, 'I'm sorry Noblewoman Templeton but really we can't.'

Ivy Templeton threw the pen she was holding down on the desk in disgust, 'so this is how you repay my hospitality, with suspicion and distrust. Now go away, the both of you. I've already been disturbed enough tonight. Leave me in peace. Reena will show you to your rooms.'

Reena who had been waiting impatiently in the doorway coughed loudly, 'yes Lady Templeton. Most certainly. That is of course my role. I can't think of anything better to do with my time than wait on wandering children day and night.'

'Oh get on with it Reena, you are a disobliging old fool,' retorted Ivy.

Reena glared at her mumbling almost incoherently, 'I used to wipe your bottom when you were but a wee little girl…' before announcing in a haughty tone, 'well, goodnight Noblewoman Templeton. I trust you will sleep peacefully with no disturbances.' Sweeping a long, graceful and highly exaggerated bow she ushered Caja and Jory out of the room.

Ivy continued to glower at them all as they departed although Caja could have sworn she heard a quiet chuckle from inside the room after they had left.

The rooms Caja and Jory were to sleep in for the night adjoined each other by a shared bathroom. Caja's room was as she expected, containing an ancient four-poster bed, with decaying ruby-red canopy and curtains, and stuffed beasts with eerie, staring eyes placed in menacing positions around the room.

Reena left them as soon as she could after setting up a table in Caja's room with a simple supper of meats, breads and cheese. Jory had managed to persuade Reena to send one of the stable hands to bring their horses in and feed them, which had relieved him immensely. Caja felt a little guilty as she had completely forgotten about them. They then sat chatting and eating companionably on her rather lumpy bed dropping crumbs and bits of food all over the worn, itchy sheets.

Jory, who always seemed to be hungry, spoke through a mouthful of cheese. 'She looked quite interested in you. I wonder why she wanted to know who your parents were?'

'Yeah, I know. I think I'm going to be something of a novelty here. I look quite different to everyone else. I guess I am from a totally different world though,' replied Caja.

'Well, I think I would quite like to visit your world if they all look like you,' replied Jory munching on some bread. He paused looking embarrassed before hurriedly carrying on, 'what's it like your world anyway?'

Caja described to him some of the things in her own world. Although she was sure Jory did not quite understand all her talk of trains, cars, computers, and iPods, he seemed truly intrigued. Their talk ventured onto their upbringings and once again they found common ground on having both lost their parents so young. They found themselves talking easily and openly about their experiences, from solitary Christmases as the only child, to imaginary friends to keep them company.

'So what d'you think of all this prophecy talk Jory?' asked Caja cautiously, 'd'you think I am the GateKeeper mentioned in that Prophecy?'

Jory took a moment to think, 'yes, I do Caja. Talwin explained some of it to me, and it seems pretty evident it's you. It's essential we find the Legacy before Menadue does. We've an important role to play here Caja,' he added solemnly. 'Without the Legacy the Twofold Power can't defeat the Dark.'

Caja looked confused, 'the Twofold Power? What is that?'

'From the Prophecy. It's the Twofold Power that must destroy the Dark, aided by the Legacy. Talwin and Ennor are not sure what this Twofold Power is yet, although I think they might have an idea. It's the only thing Merlin tells us that can destroy the Dark.'

Caja looked thoughtful and then asked cautiously, 'so…so is it true? Are your parents really on the…on the other side Jory?'

Jory's face paled. 'I've said already Caja. I don't want to talk about it.'

'But do you know if they are even still alive? What if-?'

'I…don't….want to TALK about it,' Jory interrupted in a yell. 'I come from bad stock and that's that. There's nothing I can do about it! Now I'm tired. I'm going to bed.'

And with that he jumped off the bed and disappeared into his own room. Caja was left open-mouthed and dismayed. She had upset Jory yet again. She did seem to have a knack of doing that; her and her big mouth. With a heavy sigh she cleared the crumbs from her sheets, clambered into the enormous musty bed and was soon fast asleep.

*

The sun rose the next morning illuminating the top stories and spires of Templeton Castle, seeping down through the upper floors to the bedrooms, and finally lighting up the ground-floor rooms. Caja was awoken by the bright light shining through the holes in the curtain and not long after that by a loud, clanging sound and the noise of Reena's weedy voice from the corridor yelling, 'wake up you lazy good for nothing brats!'

'Lovely,' she muttered, hopping out of bed and sniffing suspiciously at her dirty top before throwing on her clothes. She opened the door to the bathroom and yelled out, 'Jory! You up yet! I think Reena might have us some breakfast ready.'

Jory appeared from his room, his hair lopsided and scruffy, pulling on his worn shirt over protruding ribs and a concave stomach covered in raw, red lumps.

Noticing Caja's stare he said dismissively, 'oh they're the bed bug bites from my Uncle and Aunt's. Hopefully they'll clear up soon. Goodness I slept well. And boy am I hungry again.' They clattered down the worn stairs emerging into the stately hall, and made their way to the dining room adjoining the kitchen where noises of banging and muttered swearing could be heard.

Reena's head appeared from around the door. 'Up at last I see. It's true what they say. Laziness a common trait of the young eh? You two stay in there and I will bring you what I can for breakfast. Noblewoman Templeton will be down shortly.'

Jory and Caja pulled out some huge chairs and seated themselves at the even more enormous, ebony dining table. Hanging all around the room glaring at them were portraits of the Templeton's ancestors, all now long gone.

'I think that old fuddy one looks a bit like you,' said Jory with a laugh pointing to a particularly ugly looking portrait of a man with auburn curls almost exactly like Caja's.

'That is my late husband's father, Tristan the Elder,' came the stern voice of Ivy Templeton as she entered the room glaring indignantly at them both. 'It's his great hospitality that you have been enjoying, as it was he who restored Templeton Castle and brought prosperity back to the Templetons,' she carried on, her brow furrowing even further.

'Of course, Noblewoman Templeton. I'm sure your ancestors were all very…um…illus...illustrious,' stuttered Jory stumbling over the word.

'And we are very grateful for your hospitality and …um…that of your ancestors,' added Caja appeasingly.

Ivy eyed them both suspiciously and then lowered herself slowly into one of the chairs at the head of the table. At that moment they were greeted by Reena's skinny rear emerging through the twin swing doors from the kitchen. She swivelled around bearing a large tray in her hands laden with breakfast. Scowling fiercely and muttering under her breath she placed the tray on a sideboard before individually serving them all with eggs, and some odd vegetable that looked a lot like regurgitated cauliflower. She finished it all by slamming down some toast and jams on the table setting all the crockery rattling.

Caja tried eliciting a smile from her, 'thank you Reena. This looks delicious.' But this seemed to have the opposite effect of deepening her scowl even further.

After some moments of silence with Reena standing glaring and neither Caja nor Jory daring to say anything else, Ivy abruptly spoke up. 'Oh for goodness sake Reena. You're not still in a huff over yesterday. You've got a face like a smacked chicken. Do cheer up.'

At this, Reena's face darkened and giving Ivy a look of pure contempt she stated with greatly forced composure, 'well, I wouldn't want to inflict my misery upon anyone else. I will leave the rest of the serving to you, and will retire to my own quarters. Enjoy your breakfast.' And with that she departed.

Ivy rolled her eyes dramatically and started eating her food, a faint look of smug satisfaction upon her face.

They ate the rest of the meal in silence with Jory's attempts at polite questions failing to elicit any conversation whilst Caja chewed on the cream vegetable with unconcealed dislike. A couple of times, she looked up to find Ivy's gaze focused directly upon her, but the Noblewoman would instantly turn away and resume eating.

At the end of their meal Jory thanked Ivy for her hospitality, 'you've been most kind Noblewoman Templeton, a trait for which I believe your family are known. My Aunt told me she saw you and your son nearly thirty years ago when he was just a boy. Even then he was most generous to the villagers. He-'

'Do not talk of my son!' interrupted Ivy shrilly, a sharp pain evident in her taut face, 'he is dead. And I'll not have his memory desecrated by the likes of you. He was...' She gulped heavily, unable to finish her sentence, and standing up abruptly she threw her napkin from her lap onto the table and marched to the door. She turned and stated with some effort, 'I...I am glad you have enjoyed your stay. I hope the rest of your journey fares well.' And with that she stormed out of the room.

Caja winced at Jory. 'Think she's a bit sensitive about her son Jory. Probably shouldn't bring that up again.'

'I think I got that. Let's get out of here. It'll be good to get to Truro early and hopefully we'll receive a warmer welcome there.'

Before long they found themselves on their way again, both Jory and Caja happy to be away from the stuffy castle with the two bickering old women. Their horses had been well rested and fed, and they set off at a lively pace with Parsley unusually, pulling to go faster. The undulating landscape of moor and slate-grey rock went quickly past. Jory, in a chatty mood pointed out objects of interest including sacred druidic wells, much to Caja's delight, and the small 'kellies' or groves of trees where local villagers would meet with the elusive druids to ask for their sagely advice.

'The people don't go to the Druids so much anymore though,' he explained, 'they're more likely to go to a Zard or someone who trained at Ambrosius Academy now. They don't have to put up with all the rituals and sacrifices with them.'

'Sacrifices?' asked Caja curiously. 'What kind of sacrifices?'
'Bulls, goats, boars. Animals mostly.'
'Mostly?'
'Well, there have been rumours that some of the Druids made human sacrifices. But I've never heard it confirmed.'

Finally they came to a narrow cleft that ran through a low range of hills, which Jory explained was a short cut to Truro. As they passed through the granite gorge, the sounds of the birds seemed to quieten. It was an overcast day and the sky had gradually darkened with heavier clouds during their journey. The sounds of their horses' hooves on the ground suddenly appeared abnormally loud. Then Caja heard it. A muted giggle. Just like the one she had heard before, outside the stony walls of Templeton Castle.

'Jory, did you hear that?' she hissed urgently.

Jory turned in his saddle to look at her quizzically. 'No,' he said shaking his head, 'hear what? Do you hear something?'

Again another snigger, this time from somewhere just ahead and above them. Jory stared intently around this time, trying to find the source of the noise.

He turned with a worried look on his face, 'I think I should–'

But his next comment was drowned out as suddenly there were spine-tingling shrieks from all around them, and small dark creatures were jumping out from behind the boulders that made up the gorge.

'Piskies!' yelled Jory in dread, 'Caja, follow me!' He turned his horse around to head back out of the narrow gorge but Parsley had gone into a panic and was prancing around in utter terror, completely out of Caja's control, entangling his bridle and Caja in one of the stooping trees that clung onto the sides of the gorge.

There were five of the terrifying creatures and they were all squealing and advancing upon Caja and Jory with vicious and determined looks upon their faces. They were small but formidable looking, about half the size of Jory with small heads and beady coal black eyes with no discernible irises.

Their lips were drawn back revealing rows of sharpened teeth and their wide nostrils were flaring in gleeful anticipation of a fight. They were brandishing lethal looking clubs, or sticks with round metal balls on the tops covered in brutal spikes. Seeing the horse's obvious distress, one of the piskies let out a horrifying screech that ended in a bloodcurdling cackle aimed directly at Parsley who reared up in terror, throwing Caja clear off his back before ripping his bridle from the branch and tearing off at a full gallop back the way they had come. The piskies shrieked in triumph as Caja lay immobile on her back, the jubilant creatures in front of her.

Without hesitation Jory pulled Saraid to a skidding halt, and in one swift move had jumped off, and rushed to stand in front of Caja. She looked up at him groggily. 'stay behind me Caja!' he commanded, 'can you get up?' She rose shakily to her feet. 'Yeah, yes, I'm ok.'

'Saraid!' he yelled, but the piskies had already advanced on his horse, and it was now frantically copying Parsley's flight out of the gorge.

He turned back to face the piskies just as the lead one reached them. With a harsh guttural sound the creature swept his arm across to strike his club into Jory's knees with the intention of downing him. Jory managed to sidestep the blow by a fingers breadth before another club was bearing down on him and caught him solidly in the side. He grunted in pain and bent over clutching at his stomach with one hand. Another piskie, taking his chance heaved his spiked club up to clobber Jory on the head. Without looking up, Jory's other hand shot out and a sharp, wide burst of air erupted thrusting all the attacking piskies a good few metres backwards and onto their backs. They scrambled up hastily, surprise and some fear now evident on their faces. Warily they approached again, this time in a more strategic formation, coming at them from all possible sides whilst continuing to sneer lustily at their quarry.

'Pick up those rocks. They are vicious but stupid and not good fighters,' Jory whispered forcefully to Caja.

Caja had recovered enough and started piling up rocks beside her. Once again the piskies launched themselves upon them, with squeals and snarls, and Jory defended with aggressive volleys of wind that catapulted the startled piskies into the air, whilst Caja threw rocks at those trying to sneak in when Jory's attention was diverted elsewhere. Jory's strength however was diminishing and Caja's piles of rocks were rapidly dwindling. There were just too many of them. The piskies began to eye each other gleefully, sure of their impending success, with one of the piskies beginning to scale the gorge behind Caja and Jory, just out of their line of sight. Jory batted two away with a fist to one's head and a burst of wind to the other, at which point the one climbing the gorge leapt onto Jory from behind with a great yell. Jory grunted in shock and fell to his knees. The piskie had its legs wrapped around his neck and was beating him on the head with its fists, having had to drop its weapon to climb the cliff. Jory was back up within a second and started writhing around trying to dislodge the piskie with jerks and smacks to his body. Caja gaped in horror, and attempted to throw a rock at the piskie's head but it missed by a hairs breadth. Two other piskies taking the chance leapt upon her, and tackled her to the floor. One lifted his studded club high to batter her in the head.

'No! Not that one! We must bring her back unharmed,' hissed one of the piskies.

He dropped his club in disappointment and pulled out a rope from his pocket. As Caja twisted and struggled trying to free herself from the piskies' grasp, a flash of blue caught her eye from her trouser pocket and something flickered in the back of her mind, something her Aunt had said to her. Without another thought she pulled the scarf out of her pocket. As she did so, it appeared to triple in size and transform into a brilliantly luminous and pliant shield that undulated in an unfelt breeze. The shield touched those piskies closest to her and they screamed in agony leaping back in dismay and horror, falling over their feet in their haste to run away.

'A costan! How has she got a costan?' screeched the head piskie.

Caja stood up quickly and with one hand clenched on a light strap that held the rippling shield in front of her, she approached the two piskies who were now beating Jory about the head and body, oblivious to what was going on around them. As soon as she came within a few feet it was as if they could feel the advance of the costan. They peered up startled, and then immediately sprung off Jory backing away to join the others, their nostrils flaring, now in abject fear.

It was just in time. Jory was looking battered and stunned. He staggered up dazed and stared at the piskies disoriented. The shield seemed to have a trance like effect on them. They were staring at it in fascination but also with horror, their eyes glazed. Jory took in the situation and using his last reserves of strength began to chant a spell. A few seconds later and fire burst into the air around them setting the clothes alight of the nearest piskies and singeing those further back.

At this, they had had enough, and they all turned and fled wailing in pain and panic, shoving each other to make their way out of the gorge first. Jory watched for a moment to ensure they were all gone, and then turned to check on Caja who was trembling with fear, the shield still held out in front of her protectively.

'Caja, Caja? Are you all right?' he asked.

Caja answered shakily, 'where…where did they come from?'

'I'm not sure. Don't worry Caja, they've gone now and I don't believe they'll be back in a hurry. But what is that?' he stammered, exhausted from the beating the piskies had given him.

Caja stared at the remarkable object in her hand, 'I…I'm not sure,' she said uncertainly, 'my Aunt gave it to me. I think the piskies said it was a costan? Have they really gone though Jory? Have they?' Her eyes darted around anxiously for any sign of the vicious creatures.

'Yes Caja, they've gone. Come, let's find the horses. We're not far from Truro now and the sooner we get there the better. They won't come back now,' he reassured her, putting his arm around her protectively as they hobbled out of the narrow gorge.

As Caja lowered her arm the shield fluttered down, rapidly shrinking in size and turning back into the ordinary scarf that her Aunt had given her. 'S'pretty amazing,' she muttered in admiration stuffing it into her pocket, but too tired and scared to make any further investigation. The horses were waiting patiently for them just outside the entrance to the gorge.

Jory patted them in relief, 'Good Saraid. Good boys. I think we'll go around the gorge this time. It'll take a little longer. Not a route I usually take but we don't want to risk it. Hop up Caja,' he said panting a little.

Caja gazed at him in concern seeing him properly for the first time, 'but Jory look at you. We must try and patch you up first. You're bleeding all over,' she added becoming more and more distressed.

Jory glanced down at his ripped clothes, and held his hand to his face to touch the blood that was dripping down his forehead from a nasty cut in his head. 'Hmmm....I guess I should do something about this. Don't worry Caja. I'm pretty good at fixing myself up. Remember I do get myself into a lot of fights.' He said this with a wry smile, whilst taking different bandages and ointments from his pack.

After some minutes of blotting and awkward bandaging, with Caja trying to help unsuccessfully, he managed to stem the blood flow and clean himself up. He still looked in a terrible state but now also rather comical with tufts of hair sticking awkwardly out of the bandages he'd wrapped around his head.

'That'll do for now. Let's be off. I can visit a Healing Zard in Truro,' he sighed eventually, climbing gingerly up onto Saraid.

Caja for once happily climbed back onto Parsley, keen to

be away from the gorge and back safely on their way. She was more eager than ever now to get to Truro, to find the staff and return to Aunt Flora and the comforting normality of home, where terrifying creatures did not exist. She had to admit that the allure of Kernow was rapidly wearing off. But at least she had Jory. She did not know what she would have done without him.

She glanced at him hesitantly, 'Jory…thank you. For defending me there. Really thank you.'

Jory looked away in embarrassment, 's'alright,' he muttered, 'anyway we would have been goners without you and that shield'. And with that he kicked Saraid into a fast trot and with Parsley following obediently behind, they set off once again, grimly gripping on, anxious to reach the safety of Truro.

CHAPTER SIX

The young boy groaned into the silence. He was hung by his straining wrists, tied above his head to an iron ring firmly embedded into the dripping wall. His feet were only just touching the earthen floor, placing enormous pressure on his throbbing shoulders. An eerie, glowing bond was wrapped around his body, encasing his hands and feet entirely. It pulsed with a steady metallic light that seemed to have a life of its own.

The boy squeezed his eyes tightly shut, tensed his drained body and then released all of it, focusing fully on his mind, falling into the depths of his being, and finally rising above the excruciating pain of his physical body. Although in a state of deep meditation, his awareness of his surroundings was still acute, and he heard the measured footsteps many minutes before the man once again appeared at his cell door.

There was a grating as the door swung open and then silence, broken finally by the man's deliberate and low tone, 'have you come to your senses yet Willam? No one can endure pain such as this forever. Eventually you will falter… and I know how to keep you alive whilst withstanding the most immense pain imaginable…It is a talent I have,' he said with a slow smile.

With this his hand shot out and a piercing black light

emerged from his middle finger trained on the centre of Willam's bare and panting chest. Willam screamed in agony as Menadue calmly and methodically moved his hand downwards, searing the flesh in a long line crossing the recent scars of other lines that already layered Willam's torso. The putrid smell of charred flesh filled the room.

Eventually he let his hand drop away, a dark smile on his face, 'well?'

Willam lifted his head carefully, tears streaming from his agony-filled eyes, 'You'll have to do… better… than… that…' Beneath the tears his eyes revealed a single-minded resolve.

Menadue sighed, and lifted one eyebrow in quiet exasperation, 'why keep your secrets to yourself when this is all there is Willam? Human life is unimportant and meaningless. We will all die and nothing we will ever have done will mean anything; it's all so futile in the end. There is no point in enduring such pain, especially for such pitiful reasoning.'

'It is why I will endure at all costs,' replied Willam through gritted teeth, 'with our one life we must live it to its fullest…striving for the highest truth and living always to our utmost potential. I will die as I have lived, with courage and faith.'

'You foolish boy, faith in what?' spat Menadue a trace of anger lacing his voice, and with a nasty sneer he raised his hand again.

*

Jory and Caja remained silent for the remainder of their journey, moving along at a fast canter, with Jory wincing regularly and occasionally letting out unavoidable whimpers, as he was jolted around. Caja suggested they slow down but he insisted they travel as fast as possible, to reach Truro as soon as they could. Descending towards a delicate river in a small wooded valley, Caja pulled to a sudden stop with distinct fear on her face, her nerves still strained from the encounter with the piskies. 'Jory, there is someone over there by the river. Look!'

Jory twisted quickly to gaze where Caja was staring wide-eyed. There was a male figure, bent over awkwardly peering intently into the river, standing next to a wooden bridge. As they watched him in apprehension, the figure turned and immediately beckoned to them, as if he knew they were there all along.

Caja looked at Jory in puzzlement, 'well he certainly doesn't look dangerous. Shall we go and talk to him?'

They both stared at the grizzled figure who was now beckoning to them furiously. He was an old man, with dirty, mud-coloured hair, and a tangled, over-grown beard. His figure was stooped and weathered, and he appeared to be mumbling to himself although at the same time continuing to indicate to them urgently.

Jory urged Saraid into a slow walk down the slope, 'keep close to me, and we'll see what he wants. I think he's a BridgeKeeper and we have to cross the river at some point so this is probably the quickest way.'

As they drew nearer Caja whispered to Jory, 'looks like he's a few picnics short of a sandwich.'

Jory threw her a confused look before continuing towards the old man. His unusually pale blue eyes darted here and there constantly, and his fingers relentlessly fidgeted as he continued to mutter and beckon to them.

He raised his voice as they approached, 'young things, young things…w…where did you leave it? Leave it. Now, now pay for the bridge. It's a good bridge. But don't leave it be…be…behind…So young, so young… We must leave it. My…m…my Tar……Tara…It's a good bridge. A good bridge. P…pay for the bridge. ' He held out his hand expectantly towards them, eyes not focused upon them but darting around everywhere else.

Jory indicating to Caja to do the same carefully descended from Saraid emitting a whimper of pain as he did so. He then delved into his pocket for a small coin which he handed hesitantly to the BridgeKeeper. The old man stuffed the coin away into a grubby leather pouch tied around his middle and began to work on the many complicated locks of the rusty gate that barred anyone from crossing the small bridge.

Caja stood transfixed by the old man's chatter. There was something so sad about him.

'Did we leave it behind? L…leave it. Lost. G…good…bridge. It's a very good bridge. Leave it. Leave. My t…t…tar…sita….m..my tara…sita.'

His sorrowful eyes were constantly moving as he muttered on, as if searching for something. Underneath it all there was a profound grief seeping from his crushed being. He lifted his eyes for a second, they seemed soaked in torment. She wondered what could possibly have made him this way.

'Leave it…L…leave it...' Suddenly the old man stopped talking and looked up directly at Caja, 'C…Cornwall…Cornwall,' he said in a strong although stumbling voice.

Caja shook her head in surprise, 'why yes. From Cornwall. You know Cornwall? Have you been there?' she asked eagerly.

But the old man's eyes had once again glazed over and he had recommenced his mutterings.

She grabbed his sleeve, 'd'you know Cornwall? What do you know of it? Can you tell me? Please!'

But he continued to ignore her, focusing instead on the locks of the gate. She tugged on his sleeve and continued to plead, but to no avail.

Jory said gently, 'c'mon Caja. He's probably just heard the word from somewhere. Look at him. He can't help us.'

Again the man looked up sharply, this time at Jory, and an expression of unerring sympathy arose on his face as he studied Jory's battered face and body. He held out a shaky entreating arm to Jory and stuttered out with great difficulty, 'come….h…help.'

Jory looked at him uncertainly for a moment, indecision

on his face.

'I think he really means to help,' Caja whispered, 'let him. I don't believe he can do any harm.'

Jory shrugged and tentatively approached the old man's outstretched arm. As his trembling hand touched Jory's youthful arm, a shudder ran through Jory's entire body and his eyes seemed to roll into the back of his head. The old man was staring fixedly, his energies concentrated on Jory.

Caja looked on in alarm, what was he doing to Jory? Was he hurting him? But before she could even start to protest the old man had released him.

Jory stepped back with a gasp of relief shaking his head. He looked around, astonishment evident on his face. 'I feel great!' he said.

Caja shook her head, startled. Although Jory's wounds that were not covered by bandages were still visible, they now looked like they had been inflicted many days ago, and were well on their way to being fully healed.

'Thank you, thank you,' said Jory earnestly, but the old man was once again muttering and ignored him completely, focusing on his task of unlocking the gate to the bridge. Eventually the gate was open and their way was free to cross the river.

'I feel so much better now. He has Minerva's touch! He must have been a Healing Zard once. This'll make things so much easier. We'll be in Truro in no time now!' exclaimed Jory as he led Saraid across the shaky bridge.

Caja grabbing hold of Parsley's bridle followed Jory cautiously through the dilapidated gate and across the unsteady bridge. Once on the other side, Caja gave one last curious look at the BridgeKeeper, who was busily locking the gate again, before they mounted their horses and rode quickly up out of the steep valley.

*

It took hardly ten minutes to reach the rolling moors once

again where Jory began to gesture excitedly to Caja, pointing into the distance ahead, 'look! Truro! There Caja, can you see it?'

Caja who had been fully occupied in keeping astride Parsley as they cantered along at a speed she was still not yet accustomed to, squinted against the sun, peering into the distance.

'Wow! … I've been to Truro a number of times in my own Cornwall. But this Truro looks nothing like that!' she gasped.

Up ahead, not too far in the distance was a prominent city surrounded by a towering wall, made from the beautiful light Cornish slate that was also so common in her world. Rising above this were a number of gleaming towers and spires that dazzled brilliantly in the setting sun.

'The highest tower you can see with the stone chough on top is the Kernow Assembly where the Nobles all meet to set taxes and the rules of the land. Just next to it, you can see the spire of the Order of Avalon, the group of Wizards who lead all magical issues in the land. They answer ultimately to the Assembly, although some of them would disagree with that!' he added with a chortle, 'and there, you can just see it, there the …Kernow Library!'

He was pointing so fast that Caja could not see which was which.

'So what d'you think Caja? It's quite impressive isn't it?' asked Jory obviously keen for her approval.

'It's amazing,' said Caja enthusiastically with no need for exaggeration. For Truro was indeed a breath-taking city in this land. The soaring towers and lofty spires were made from a myriad of multi-coloured crystals and stone, verdant greens, and glacial blues to soft hues of ruby leading to a riotous display of colour. The grander buildings were set amongst the traditional, stubby Cornish stone buildings which served as a blank canvas to emphasize the beauty of the more elaborate and colourful architecture. Outside the walls of the city was a neat, bustling port situated upon the River Truro, which curved its way out to the sea.

'Ah, it will be good to be inside the city walls. We'll be safe there,' sighed Jory with some of his tension dissolving.

They cantered down to the outskirts of the city and began to follow a wide track, eventually approaching one of the high gates set within the stone-walls.

'Are they what I think they are?' asked Caja excitedly as they stopped in a small queue forming in front of the enormous gates.

Monitoring the people coming in and out of the city were two men and two women standing a pair abreast on either side of the gates. To Caja the imposing figures appeared gigantic and stern, made bigger by the heavy chainmail shirts they wore emblazoned with a small blackbird with a distinctive, tangerine beak.

'And are those massive swords real?' she asked in astonishment.

'Yep, they're real broadswords,' answered Jory grinning. 'And yes, they're knights. Those are Knights of Kernow, commanded by the Kernow Assembly. You can tell by the blackbird, or chough as it's called, on their shirts. It's the emblem of Kernow.. The Assembly have the largest force with Knights coming from all the different Nobles' forces, although some say Noble Kilmar now has almost as many.'

The knights checked Jory and Caja's packs and waved them through, and before they knew it they were leading their horses through the thronging streets of Truro. Caja was fascinated by everything around her. She realised she hadn't seen many of the people of this world but now, to her delight, she was surrounded by them. Many of them were dressed in similar clothes to that of Jory, but there were also others in lavishly coloured cloaks, impressively tall hats, or women in shimmering robes being held out of the mud by their maids. They rounded a busy corner, squeezing past a pudgy woman with a mysteriously bulging sack that appeared to be kicking, and entered an immense square surrounded on all sides by dignified buildings topped by the kaleidoscopic-coloured towers that they had seen from afar.

'This is Tintagel Square. The most important square in Kernow. See, there is the Kernow Assembly, and next to it, the tower that's changing colour, that's the Order of Avalon.'

The towers were magnificent, made from an undulating material that Caja had never seen before.

'Come, we must carry on to Blake Manor. It's not far from Tintagel Square. Only a little further. We'll go past Ambrosius Academy. I've always wanted to see inside. I'm going to be starting there next year. Can you believe it?' Jory shook his head in wonder, as they crossed the bustling square leading their horses by the reins.

'It sounds wicked. I'd love to see inside it too. Does every one who can do magic go to Ambrosius Academy then?' asked Caja tugging Parsley along behind her. The reluctant horse was pulling his head backwards and staring longingly at a big bucket of carrots that an old lady was peeling on the corner of the square. 'Oh come on Parsley. You shall have a good feed soon enough. Come on!' she added as Parsley continued to resist any forward movement dragging his feet along unwillingly.

Jory glanced back with a grin of amusement. 'Yes, the Order of Avalon search out everyone who can connect to the Telluric and ensure they attend Ambrosius Academy for at least a few years. Well, except the Druid children of course. They tried to make them go to the Academy for awhile but that was a battle they were never going to win! They're a stubborn bunch those Druids.'

'So what will you do at the Academy? Is it like school?' asked Caja intrigued.

'It's a bit like a school. But not really. The main role of the Academy is to research Telluric Magic. They're always finding new things you can do with it. But they also train those like me to use our magic. Otherwise it could be dangerous. You start as an Initiate, and you're not meant to leave until you become a Zard. There are the Junior Zards, and if you're good you can train a bit more to become a Senior Zard. They tend to specialise in different areas. There all sorts of different Zards, Healing Zards, Kindred Zards, Prosaic Zards and Cabalistic Zards. After that, a very few stay on to do the serious training and become a Wizard. The only Wizards I've ever met are Ennor and Talwin,' added Jory, a look of pride on his face. 'Most others stay as Zards, and work in the cities or villages selling their skills, as Healing Zards or in the Order of Avalon.'

'But what happens to those who have this Telluric Magic but don't attend the Academy? There must be some the Order don't find,' asked Caja.

'A few do slip through the gaps.' Jory gave a sigh. 'If I hadn't met you, and ended up going to see Ennor and Talwin, that might've been me. They told me magic is dangerous without training and often those who don't get any help end up in Yeghes Hospice… or even worse in Morghase Prison. At least something good came out of me coming across you hey?'

Caja grimaced at him gloomily, 'I've brought a lot of trouble into your life haven't I? If it wasn't for me you wouldn't be traipsing across the country being attacked by horrible creatures.'

Jory glanced at Caja's downcast face, 'hey it's not all that bad. If it wasn't for you I would still be at Villant Farm being yelled at by my Uncle and Aunt with nothing but a life of menial drudgery ahead of me. Now there are all sorts of opportunities for me. Even Ambrosius Academy! And look there it is!'

Whilst they had been talking they had exited Tintagel Square and taken one of the busier roads heading northwest. Jory stopped and stared in admiration through two proud gates at a vast building flanked by a pair of soaring towers set a good half-mile away. In front of the building was an extensive grassed space, with four identical houses arranged around it. Milling around on the grass closest to them were a few young students, some playing a complex game of ball amongst themselves, and others relaxing on broad benches set amongst the trees. The students were all dressed in long, light green or red cloaks although many of them had discarded them in the warm, autumnal sun.

'That could be me one day,' said Jory wistfully staring through the bars of the tall fence at the playful students.

'They all look a bit like Christmas ornaments in red and green,' said Caja with a grin.

'Christmas? What's that?'

But Caja was prevented from answering by the sudden yell of 'heads!'

Jory quickly stepped out of the way but Caja was not so fast. She stayed rooted to the spot in indecision, and then yelled in surprise as a small cricket-sized ball smacked her directly on the forehead.

'Yowch!' she cried bending over and rubbing her head in pain. Luckily the ball was not as hard as a cricket ball.

Jory snorted in laughter and bent down to pick up the offending ball.

'Good shot!' he yelled as two of the younger students, a girl and a boy dressed in ivy-green approached him.

Caja glowered at him and continued to rub her head frowning.

'I'm so sorry,' said the younger girl to Caja as they approached, 'Ralph's such a terrible thrower. He was meant to be aiming for Michel over there.'

'Well no I wasn't actually Rae, I was aiming for you. Guess that still makes me a bad thrower though hey?'

Rae gave him a shove.

'That's ok. It really didn't hurt that much,' said Caja dropping her hand from her head. 'Are you students at the Academy then?' she added curiously, her attention diverted as she examined these new young people in front of her. They both had identical smooth, black hair, hazel-green eyes, and tiny, upturned noses.

Ralph nodded his head slowly, 'duh yes. We certainly wouldn't choose to wear these outfits for fun.'

Rae gave him another push, 'yes, we're both Initiates at

Ambrosius. My name's Raelyn and this is my rude twin brother Ralph. But most people call me Rae.'

'Hi, I'm Caja and this is my friend Jory. Jory's actually coming to Ambrosius Academy next year.'

Jory glared at her in annoyance, as Raelyn and Ralph turned to stare at him in interest.

'That's great. When you coming? How come you didn't join in September?' asked Raelyn.

Jory paused for a moment, thinking. 'I'll probably start in the New Year, in January. Couldn't start before. So how is it?' He had no intention of talking any more about himself or even worse his family.

'Overall it's pretty good. Some of the Guardians are great, some are real taskmasters, really strict.'

'Guardians?' said Caja questioningly.

'Yeah, they're like our teachers,' explained Raelyn, 'although they aren't just teachers as some of them work in the research towers and many don't even teach at all. They're Guardians of Telluric Magic for the whole of Briton. There are some pretty tough ones but I love it here. We're learning so much about Telluric philosophy and history, and all sorts.'

Ralph rolled his eyes in bemusement. 'Yeah, Raelyn really likes to study. What a geek.' He turned to Jory, 'so are your family magical? Does it come from your parents?'

Jory's smile faded, 'I don't know my parents. But yes I've magic in my family… In fact my Great Uncle and Aunt, Ennor and Talwin, are Wizards,' he added brightening considerably.

Raelyn gasped in amazement, 'you know Ennor and Talwin Quintrall?'

Jory looked at her nonplussed, 'well yes, we've actually been staying with them for the last few days.'

Both Ralph and Raelyn looked astonished at this.

'Ennor and Talwin Quintrall are our idols. All the students look up to them, although we've never actually met anyone who knows them,' whispered Raelyn in awe.

'They're known as two of the greatest Wizards to have

ever graduated from Ambrosius Academy,' continued Ralph, 'although others would argue Menadue Enfer was the greatest, after Merlin of course.'

'Menadue? I've heard of him. Who's he?' queried Caja, curious to hear what they would say.

Ralph was keen to answer. 'He was one of the best Wizards to ever come out of Ambrosius. They say he had more power than all of the Guardians by the time he was sixteen! Although there are rumours about him…' He paused. 'But no one knows, and anyway he disappeared many decades ago, so I guess we'll never know.'

Caja and Jory shot each other knowing looks.

'Many of the Guardians use Ennor and Talwin as examples for us. They were so talented. Although not all the Guardians like them,' added Raelyn with a meaningful look, 'there are some who do not like to hear their names spoken and…'

'Yes, but those Guardians are just aligned with the Order and talking rubbish,' interrupted Ralph. 'We've heard so many amazing stories bout them. What are they like?' he asked staring at Jory eagerly.

By this point, Jory's whole body had begun to swell with pride. 'Well, aye, they're pretty talented I guess. And…'

'When you come here, could you get them to visit us?' interrupted Ralph.

Jory frowned, 'well…I guess so. We'll actually be meeting with them in a few days from now.'

'Wow,' said Ralph dreamily, 'that's just so amazing that you're related. I can't wait for you to start at Ambrosius!'

Jory responded with a delighted grin that he attempted to conceal with a more composed look.

'I didn't realize they were so renowned,' commented Caja in reverence.

'Well not everyone thinks like we do, ' explained Ralph, 'you have to be careful who you talk to about them.'

His explanation on the matter was cut short however, by a harsh shout coming from behind Ralph and Raelyn.

'Hey you there! The Bryants. What do you think you're doing?' An older man with swishing, grey robes was walking quickly towards them, an angry expression on his face. He had shoulder-length hair coloured in a curiously striped pattern of grey and white. His nose was long, his eyes dark and poky, and his mouth almost non-existent, hidden as it was under the long hook of his nose. The more Caja stared at him, the more he began to resemble…well….a badger.

Ralph raised his eyebrows at Jory and Caja, and turned to reply, 'Ah Guardian Brock, we were just talking to-'

'Local riff-raff. Yes, I can see that. You know you shouldn't be fraternising with the locals during Academy hours. There'll be consequences for this Ralph and Raelyn Bryant. And as you've been in trouble many times before this will almost certainly warrant some form of detention or perhaps even a….'

'But they're not just locals Guardian Brock. Jory here will be coming to Ambrosius Academy,' interrupted Rae.

Guardian Brock looked Jory up and down with a sneer, 'really? We do seem to be getting all sorts these days. The quality of our intake does seem to be slipping tremendously.'

'Now look here…' Jory started but Caja placed a calming hand on his arm and started talking over the top of him, 'Guardian Brock. We do apologise for disturbing your students. We've been travelling for some time, so do excuse our attire. We're here to stay with Noblewoman Blake at the Blake Manor.'

At the mention of the Noblewoman, Caja saw a distinct brightening in Guardian Brock's eyes.

She continued on hopefully. 'As Jory here will be coming to Ambrosius Academy next year we were hoping to pass by and possibly see inside. Ralph and Raelyn here were just helping us. Is there any chance we can have a look round?'

Guardian Brock surveyed Caja for a moment, a look of uncertainty on his face. 'Certainly not', he eventually said, 'open days are over. You'll have to come back-'

'Ah Guardian Brock, but we do have a policy whereby

new students can come and take a tour of the Academy, if a Guardian is free and offers to provide his services,' came a deep voice from behind Guardian Brock.

Guardian Brock let out a blast of frustration before turning resignedly around. 'Ah Guardian Quinn, I didn't hear you coming. Very stealthy you are…despite your size.' The last was added in an undertone.

'I do apologise. I didn't mean to sneak up on you. So this must be Jory Hobart,' said Quinn studying Jory attentively.

'My good friends Ennor and Talwin told me you would be coming through Truro. I'm more than happy to give you a tour. How does tomorrow morning sound? Are you here for long?'

Guardian Quinn was a short, stocky man with fluffy, brown hair and kindly eyes, and although not fat was certainly very well-built.

Jory had lightened immeasurably at Guardian Quinn's words. 'Why that'd be great. I would love to. We're staying over at the Blake Manor but I'm sure I can take some time off tomorrow morning to come and see the Academy.'

'And who is your friend here? Would she like to come along too?' asked Quinn.

'This is my friend Caja Delaney from Albion. I'm sure she'd love to come along too wouldn't you Caja?'

Caja thought for a moment, struggling between her desire to find the Legacy and return home, and her innate curiosity. Finally her curiosity won. 'Well yes, I would love to see inside an Academy where they teach magic. My friends at home would be so jealous,' she added quietly. What would Aggie and Luke say if they could see her now?

After setting a time and place to meet, they said their goodbyes and set off for Blake Manor. Guardian Brock left with a gloomy look on his face, whilst Ralph and Rae mumbled hurried promises of spending lunch with them after their tour tomorrow.

It took them only another ten minutes of slow riding to find themselves outside the gates of Blake Manor. In contrast to Templeton Castle, the building looked much more warm and welcoming with wide-open gates revealing a well-swept, perfectly-straight driveway leading up to the grand Manor, which was situated quite high, looking out over the Truro River.

'Blake Manor is one of the oldest Noble residences,' explained Jory as they rode up the driveway, 'the oldest part is older than Templeton Castle although you wouldn't know it from the outside.'

Caja nodded her head in agreement. Blake Manor was certainly better-kept than Noblewoman Ivy's Castle. It was a sprawling Manor of two stories with more and more of its various wings coming into view as they approached. It looked like various sections had been tacked on by different generations, with disparate styles contrasting starkly with each other.

This time Jory rang the doorbell which pealed with an elegant sound. They both looked at each other encouragingly. The door was opened with a sharp clang by a stern, middle-aged man, all pristine, smooth lines, and slicked down hair.

There was no smile with his greeting. 'The Blake Manor. How may I be of help?'

Caja went to open her mouth, but Jory seeing her mischievous look got there first. 'Good afternoon, Noblewoman Blake is expecting us. I'm Jory Hobart and this is my companion Caja Delaney.'

The stern look did not disappear, 'Noblewoman Blake left me no such information. I am her personal manservant, Bolton. I cannot let anyone into Blake Manor without her authority.' He stood staring at them clearly expecting Jory and Caja to turn around and depart.

'Ah, well the message may only have come in recently. Can you please go and check,' persisted Jory pleasantly.

Bolton gave them a grimace and then reluctantly retreated back inside firmly shutting the door behind him.

'I wish people would stop shutting doors in our faces, it doesn't seem too much to ask,' Caja moaned. They waited patiently.

Abruptly the door opened again, 'it appears you are right. Do come in,' said Bolton with an intense look of disappointment. 'You can wait in the drawing room. Noblewoman Blake is expected to return at any moment.'

He led them into the house and to a large, fussily decorated room with rigid, uncomfortable chairs, and several musical instruments displayed on stands that looked like they were never played.

'Please sit. Arnold will be in shortly with some refreshments,' said Bolton, promptly vanishing again.

Arnold entered moments later with a rattling tray filled with an extensive assortment of cakes, biscuits and cold beverages.

'Is this all for us?' asked Caja impressed.

Jory's eyes lit up at the generous spread, and he quickly started tucking in. 'I could probably tackle most of it if you're not feeling hungry,' he responded helpfully.

They had made good inroads into the spread between the two of them, when they heard the peel of the door bell once again.

'Maybe that's Noblewoman Blake?' queried Caja.

'Don't be silly Caja. Why would she be ringing her own doorbell?'

Caja reddened, 'um…maybe she's forgotten her keys?'

Jory threw her a bemused look and carried on stabbing heartily at an enormous slice of cake he had served himself. A moment later the door flew open and Gorran stepped in.

'Gorran! We didn't expect to see you here so quickly!' exclaimed Jory in surprise. 'It's great to see you again so soon.'

Caja's eyes beamed as she gave him a shy grin.

Gorran approached with a wide smile, 'Jory, Caja. It's good to see you both again so soon. I hear we've much to do.'

Jory clapped him heartily on the back, happy to see his friend. 'Aye, there is. How d'you get here so quickly though?'

'Natan and I set off for West Wivel to see Nobleman Salisbury but then we met him on the way before we'd got there. He was out with a contingent of his knights to investigate reports of one of his villages being ransacked. We tried to convince him of the threat of Kilmar but he was reluctant to believe us. He doesn't believe that Kilmar would do such a thing. And to make matters worse, the Order has spread rumours about Ennor and Talwin which doesn't help. As Talwin left the Order under such difficult circumstances many believe them. Is Noblewoman Blake here yet?'

Jory frowned at this new information replying, 'no, she's not arrived yet. We've been making ourselves comfortable. Tremendous food here. Although that Manservant seems a bit unfriendly.'

'I know, he didn't seem overly happy to see me either. How was your trip?'

Caja shuddered, 'we were attacked again. This time by these horrid, little creatures, called... picksies.'

'Piskies,' amended Jory looking grim, 'I don't know how they found us. We were ambushed. It seems they knew exactly where we were heading. Although maybe they weren't sent by Menadue. Maybe Kernow is just so full of these creatures nowadays.'

Gorran was shocked. 'That's bleddy terrible! Those piskies can be dangerous creatures. Thank Taranis you're both ok. How did you manage to get away?'

Caja answered shortly, 'Jory did pretty well with his magic, and between us we managed to fend them off and get away.' She was not sure why, but she was reluctant to tell him about the costan that she now kept on her at all times.

'They're vicious, but they're not the brightest,' added Jory.

'That's true. It looks like you may need to be armed for any future trips. I'll look into it for you,' said Gorran looking concerned. 'And you should have someone with you. To help. I will gladly help wherever possible. You shouldn't be facing these dangers alone.'

'Thanks Gorran,' replied Jory relieved to have his support.

'Anyway I'm here to help you now and entirely at your disposal. There's nothing I won't do to stop this evil that's taking over our land. Now tell me, what can I do?' asked Gorran, looking earnestly at them both.

Jory replied gratefully, 'well we're searching for something from the Prophecy. Something that will help us in the fight...'

Gorran interrupted, 'ah Merlin's Legacy. Ennor and Talwin have told me of the Prophecy. Is it the Legacy that you now hunt?'

Jory nodded eagerly, 'yes, yes. Ennor and Talwin have found it's-'

'Jory!' blurted Caja, 'remember what Talwin told us.' She glanced apologetically at Gorran.

Jory glanced from Caja to Gorran, 'but Gorran is my friend Caja. He can help us. Surely we can tell him?"

Caja frowned at Jory reluctant to discuss the issue in front of Gorran.

Gorran turned an understanding gaze onto Caja, 'I understand Caja, of course. It's important that you trust no one in these times. You must do what Talwin says. But I hope sincerely that I can still help, otherwise my journey will be a wasted one.'

'Of course Gorran. Of course. I'm sure you can still help us. Let's start now, right away! We've some papers that Talwin gave us that will help us to find what we're looking for.'

Before Caja could say anything more, Jory had retrieved them from his shirt pocket and added, 'she said there was some mention of the staff in….oh.'

Caja threw her head back staring up at the ceiling in exasperation. 'Well I think he knows now Jory.'

Gorran regarded them both calmly and with a reassuring air said, 'don't worry Caja. You can trust me. I'll never say a thing. I swear to you both on the life of my mother.'

Jory looking relieved mumbled, 'yeah he probably would have guessed anyway Caja. And he is my friend.'

Caja's voice was accepting. 'I suppose it can't hurt. And

it'll be wonderful to have your help Gorran.' Her sincere and radiant smile was not lost on him and he gazed at her, disconcerted for a moment.

'Thank you Caja,' he said softly.

Jory's voice was suddenly loud. 'Right, right now that's all sorted, so let's get cracking. Let's see what we can find out from these papers.'

'Yes, yes. Good idea Jory,' replied Caja suddenly keen to start their search and move closer to returning home.

'So, we're searching for a staff. Don't worry I don't need to know who's although I think I could have a good guess,' said Gorran smilingly.

They all stared as Jory flattened the crumpled pieces of paper on the small table he had been eating off. There was a cut-out article and a page of Bentley Blake's last Will and Testament.

'See, it was this article that alerted them to the staff in the first place,' Jory explained.

Blake Manor Auction Disrupted

Many folk were in attendance today at the Blake Manor auction as numerous Blake artefacts were sold to pay off the debts of Nobleman Bentley Blake, allegedly brought about by the incurrence of excessive losses at gambling with certain, disreputable local characters. The proceedings were interrupted however, by an irate Nobleman Blake who stormed in and declared that the item currently on display was not for sale and in fact should never have been in the auction.

As one eye-witness stated: 'He was bellowing all over the place. Making a right to-do.' "How did that get there!? The Blakes will never sell that. Never! We were given that to protect, and protect it we will for as long as there is a Blake left alive! It will not leave this estate!"

Stamping up to the dais, Nobleman Blake, grabbed the item in question, an ordinary looking oak staff with a rather crudely carved neck in the form of a raven, and marched out the room muttering furiously under his breath.

'It was quite a commotion. We all wondered what he was talking about and what had made him so angry. It seemed quite strange to be so

concerned about such a common-looking item,' said one witness.

'Talwin was intrigued as to why Nobleman Blake had been so angry over the incident and wanted to know what had happened to the staff. She found it mentioned in a private version of his will that Helena sent to her.' Jory brushed some crumbs off the other paper and pointed to one of the highlighted entries under 'personal items' in the Last Will and Testament of Bentley Blake. *Unknown Oak Staff with raven carving*, and then scrawled next to it in Bentley's handwriting, *The Legacy of Merlin, entrusted to the Blake Family for protection. Edward you'll find the directions to its whereabouts in my personal bureau. If you wish to preserve our family honour you must ensure it is kept safe.*

At that moment Bolton entered the drawing room. 'Cook wishes to know if you have finished with the refreshments and whether you'd like anymore?'
'No, we're fine thank you,' said Gorran with a polite smile, 'I say Bolton, would you happen to know what became of Nobleman Bentley Blake's personal bureau?'
Suspicion lit up Bolton's eyes, 'what would you be wanting to know that for Master Gorran?'
'We've Noblewoman Blake's permission to search for a certain item. Unfortunately we can't share any further details with you.'
Bolton gave him a sour look, then a vaguely malicious glitter flittered across his eyes. 'Yes Master. Nobleman Blake's bureau is now being used by Helena Blake in her private chambers.' And with that he abruptly departed.
'Well, we can't really go rooting around Noblewoman Blake's rooms can we?' said Caja dubiously.
'I don't see why not. We won't go through anything else. Just the bureau. And I'm sure she'll understand if we explain this to her later. It's crucial we find the Legacy before Menadue, especially as he seems to be pre-empting your every move. It's vital we get to it as soon as possible,' persuaded

Gorran.

Jory pondered this for a moment, 'I guess you're right Gorran,' he said slowly, 'it's important we find the staff as soon as possible. Talwin did keep saying that.'

Caja looked unsure, 'well I guess we can have a quick look. It's a shame Noblewoman Blake isn't back yet.'

Gorran leapt up and headed out the door, 'c'mon, there's no time to lose!'

The other two followed him, excited to be starting their search. They clambered up the enormous staircase and found themselves faced by a long corridor with a multitude of uninviting, closed doors. Gorran looked around uncertainly.

At that moment one of the doors opened and a young chambermaid appeared, 'Are you looking for something Masters…and Mistress?' she asked in a timid voice.

'Yes. Can you point us in the direction of Helena Blake's personal chambers,' Gorran asked respectfully.

The chambermaid looking thrilled to be addressed directly by Gorran, directed them down the corridor to a doorway about half way down.

'Are you sure about this?' muttered Caja as they entered Helena Blake's personal sitting room which was connected to her bedroom and bathroom.

'There! That must be it!' said Jory pointing to a neat desk in the corner of the room. He hastened over to the object of his attention, and immediately began to open drawers and rummage through them.

Gorran put a hand on Jory's arm. 'We should do this methodically Jory. And try not to make too much of a mess. After all, these are Noblewoman Blake's personal papers.'

'Aye, yes of course Gorran, you're right.'

Gorran indicated to Caja, 'Caja, you can start with these papers from this drawer here. You can sort through them there. Jory and I'll look through the main desk.'

Soon they were all quietly sorting through the vast mass of papers, exclaiming every now and again at objects of interest.

Sifting through the stack of documents assigned to her,

Caja found that she could easily read them all, although she figured they were not actually written in English but in Kernewek. The Nexus Bond between the two worlds allowed her to understand it all. It still amazed her. She found many tedious documents on household matters, and some on the more interesting affairs of Truro, such as minutes from meetings of the Kernow Assembly of which Helena Blake, as a Noble, was a member.

Jory had taken out a whole pile of papers and was busily creating chaos in the middle of the room, whilst Gorran was carefully reading through various bound notebooks at the desk.

'What on earth are you all doing in here?' came a furious voice from the doorway, instantly changing the peaceful atmosphere to one of tension.

Jory and Caja froze, gazing at the woman half hidden in the doorway who Gorran was now approaching in a deferential manner. 'Our sincerest apologies Noblewoman Blake. I'm Gorran Kane, and these are my friends Jory Hobart and Caja…' he paused a moment, obviously trying to remember Caja's surname.

'Delaney, your honour,' added Caja with an ingratiating look. Your honour? Where did that come from? Her cheeks heated up in embarrassment.

Noblewoman Blake fully entered the room, the furious look still upon her face and Caja gasped. Although beautiful, half of the Noblewoman's face was a horrendous mass of shiny scars that pulled her left eye awkwardly down and distorted the thin eyebrow above. The scars extended to a misshapen ear surrounded by patches devoid of hair. The right side of her face however was smooth and clear although Helena Blake had obviously passed the first flushes of youth. Her irate air became even more ominous as it turned upon the dazed Caja who was staring without restraint. Caja quickly looked away remembering Talwin's warning.

'We were sent by Ennor and Talwin Quintrall on urgent business, and we felt we had to start our search as soon as possible. We didn't feel we could wait as the fight against Menadue is so, very crucial,' continued Gorran politely. 'We hope we've not offended you in any way and offer our sincerest apologies. We certainly meant no harm, and we'll ensure we leave everything exactly as we found it.'

There was an uncomfortable silence for several, excruciating minutes as Noblewoman Blake continued to stare at them all severely. Eventually she shook her head, 'yes, Ennor and Talwin did tell me of your impending arrival and our fight against this threat is indeed almost certainly one of the most important trials we'll ever have to face. I know what you're looking for. But what on earth made you think you'd find it in here. Really! These are my private rooms.' Her face was softening somewhat, although there was still a stern look in her eye.

'Oh, um…well…we had a clue to look in Bentley Blake's bureau and we believe this is his bureau?' spoke up Jory somewhat reluctantly.

'No it is not.' A look of understanding flittered across her face. 'what would've made you think it was?'

'It was-' Gorran started.

'No need, no need,' interrupted Helena, 'I think I understand. Bentley Blake's bureau is downstairs in his study, where it's always been.'

Jory and Caja's faces fell in confusion as Gorran nodded with a grim but half-amused understanding.

'Now out you go. There's no need for you to come in here again, although if that changes, I trust you'll discuss it with me first. We'll be having supper soon. I suggest you go and ready yourself and join me in the dining hall when the gong sounds.' She ushered them all out of the room, brushing aside their attempts to right their mess, and carefully shut the door behind them.

The long, empty corridor was dark now as the evening approached. As they trudged along it, a little chastised by their encounter, Gorran expressed his apologies, 'I'm sorry Jory and Caja. That was completely my fault. And I shall explain that to Noblewoman Blake as soon as I get the chance.'

Downstairs, in the great hall, they spotted Bolton leaning casually against one of the stone statues, smirking at them.

Gorran called out to him with a raising of his eyebrows as they went past. 'It appears you were misinformed Bolton. Bentley Blake's bureau is in fact in his office, not in Noblewoman Blake's personal sitting room.'

Bolton assumed a face of surprise staring at the ceiling ponderingly, 'now I do think you are right. What could I've been thinking? I hope I didn't cause you too much trouble young sir.'

Gorran gazed at him for a moment with a half-smile, 'no, you're all right Bolton. No harm done.'

Bolton's face fell in disappointment. 'Right. That's good. I guess you'll be wanting directions to Bentley's Blake's study instead then?'

'That would be most helpful Bolton.'

Bolton gave them a set of complicated instructions to the study that seemed to involve a maze-like number of turns before adding enigmatically, 'bit neglected that wing of the house. No one goes there much these days, because of its past.'

'Its past? What of its past?' Gorran asked.

Bolton looked at them for a few moments before answering, 'well it's where Bentley Blake spent most of his time, with his rather unsavoury friends.'

'What do you mean by unsavoury?'

Again the pause, and then Bolton added with a huff, 'well you might as well know. They're still common enough in these parts. Bentley Blake spent much time with smugglers.' At this, as if fearing he had said too much, he promptly turned on his heel and slipped through a barely visible door behind him.

'Smugglers,' said Jory grimly. 'That adds an interesting element.'

'It certainly does,' affirmed Gorran seriously.

CHAPTER SEVEN

Ennor sighed wearily. Their trip to North Kernow had been extremely tiring and for the most part utterly futile. Talwin was riding despondently next to him on her dappled pony, Pasco. They had travelled first to the Hundred of Trigg and to Nobleman John Kilmar's home, Kilmar Castle. He had kept them waiting for many hours and then had eventually deigned to see them, with a sarcastic sneer permanently fixed upon his face.

Ennor and Talwin knew John Kilmar well from meetings of the Kernow Assembly and Order of Avalon, and had always considered him an arrogant and cruel Noble. He treated his subjects with scorn and was known to tax them the hardest, with no reprieve for those who could not pay. Talwin had predicted that he would be the first to join the Dark side when the time came, and it seemed her forecast had come true. He would not admit it as such, and evaded all their questions of Menadue, claiming that he knew nothing of him, but the state of Kilmar Castle alone revealed that Nobleman Kilmar was dabbling in dark affairs. Wolves were glimpsed in the grounds of the castle as they approached, and the staff of the castle seemed to have been replaced with a group of mean-looking men and women with callous expressions and unnerving, unblinking eyes.

As they were led by a mute servant into one of the dank backrooms to wait, Talwin whispered to Ennor, 'it seems the dungeons are in use again.'

Ennor glanced downwards at the sound of very quiet but desperate wailing coming from deep underneath them, and nodded silently.

They did not speak as they waited, not willing to trust the walls around them. Although the oppressive feel of hostility pressed in on them, they knew that John Kilmar would be reluctant to risk harming them as he was not a Telluric, much to his disappointment, and was extremely wary of their magical skills, particularly when they were together.

Ennor and Talwin Quintrall inspired a certain respect amongst all the Nobles of Kernow, as they were all aware of their reputation as two of the most powerful Wizards Kernow had ever known. Eventually they were shown in to see Kilmar, who was lazing on a chaise longue, in his musty drawing room. The conversation started badly and ended up no better.

After evading all their questions for several minutes with a half-smile, John Kilmar's frustration began to show, and he swiped his hand at them as if swatting a pesky fly. 'Do you propose to question me all day?'

'We wish to find out whether the rumours are true that you're betraying Kernow and the laws of the Kernow Assembly that you, as a Noble, are a signatory to, and have a responsibility to uphold!' replied Talwin angrily, her patience beginning to wear thin with his constant evasions.

'And why would I do that? As I've said, I've no idea what it is you're rambling on about. Cuthbert Bramby is a good friend. And I've never met this Menadue fellow. The Kernow Assembly has agreed that there is no threat. Are you doubting the capability of the Assembly?'

'Of course not,' Ennor responded wearily. 'We know the Assembly work to assure the safety of Kernow and its inhabitants. But we do believe they have been misinformed and that a great threat exists. And we believe you may now be part of that threat!'

John Kilmar let out a contemptuous chuckle. 'Believe what you want Ennor Quintrall. Now if you don't mind, I've much to do.' Again another shrewd grin, 'I hope you do not think it rude of me if I ask you to leave, but I've far more important matters to attend to.'

Ennor and Talwin left without another word, convinced now of the futility of any attempt at persuasion and aware that this was almost certainly the last time that they would encounter John Kilmar with any pretence of cordiality.

They rode on, leaving the Hundred of Trigg, passing through the Hundred of Lesnewth, and into the Hundred of Stratton which was run by Nobleman Bramby.

Cuthbert Bramby had been more welcoming, although there was a caginess to his general demeanour that worried them both. On the outside his attitude was as accommodating as they could have wished, but it seemed that he was saying what they wanted to hear, and was all too eager to see them leave.

'Yes, yes. I understand that there is something going on. I've witnessed it in my own lands. Many of my villages have been attacked by various dark creatures, as well as outlying farms,' he agreed his gaze distracted by some of his sheep outside in the fields.

'But Cuthbert, we need to know where your allegiance stands. Your support is vital. Has Kilmar approached you at all?' urged Talwin.

'Kilmar? No. No. Why would he approach me?'

'We've heard rumours Bramby. Reliable rumours that Kilmar has gone to the Dark side and is trying to persuade you too. We can't let Menadue gain control of these lands. He'll destroy them all. He can't be trusted. He'll not keep any of his promises.'

Bramby looked at them for a moment in befuddled interest, 'no, I'd never do that. Why would you think that of me? Besides, isn't Menadue that wizard who did so well at

Ambrosius Academy but left Kernow decades ago? Why would he be doing all this? Are you sure this is all him?'

Ennor's stare was serious and unblinking, 'yes, we are sure Cuthbert. It's Menadue. He has returned and is now a great threat to the very existence of our land! We are certain of it,' he repeated.

Talwin continued on, 'there will be a motion coming soon in the Assembly, to do something about Menadue. Can we count on your support?'

Cuthbert Bramby had nodded abstractly, avoiding their eyes, and seeing they could get no more from him Ennor and Talwin made their goodbyes and rode south again, now onto the Penwiths'. It was now more urgent than ever that they ensure Penwith would support their cause in the Kernow Assembly.

*

For Caja, Jory and Gorran the evening had infinitely improved after their calamitous start. Although fairly distant, Noblewoman Helena had proved a knowledgeable and fascinating host, and she warmed considerably as the evening wore on. She had been involved in many of Kernow's recent, important historical events, and told lively tales of the different Nobles and the Kernow Assembly that left them all in tears of laughter. Caja listened enthralled to all the stories of this new land, although at first she found it hard to look at the Noblewoman's face without becoming transfixed by her deformity. As she found herself relaxing however, and becoming more engaged in the entertaining stories, she found the scars no longer distracted her.

'Noblewoman Blake, may I ask you a question?' asked Jory politely at a lull in the conversation.

'Yes, you may Jory,' replied Helena with a smile.

'Are your family magical?'

Helena looked down at her plate, 'no, no the Blakes have not been Tellurics for a long, long time. But we tend to hold our own, through other attributes. And I've always got a Zard at the Manor to help me with any Telluric needs. Hicca is around here somewhere.'

Caja chirped in, 'so not all the Nobles are magical? Which ones are?'

Helena smiled at her curiosity. 'Well, they all used to be many centuries ago Caja. Now it's just the Templetons, the Penwiths and the Salisburys. Although it quite frequently skips whole generations, which can cause tremendous resentment, and then pops up again. The Kilmars used to be quite a powerful Telluric family but it disappeared a few generations back. The current Noble can't bear it. He would've loved to be a Telluric although he pretends he doesn't care. Which is probably why he's such an unpleasant ass. Now, the Templetons on the other hand, have had some really impressive magic in their family. Up there with the best. Ivy's son was particularly powerful. It's unfortunate he did not survive. He could've been a great help to us,' she added expressionless.

'What happened to him Noblewoman?' asked Caja.

Her voice sharpened, 'he was killed in a duel over a woman, purportedly. Anyway enough of that, let's move on to what you're here for. What have you found out so far?'

'Um….we've been looking at the papers. Um…' started Jory, hesitant to tell Helena everything.

'Now don't you worry Jory. Talwin has told me everything. I know what you're looking for. It amazes me to think it might have been somewhere in this house all this time. But they didn't mention that you, Gorran, would be involved?' At this she gazed at Gorran with an acute stare.

He returned her stare a little uncertainly, fingering the long-stemmed cross that always hung around his neck, 'I know. It's a bit of an impromptu thing. I had some unexpected time on my hands and wanted to come and help Jory and Caja. I'm sure Talwin and Ennor would approve of my being here. After all, the task is so important.'

'And he does know everything now. It…well…it kind of

came out by mistake,' added Jory.

Noblewoman Blake continued to stare at Gorran, 'I guess it can do no harm. It may even be good to have your help. Now, where were we?'

Caja pulled out some pieces of paper, 'we have these that Talwin gave to us. We need to look in Bentley Blake's personal bureau. Which we thought we were doing when you found us,' she added in a whisper.

Helena smiled lightly, 'so have you found out where Bentley's bureau is?'

'Yes, Bolton told us. It's at the end of the west wing right?' asked Jory uncertainly.

'Yes, yes it is. I'm afraid the house is a bit of a warren. I've not been in grandfather's study for years and there are some rooms I think I may never have entered. Here, you may find this useful.' At this she handed Caja a tattered looking map. 'It's not a great map of the house but it'll give you a general idea of where you are. It's so easy to get lost.' At this she stood up, 'if there's anything else you need, just let me or Bolton know. I will retire now.'

They chorused their thanks and goodnights, as Helena made her way to the door turning around at the end to add, 'and do call me Helena. I do find this Noblewoman business so tiring.'

*

They all awoke early, eager to carry on their search for the staff, although it took them quite some time to work through Bolton's instructions and finally find the study. They passed through many unusual rooms along their way including a circular room with life-like, sprawling trees carved into the walls, and a small room crammed full of abandoned, lonely toys. Luckily they had the map that Helena had given them otherwise they would never have found the bureau. After retracing their steps many times they eventually reached the ballroom, which according to Bolton led directly onto

Bentley's study. The ballroom's only source of illumination was light from the previous room, revealing a shiny marble floor and high ceilings. There did not appear to be any furniture in the huge room, and their shoes clacked disturbingly noisily as they crossed the highly polished yet dusty floor.

'Which way now then?' asked Caja. Her voice bounced off the stark walls and floor.

'It's this way. Follow me. There should be a door over here,' responded Gorran confidently, striding loudly to the other side of the room.

There were two doors exiting from the ballroom, and they opened the left one first, exposing a cramped and grubby study filled with decades and possibly centuries' worth of books, papers and those odds and ends that are collected over a lifetime. In the corner of the room, barely visible, was a laden desk.

'Well, this looks promising,' said Jory excitedly. The others nodded in agreement.

They entered cautiously, careful not to knock over any of the piles of clutter that were ranged haphazardly around the room. Along one wall was a long and narrow panel, around head height, with illustrations tracing the history of Kernow.

'This must be it! Look,' exclaimed Gorran pointing eagerly to the engraved initials 'BB' clearly carved into a panel on the front of the desk.

'Right, time to get to work at last,' said Jory with relief.

'Let's start again like last time. Caja you check the bottom drawers. Jory the middle, and I'll do the top and shelves. Put aside anything, and I mean anything that looks like directions or a map of some kind,' instructed Gorran.

They purposively set to work, rifling through all sorts of musty documents and disused items. Caja quickly found that many of the documents had to be treated with care, as they were so ancient that they crumbled into dust if handled roughly. She often found herself distracted from the task at hand as she became engrossed in the stories she came across.

One of the documents detailed the agreement that the Blakes had reached with the Templetons after the Templetons had aggressively taken over the southern Hundred of Kerrier. Relationships between the Nobles had been very tense during this period, and the Kernow Assembly did not have the power to stop the takeover. There were even a few antique looking documents that related back to the period when King Arthur ruled. Caja read in fascination about Arthur's Knights of the Round Table, a select group of fighters who had been known for their collective strength and invincibility.

After a number of hours of searching, the three had come up with a pile of possible documents related to the staff. As they were about to commence re-examining this smaller pile, they heard the distant gong of the breakfast bell.

'Well, I don't know about you lot, but I'm starving. Anyway Guardian Quinn will be here soon for our tour Caja. I wonder if he'll allow Gorran to join us. Gorran would you like to come?'

Caja looked eagerly at Gorran who responded with a warm yet apologetic smile, 'no, no. I'll stay here and continue looking for the staff. I've no need to look around the Academy. It's not like I'll ever be going there.' He gave a joyless laugh. 'You go, enjoy yourselves. But don't take too long. We all need to be spending as much time as possible looking for the staff.'

Although she had met him only once, Caja found herself looking forward to the arrival of Guardian Quinn. Just after the clock struck nine, they heard the sound of the doorbell, and the slow tones of Bolton welcoming Guardian Quinn to Blake Manor. They rushed out into the hall to greet him as Noblewoman Blake swept down the stairs, her arms outstretched in a warm welcome.

'Byron, how good it is to see you. It's been some time.'

Guardian Quinn's full smile radiated from his eyes as he surveyed Helena Blake gracefully walking towards him, 'Helena, it's good to see you too. You are looking as beautiful as always.'

Helena gave him a rueful smile. 'Thank you Byron. I hear you're to be Tour Guide today?'

'Indeed, indeed. Ah, Jory and Caja, how are you both today,' he exclaimed pumping both of their hands. 'And how are you faring at Blake Manor?'

'Good, excellent, thank you Guardian Quinn. Although, we're very much looking forward to our tour today,' replied Jory enthusiastically.

As they headed towards the front door, Helena and Byron fell into discussion about the recent events.

'I hear you've been up North. Can you tell me how it's going up there?' asked Helena.

Byron recounted the concerns about Nobleman Kilmar and Bramby before asking, 'and what of Penwith. Have you spoken to him?'

'Yes,' sighed Helena. He's a hard man to convince. He's insisting that Ennor go see him before he makes any final decision about providing his support. I don't think he can be convinced by a woman's word. I've sent a message to Ennor and hope he'll be able to convince him.'

Byron shook his head, 'the stubbornness of that old man. I know his son, Oliver, quite well. We were at Ambrosius together. Did you get to talk to him?'

'No I didn't see Oliver at all. Old Man Penwith was rather hesitant about divulging his whereabouts.'

After some further murmured conversation, Guardian Quinn gave Helena a peck on the cheek exclaiming, 'well Helena, it's been a pleasure as always. Unfortunately though, we must get going. There's much to get through!' With this, he ushered Caja and Jory out of the doorway.

It was a chilly morning although the sun was intermittently peering out from behind the scudding clouds. They went on foot to the Academy and were there within fifteen minutes.

'So we'll start with the main building, Kowetha Hall as it's called,' explained Guardian Quinn as they approached the large building that Jory and Caja had seen through the gates.

The splendid two-storied, stone building formed a blunt C shape with a tall tower in the centre and two smaller towers at either end. Within the middle, surrounded by the building was a tranquil blue pool from which the statue of a Wizard emerged, his cloak gliding out behind him, and his hand stretched towards the sky with a gently spinning, floating orb balanced a few centimetres above his cupped palm.

'The founder of Ambrosius Academy. Merlin, himself!' Quinn exclaimed proudly as they passed the statue.

As they hurried past, Caja stared in fascination at the orb in Merlin's hand, which was continuously changing through a kaleidoscope of colours. Merlin himself was not at all as she expected, with a short, dark beard and carefully trimmed hair, hidden underneath a short conical hat. His face was set in a stern expression, and he had a rather hooked nose and remarkable, piercing green eyes, even in his statue form.

'From his younger days, of course,' added Quinn noticing Caja's inquiring look, 'he wasn't always the old, wrinkly fella we all seem to remember him as.'

They entered the main building by the imposing front doors, and immediately turned to the left, hurrying down a wide, empty corridor with heavily-framed, portraits aligned along the walls.

'Now as you might already know, everything here is arranged around the four main strands of Telluric Magic; earth, water, wind and fire. This gives us our four main subject matters, Earthcraft, Watercraft and so on, and corresponding teaching rooms.'

At this Quinn grandly opened one of the many doors placed evenly apart along the corridor.

Caja gasped. The sounds hit her first. Cascading water as if they were stood right next to a waterfall. Then the sights assailed her. It was set out like a normal room for teaching with rows of desks and a main one in front. But there were no walls. Instead of walls there was water. Water in every form imaginable. One wall revealed a huge waterfall descending from a peak and culminating in a large frothing pool below. Another wall encased a fast flowing river, its water rushing perilously close to the desks and splashing them with its ferocity. The third wall portrayed calmer turquoise waters lapping at a tropical beach whilst the front wall was an enormous chalkboard with gentle falls rushing behind.

'Don't worry, it's not always this noisy. The rooms appear to let go a bit when there's no teaching going on. Sometimes they're all just puddles. You do get used to them,' said Quinn hurriedly shutting the door. 'Next stop the Firecraft room!'

Caja couldn't wait to see what was next. The Firecraft room was just as fascinating although the impact was less dramatic. The room was laid out a classroom manner with the desks arranged in a semi-circle. However the whole room appeared to be inside an enormous cavern, with flickering flames dancing on the rocky walls around them, and the atmosphere was warm, dark and intimate.

Quinn seemed much more pleased with this one, 'it can actually be quite dangerous to see the Firecraft room in its full intensity. It's pretty rare though and we tend to use another room if it's in full flow.'

The Earthcraft and Windcraft rooms were set out in similar ways. The Earthcraft room Quinn declared as his favourite as it was where he himself taught. Today the desks were set out on a slight hill in the midst of a wonderfully green field, with trees beckoning in the distance and lush green grass swaying in a soothing wind. But both Jory and Caja loved the Windcraft room best, which was floating high up in the sky perched on an invisible platform with birds sailing merrily past, and the whole room occasionally driving right through wispy clouds that left a damp residue on their faces.

The Telluric history, philosophy and law rooms were not quite as exciting although they were still far more enthralling than any classrooms Caja had ever known. The Telluric lawroom was set out like a courtroom, whilst the philosophy room appeared to be floating in a still, hushed space, with stars glistening in its vast expanse. The history room meanwhile was surrounded by high bookcases crammed full of books that seemed to go back into the distance forever.

As they stood in the history room with Quinn explaining some of the main teachings of Telluric history, which Jory appeared to be ignoring entirely, Caja whispered in his ear, 'you're so lucky to be coming here Jory.' He nodded silently.

As Quinn's tour of Kowetha Hall drew to an end, Caja asked, 'Guardian Quinn, it seems awfully quiet around here. Where is everyone?'

'They're all in the main auditorium where Dean Campbell's giving a speech. I thought it'd be a good time to look around. Come, we can have a quick peek at the Ambrosius Auditorium, before heading outside.'

With that he led them back to the main corridor and to two large doors with smaller windows cut into them covered by wooden shutters around head height. He carefully opened one of the shutters and they all took turns to peep into the auditorium. It was packed full with the Guardians in their ash-grey robes, and a smaller number of students in their green and red robes ranging in age from as young as twelve to twenty years old. The auditorium was laid out in an amphitheatre setting with rows of seats set out progressively higher as they moved away from the main dais. On this dais, Dean Isobel Campbell was talking earnestly to her audience, although Caja and Jory could not hear what she was saying.

'The Guardians are the ones dressed in grey, the students are in the more colourful cloaks, green for the Initiates and red for the Zards,' explained Guardian Quinn. There were many more grey cloaks than red, and only a few green.

Guardian Quinn then led Jory and Caja outside to some enclosed, grassed areas, which he explained were for teaching Telluric Combat. There were complex nets, small sheds full of all sorts of protective equipment, and what seemed like an assault course. As they were walking around the sparring grounds, there was a loud clatter from one of the smaller towers of Kowetha Hall, and a lime-green gas started pouring out from one of the upper windows.

'That's one of the research towers where the Guardians work,' explained Quinn distracted for a moment. 'Guardian Bowers is in there working on some new and very significant research.'

By this time it was noon, and a large gong had started to clang noisily announcing lunchtime. Students were emerging like ants crawling out of the buildings, and charging towards the four dwelling houses.

'I told Rae and Ralph we'd meet them in their house for lunch. Then you can get an idea of what life's like in one of the houses. They're both in Earth-Dwelling, one of the less rowdy houses, even with Ralph in it,' said Guardian Quinn leading them out of the main building and down a wide path to one of the lodging houses on the left side.

All the houses seemed identical from far off but as they approached they could see that each house, although built out of the same Cornish stone, was tinged in a slightly different colour, the Earth-Dwelling a natural burnished brown, the Water-Dwelling an icy blue, the Wind-Dwelling an ethereal wispy white, and the Fire-Dwelling, as expected, a light but fiery orange.

Ralph and Rae were waiting for them on the Earth-Dwelling steps and gave them a joyful welcome.

'So Guardian Quinn are you sitting with us today?' asked Rae happily as they entered the house.

'Yes, Rae, although Ralph you must promise not to eat all the dessert this time.'

Ralph replied with a cheeky grin, 'I'll try not to Sir.'

The hallway of the house was crowded with an ungainly queue, with the Guardians dressed in their different shades of grey at the front, and the colourful red and green students vying behind them. They were all lined up to enter the dining hall which lay just off the entrance hall. There were six tables laid out and room for seven people on each. After only a few seconds wait, everyone began to surge into the dining room, and Ralph and Rae led them all to a table near the back.

'So how do you two know each other?' enquired Rae to Caja once they had sat down and started upon their food. The tables were all filled, and the room was full of chatter.

'Um…well….you see….' fumbled Caja hesitantly.

'Family friends,' blurted in Jory, 'Caja is staying with my family in Trethewyn for a while. Come to see what real down-to-earth folk are like, haven't you Caja?'

'Yes, my parents decided I needed a little break,' responded Caja smiling 'to spend some time with our simpler relatives here in Kernow. Uncle Carson and-'

'Cardew,' interrupted Jory.

'Cardew. And Aunt Urma-'

'Ursula,' interrupted Jory again.

'Ursula,' continued Caja with a smile, 'although my nickname for her is Urma…They've been very kind to let me stay and experience the humbler things in life.'

'I see,' said Rae nodding unconvincingly and looking slightly puzzled at the smirks Caja and Jory were giving each other. Probably the usual family dysfunctions going on there she thought.

They nattered happily over lunch, with Rae describing their life at Ambrosius Academy and Ralph interrupting on a frequent basis with his own opinions. Students could choose which house they went into when they arrived, often choosing the one that corresponded to their Telluric strength.

'I'm a bit better at Earthcraft although I'm not particularly good with any of the strands,' said Ralph munching happily, 'in fact, it could be said that I'm equally bad at all of them. Whereas Rae here, is awesome with transforming things. Which generally comes from someone who is good with Earthcraft.'

'No kidding! That must be awesome,' said Caja, adding with a snicker, 'Jory here, can produce particularly strong wind.'

She laughed even louder when Rae and Ralph both let out

identical seal barks of laughter attracting the attention of those around them.

Jory grimaced at them putting his hands over his ears, 'it seems you all have something in common.'

Once the racket had died down Rae continued on. 'Well the Wind-Dwelling is a pretty good house to be in. The Fire-Dwelling, as you could probably guess, contains quite a few fiery characters, and there's a lot of arguing.'

'They do very well in the Telluric Contests though, pretty strong some of them,' commentated Ralph, 'although they used to set their dwelling on fire all the time with their arguments, but now there are so many protective wards around it that it's virtually indestructible. The Guardians got sick of having to rebuild it.'

'The Water-Dwelling has almost the exact opposite feel to the Fire-Dwelling. They're much more airy-fairy there. Off on another planet half the time. We're probably closest to those from the Wind-Dwelling, although the earth students tend to be more grounded than the wind.'

'Wouldn't guess that from me though would you?' said Ralph grinning.

All the houses contained a different mix of student Initiates and Zards, as well as the Guardians, whereas trainee Wizards moved into the research towers for their last year for the rigorous Wizarding exams.

'You rarely see them. They're locked away in the research towers day and night beavering away. They appear for some of the Academy events though,' explained Rae.

'Yeah, you usually see them at the Winter and Summer Solstices, and sometimes even Harvest,' mused Ralph.

'Solstices? What are they?' asked Caja, 'are they like Christmas?'

'Chriss what?' asked Rae.

Ralph looked similarly blank. Jory gave her a warning look.

Caja ignored him. 'Uh, Christmas. You know celebrating the birth of Jesus? Santa Claus? With Rudolph the red-nosed reindeer?'

'Never heard of it,' replied Rae shaking her head.

'Me neither,' added Ralph.

'Sorry can't help,' added Rae with an apologetic shrug. 'I've never heard of reindeer in a festival!'

Jory gave her a forced grin, 'I think the customs in Albion may be different to the customs we have here.'

Caja nodded slowly, realization dawning on her face.

'Is this Jesus a good friend of yours? Is that why you celebrate his birthday?' enquired Ralph helpfully.

Caja chortled at this, but stopped as Jory frowned at her announcing, 'yes, Caja's family does have some weird customs. It's most likely something just your family does, right Caja?' he added with emphasis.

'Of course, yeah just a little thing our village does. Thought maybe it would be celebrated elsewhere,' she said smiling, 'silly me. But do you do anything in the winter? You know, just have a day where you give each other presents and eat until you feel sick?' she added wistfully.

Ralph nodded his head vigorously, 'why yes, sounds like Winter Solstice to me. Best day of the year. Surely you celebrate Winter Solstice?'

'Oh yes, we just do things a little differently where I'm from.' Caja nodded her head energetically, 'what's it like here?'

'We celebrate Winter Solstice at the Academy at the Midnight Dinner and then again at home with our families. We decorate our homes and trees with snow garlands and illuminate everywhere with light, give each other presents, eat too much and drink pear cider all day long!' exclaimed Ralph. 'I love pear cider,' he added dreamily.

'Your parents let you drink pear cider?' exclaimed Caja.

'Yeah why not? Not like gallons of the stuff. Although Kitto did throw up one year because he drank all of Zephyr's cider as well as his own at the Midnight Dinner.'

Noticing Caja's intrigued look Rae explained further, 'Winter Solstice is held in midwinter, on the shortest day and longest night of the year. To celebrate our bond with the earth around us. What about the Summer Solstice Caja? Do you celebrate that?'

Caja stuck out her bottom lip nodding carefully, 'oh yes, definitely. We really like Summer Solstice…um…celebrations.'

Rae looked at her doubtfully. 'Well here, we light bonfires on all the hills, and dance until late into the night. It's held on the longest day of the year so even the little'uns can stay up late. It's not such a big celebration as Winter Solstice, but it's a lot of fun.'

Caja nodded happily, 'it sure does sound like a lot of fun.'

The lunch was over all too quickly for everyone's liking, but both Jory and Caja were eager to return to Blake Manor and continue their search. They made their farewells and hurried away, with Jory making promises to seek out Rae and Ralph when he returned to attend Ambrosius in the January.

'Let's get back onto it straight away. We've lost enough time as it is,' exclaimed Jory as he pushed open the front door.

He took a step in and immediately jumped as he found himself unpleasantly close to Bolton, who appeared to be standing motionless on the other side of the door.

'Master, Mistress. I hope you had a good morning,' he droned with no hint of a smile.

'Uh Bolton. Yes, lovely thank you,' replied Jory sliding around his inert form as quickly as he could. Caja did the same as Bolton made no attempt to move.

'And what of your plans now?' he enquired in the same sombre tone.

'Busy busy. Lots of plans. Lots to see and do here hey. It's such a big house,' replied Jory.

Bolton's face did not change, 'do you require my assistance?'

'Oh no, no. We're fine, absolutely fine,' they both started to speak at once, keen to get away from him as fast as possible.

'As you wish Master…Mistress,' Bolton replied with another of his grimacing smiles.

'Well, thanks again Bolton,' added Jory turning away to find Gorran striding towards them.

'You're back. Come quick. I may have found something,' Gorran said in a quiet voice glancing at Bolton, who was still staring at them in eerie silence. 'Come, follow me.'

Caja and Jory followed Gorran gratefully, trailing him through the complex maze of rooms and gloomy, cavernous ballroom until they reached the study where Bentley's bureau was located.

'See here, I've been trying to find out if there's a secret drawer in the desk, and I find if you tap just here.' Gorran gave a sharp rap to the side of the desk. 'Does that sound hollow to you? And if you open the drawer nearest to it, it seems like it's too small for the desk, doesn't it?'

Jory tapped the desk experimentally, and then examined the drawer. 'Yeah, I think you're right Gorran! Now we just have to work out how to open it. Here, we could try prising it open where the joins are!'

Gorran and Jory quickly set to work with a small penknife inserting it tentatively into different areas. Caja, realising there was no room to help them, set to work hitting the desk sporadically at different places, with a heavy, mouse-shaped doorstopper that she had found by the door.

Jory glanced at her with some amusement, 'what are you doing Caja?'

She continued on, commenting, 'well, obviously I'm looking for a secret catch. If I…' There was a loud clicking sound and a small drawer shot straight out smacking Jory who was bent over right in the head.

'There, see!' said Caja in triumph grinning.

'Yes, good job Caja,' responded Jory rolling his eyes and rubbing his head, but staring at the newly-opened drawer with great interest.

Gorran was not smiling, but was hastily reaching into the

drawer, a look of concentration on his face. He delicately pulled out an ancient looking piece of parchment folded in half. Painstakingly, with just the tips of his fingers, he uncurled the yellowed and crisp parchment. Caja and Jory hurried over to stand on either side of him, peering over his shoulders.

He crinkled up his eyes as he attempted to decipher the faint and elaborate script written upon the paper. 'I think…this…is it,' he said slowly, 'the instructions on how to find Merlin's staff. See here, I think that says 'Legacy bequeathed' although the "g" is all weird and here it talks of a 'gryphon'.'

The instructions had not entirely survived the turmoil of time, and parts of the ink had evaporated from the page leaving missing entries and half words.

Here lies the …
……which the Blu…
Comprising…. Legacy bequea……
Take the gryphon……..disclose…
…… Owlers' Cave.

Jory stared at the paper, 'well, there doesn't seem too much to it. It all seems quite simple really. We need to find the cave. This Owlers' Cave.'

'So how do we do that?' asked Caja, 'and what's an owlers' cave?'

'Owler is an old word for smugglers,' explained Gorran, 'the staff must be hidden in one of the smuggler's caves.'

'But first, I think we need to find this gryphon,' continued Jory.

'What's a gryphon?' asked Caja.

'I believe he's talking of a griffin. A mythological creature with the body of a lion and the head and wings of an eagle. You've heard of it Jory?' asked Gorran.

'Yeah, I believe there's even a statue of one here in Truro. Perhaps that's it! Perhaps we have to go there!'

'Maybe we don't have to go so far. Does a griffin look like this?' came Caja's quiet voice from the other side of the room. She was wiping the dust away from one of the carved murals that protruded from the wall. It was a creature with a sweeping, feline tail, the mammalian body of a lion but with outstretched wings, and the regal head of an eagle.

'Well done Caja. You're good at this! That's definitely a griffin,' said Gorran evidently impressed.

Caja beamed happily. Gorran took charge, spending some minutes attempting to twist the griffin's head and body this way and that. Nothing happened.

He stopped and sitting down on a box nearby said closing his eyes, 'let me think for a minute.'

They were all silent for several long minutes with Caja finding the forced stillness very difficult. Her foot began to bounce rapidly up and down, until eventually Gorran's eyes opened suddenly and he stood up.

'I think I might know of a way,' he announced slowly, and stepping towards the griffin he gripped the head with his left hand whilst putting pressure on the neck with his right. He held this position perfectly still with patience for several seconds, until a loud knocking noise could be heard. He let go, and the knocking continued louder and louder. There was a wrenching sound and Jory had to step back suddenly as the stone flagstone below his feet began to move sluggishly backwards, revealing a large yawning hole in the floor.

'Wow, that's impressive,' exclaimed Jory peering down into the depths of the dark hole.

'I've come across this sort of device before in my work with the druids. Look there are steps down there,' said Gorran, indicating a set of perilously, steep steps descending down into the darkness.

'Is that where we're meant to go?' asked Caja nervously.

'It sure looks like it Caja,' replied Jory.

'Don't worry Caja. Jory and I can go if you like and you can wait here,' offered Gorran.

Caja shook her head vigorously, 'no, no. I'm coming.

Besides, Talwin has said that it's gotta be me who releases the staff. You might need me.'

'Jory, how are you with glowbulbs? I can go and get some torches from Bolton if need but it'd be-'

'Oh I'm pretty good actually, it's the first thing Ennor taught me. Lead the way Gorran. We haven't much time until supper,' responded Jory, eager to get going.

With that he mouthed some complex sounds, and with a twist of his hand, and a slight strain in his face produced a bobbing bluish light with little wings that hovered a few feet in front of him.

Gorran smiled at him, 'that should do it Jory. Come on, follow me.' And he swung one leg over the hole to start his descent. The steps were slippery and steep but a ragged rope attached to the side of the earthen wall helped them down. Concentrating hard, they all descended slowly for some time in total silence. As they climbed further and further down with Jory bringing up the rear, a noise above them, seemingly originating from the study, made them all suddenly halt.

'What was that?' whispered Caja.

Gorran held up his hand, 'shhh, quiet for a moment.' They all listened keenly, clinging onto the rope. After some seconds of silence Gorran said, 'come, let's keep going. It was probably just the old house creaking. Careful now though. We mustn't rush.'

Eventually Gorran reached the bottom first, with Caja soon after, and Jory last. There was an earthen tunnel leading out into the gloom ahead of them. Jory's glowbulb was now floating in front ahead of Gorran, and they set off down the tunnel with Gorran again leading.

'Careful now. We'll go slowly. And tell me if you see or hear anything,' he directed quietly.

After a good ten minutes of following the slightly meandering tunnel, they began to hear the distinctive sound of flowing water.

Gorran slowed, saying softly, 'I think I can see something ahead. Quiet now.'

As they approached cautiously, the sound of a large volume of rushing water became louder and louder. Eventually the narrow passage petered out opening onto a narrow ledge on which they were all just able to squeeze. Running vigorously in front of them was a powerful underground river smelling strongly of the salty sea. As Jory directed the glowbulb around, glittering lights sprung out from opposite them.

'I think there's a cavern over there,' yelled Gorran over the mighty volume of the water, 'send the light over there Jory, over that way.'

Jory strengthened the light of the glowbulb and it flew across the river.

They all gasped. Opposite them, across the torrential water, was a spacious cavern. Although covered in all sorts of debris, the shine of precious objects was still discernible from where they stood. As Jory's illumination sailed across in a wide arc, they caught glimpses of all sorts of objects stacked together. There was a sword encased in its scabbard leaning against the wall, and a number of large moss encrusted chests as well as many items that were too covered in dirt to tell what they were.

'Well I think we may have found Owlers' Cave!' yelled Gorran over the sound of the water, and then urgently pointing to the left of the cavern. 'Back there Jory. Direct it over there.'

Under Jory's efforts the glowbulb soared across to the left of the cave, and there, leaning against the wall in the corner, stood a tall mildewed staff constrained by peculiar clasps that fastened it tightly to the wall.

Caja gasped in awe, 'I think we've found it. Merlin's Staff. Gorran, Jory what do you think?'

There was a moment's silence as they all took in the enormity of their find.

'I think you may be right Caja,' responded Jory with the same reverence.

'Oh finally! A way home!' exclaimed Caja excitedly, 'but

how do we get across?'

Gorran who had been studying the flowing water, suddenly cried out, 'look over there! I believe there's a submerged bridge crossing the river.'

'So there is. I see it!' exclaimed Jory pointing to the dark shape of what looked like a plank that could just be glimpsed about a foot under the waterline.

'How are we ever to cross on that though?' groaned Caja, 'the current's so strong!'

Gorran frowned deep in thought, 'Jory do you know the tide times? I do believe we're at the turning of the highest tide right now. The River Truro is strongly affected by the tidal currents. If this is the highest point we should easily be able to cross when it's low tide. That's probably why the bridge is underwater now.'

'Yes, it's true,' answered Jory. 'It's high tide right now. We'll have to wait until early tomorrow morning when the tide is low, and then I believe we'll easily be able to cross it.'

Caja could have screamed in frustration. She was so close to returning home, but now she would have to be patient again, and wait a whole night before they could even find out if it was the right staff.

Gorran seeing her disappointment gave her a look of sympathy, 'I'm so sorry Caja. I know how much you want to go home. Believe me, I understand what it's like to be far away from home. But you know, Jory and I'll always be here for you,' he said softly.

Caja smiled gratefully. It was such a relief having Gorran there to help.

Jory agreed. 'Yes, it's true Caja. There's nothing we can do about the tide now. And it'll be morning before you know it. Anyway, we'll have to wait for Ennor and Talwin before we can do anything. C'mon, let's head back to the Manor.'

'Yes, it's almost supper now anyway. And Noblewoman Blake will be wondering where we are. Come, we must tell her what we've found,' said Gorran setting off back the way they had come.

To their disappointment Noblewoman Blake was not at supper. Bolton explained she had been called away unexpectedly with Hicca but declined to tell them where she had gone. He insisted on staying in the dining room as they ate, throwing them all disapproving glances, thereby preventing them from talking any further about their discovery. Realising how tired they were after their day's activities, they headed straight to bed after dinner, with Bolton exasperatingly following them, claiming they needed help in finding their rooms. They could hear him hanging around outside, obviously reluctant to leave them, and before they knew it they were all fast asleep.

*

Menadue turned his head wearily, 'I have not seen you for some time. I trust you have good news for me.'

'Yes Master,' said the tall visitor dropping to his knees in a low bow, 'I have great news to report. I know where you can find the GateKeeper. She is currently with your dispatchers' boy and-'

'Oh really?' said Menadue in feigned astonishment, 'well of course I know that, I sent you to him!' he spurted out angrily.

'Yes, well what I meant…yes of course. I'm sorry Master,' muttered the visitor uncertainly, unnerved by Menadue's probing gaze. 'I've seen them. And they've not only discovered what Merlin's Legacy is, from the Prophecy. They've actually found it.'

Menadue stopped the monotonous tapping of his slender fingers upon the arm of his chair, and looked around. 'Now, that is indeed intriguing news. So the GateKeeper has already found it. I am impressed. Ennor and Talwin must have helped them. So, what is it exactly?'

The visitor smiled, content to have his Master's approval, 'it is Merlin's staff, Master.'

'Ah, as I guessed,' replied Menadue with no sign of

surprise. 'Have you yourself seen it, grasped it in your hand? What of the GateKeeper? Has she touched it?'

'Well, no, not exactly. They've found the cavern in which it is located. I could see it, but could not reach-'

Menadue rose unexpectedly, his obvious anger halting his visitor's flow of words, 'and why did you not verify its identity before you came to me. How do you even know that it's Merlin's staff?'

'I believe it is Master. It fits all our descriptions of the staff. I couldn't access it because of the high tide but I can reach it tomorrow before they awake,' he explained in a hurry.

Menadue's eyes closed fractionally, 'hmm... yes, this will work further to our advantage I believe. They've done all the hard work for us. It will be easier to take the staff after the GateKeeper has released it, rather than having to go through the arduous, although admittedly not without its fun, process of forcing her. You must wait until she has the staff in her hand and then call me. You have done well.'

'Thank you Master. Thank you. And what of the boy? Will you-'

Menadue interrupted him with an impatient glance, 'I will do what I like with the boy. You may leave now.'

The visitor walked carefully to the door, conscious of Menadue's dislike of noise. As he turned the handle of the rough-hewn door he risked a quick glance behind at his Master, reclining with a faint look of satisfaction on his face. Growing in confidence, he heaved a subdued sigh of relief; so far it was all going as planned.

CHAPTER EIGHT

Willam knew that his body was beginning to fail. He had only stayed alive this long because of his exceptional strength, but he knew he could not take much more without any form of nourishment. The excruciating torture had continued for days, with Menadue growing increasingly furious at Willam's silence. After his initial replies to Menadue's questions, he had refused to respond, and Menadue's rants had grown in fury and volume.

Today however, he seemed calmer, and this worried Willam. He knew his only chance of survival rested in Menadue still needing him.

'Willam, my young fool. Ready for a little more fun today? I must say I have quite enjoyed our times together but it looks like it will not be for much longer.'

Willam raised his head agonisingly slowly using the little strength he had left, 'your…h…hospitality has been most g…generous.'

Menadue released a gravelly chuckle which did not touch his eyes, 'managed to keep your sense of humour I see. Most impressive. Yes, I must give you that, despite your utter folly. You have lasted longer than I expected.'

'My m..m..mother always said I was stubborn,' retorted Willam.

'Yes, that is certainly true. Not that it matters anymore Willam Renlim. Today not only will I have the GateKeeper, but also Merlin's Legacy in my possession.' He stared gloatingly at Willam evidently expecting him to be taken aback by his words.

It was Willam's turn to let out a low chuckle, which he did despite it draining him of most of his last reserves of energy. There was still so much of the prophecy that Menadue did not understand. Although he understood that revealing parts would save his life, he knew at the same time that he must keep it from Menadue at all costs. Menadue's mouth turned up in an angry grimace at Willam's response, and turning sharply he departed the cell without another word.

*

Caja had lain awake for hours, desperately waiting for the sun to rise, eager to reach the cave and find out if it was the staff they were looking for. Finally it had deigned to make its appearance, creeping over the horizon to the east at which point she had fairly leapt out of bed and hurried to awaken Jory and Gorran. At her insistent knocks they had emerged from their room, half-dressed and grumbling.

'Yes, yes Caja,' mumbled Jory to her repeated questions, 'the tide should be right now. We'll be able to get to the cave. Just give us a moment to get ready and we'll meet you downstairs.'

Caja waited impatiently, sitting at the bottom of the great stairs drumming her feet upon the ornate paving stones. After what seemed an interminable amount of time, they both appeared again fully dressed and looking more refreshed.

'Come Caja, we can go now. Try not to make too much noise, we don't want to awaken the whole house,' whispered Jory as they approached her.

They stealthily crept into the drawing room heading for the opposite door. The roomy salon was still only outlined in shadows by the newly awoken sun, and they had to be careful not to bump into any of the furniture. As Gorran, who was at the back silently closed the door to the drawing room behind him, the shadow of a man slid in through the other door and crept furtively after them.

Eventually they reached the study, and Gorran gripped the griffin head once again opening up the hidden trapdoor, which they had carefully closed the night before. They moved faster this time, prepared for the darkness that greeted them. Down the steps they crept, their footsteps sounding loud in the enveloping silence, and onward through the tunnel to the narrow ledge. This time, the flickering glowbulb revealed much less water slowly drifting along the passage, easily exposing the narrow bridge. They tentatively stepped onto the slippery plank and walking with extra care, made their way across to Owlers' Cave.

Gorran immediately went up to the staff and reached out tentatively to touch it. 'Hmmm. So this is the great Merlin's staff. A little disappointing. I don't feel much from it.' He gave it an experimental tug. It did not budge an inch. 'Looks like it's firmly held there.'

Jory looked to Caja, 'come Caja. See if you can move the staff?'

But Caja was engrossed in a beautifully forged although rusty sword lying nearby and didn't hear Jory's question. 'Look at this. Its engraved with the initials LA and then I can't read the rest. Do you think this could possibly be Lancelot's? And look at this!' She picked up a heavy looking sceptre patterned with a complex constellation of stars, 'what is it?'

Jory approached her, eyes wide in interest. 'It looks like a druidic instrument to me. They use sceptres such as these in some of their ceremonies. Wow, there are some real treasures in here!'

'Come on you two! Don't get distracted now. We're here for one thing and one thing only. You can look at everything else once we've confirmed it's Merlin's staff,' said Gorran in an unusually stern voice. 'Caja, as the GateKeeper, you must see if you can release it.'

'Yes, he's right Caja. Try and release the staff,' admitted Jory reluctantly.

Caja approached warily, unsure of what was meant to happen. She stood in front of the staff for a moment staring at it. It looked quite ordinary to her. Not some object of great power. She hoped with all her might that it would be able to take her home. Taking a great breath she reached out her hand towards the staff but abruptly stopped at a noise behind her.

'What are you doing?' she asked Gorran perplexed. He had taken out the cross that he wore from around his neck and was fumbling with it rapidly, his eyes closed.

They snapped open. 'Nothing Caja. Come, we must be quick. Take hold of the staff,' he retorted sharply.

Caja, confused at his severe tone, turned warily and without another moment's hesitation grabbed hold of the staff. There was a sudden sharp bright light and a crack as if the rock cave wall had split open as the staff came away easily. Caja started in surprise but then gazed at her hand in wonder. The staff had changed from a common everyday tool to an enchanted object, emanating a warm, white glow that appeared charged with tiny, static lights. The carved raven that wrapped the top of staff had come alive, flapping its wings languorously, and dazzling patterns emerged covering its entire length. She stared mesmerised at its brilliance.

'I have been looking forward to meeting you GateKeeper,' said a low voice from behind her.

Caja froze, and in what seemed to take several minutes, but in actual fact took only seconds, turned to face this unexpected, new voice. Jory was standing aghast, his hands frozen in shock, an expression of horror upon his face, staring at the gaunt dark man in front of him. Gorran was behind him holding his cross tightly, and bowing obsequiously to the tall stranger.

'G…Gorran?' she stuttered questioningly.

The man smiled a lazy, predatory smile that did not reach his eyes.

'I do love a good betrayal. Not quite who you thought he was?' He raised his eyebrow inquiringly at her, his smile widening. 'Allow me to introduce myself GateKeeper. I am Menadue Enfer.'

Gorran appeared to be struggling intensely with himself.

'Gorran?' she whispered louder but barely able to say his name, 'you wouldn't….' She knew the answer before she had finished the question from the fleetingly agonized expression that traversed Gorran's face.

And then he bowed down to his knees. 'Master, it pleases me to serve you,' he intoned with a blank look now in his eyes.

Jory's focus was riveted on Gorran, his mouth open wide, outraged at the extent of his betrayal. 'But I thought you hated dark magic! I thought you were on our side! I thought you were my friend!' he yelled.

Gorran did not respond but continued kneeling staring up in reverence at Menadue, waiting for his response. Jory made to lunge at Gorran, his face a mask of furious anger but was hurled back and pinned against the hard cavern wall, chained by invisible bonds.

'Now, calm down Jory Hobart. What would your parents say?' said Menadue with a chuckle, his hand extended slightly.

Jory's face contorted into a look of bestial rage, aimed now at Menadue. He opened his mouth to let out a torrent of incensed words but found he could not speak.

Again, the contemptible laugh from Menadue, 'I've heard of your temper. Unable to control yourself are you boy? Perhaps you are more like your parents than I thought. Anyway I'm not here to listen to your drivel.' He turned slowly to Caja, 'we've not had one of your kind on our shores for many, many years Caja.'

Caja stared at him dumbstruck. She knew his face.

It was the pale face that had flickered through her mind,

many days earlier. The same feeling of dread returned but she could not stop staring. There was something enticingly hypnotic about this striking man; he exuded such a strength of presence she found it hard to arrange her thoughts.

'You're...how? How did you get here?' she stammered.

'You'll probably be able to figure that out yourself Caja,' said Menadue musingly, 'there are much more diverting matters we can talk of. There is so much I wish to know of your land. That is why, well let me be honest now, one of the reasons why, I would like you to come with me.'

His powerful stare rendered her virtually immobile, her thoughts scattered and unobtainable.

'First hand me the staff Caja. To know it still exists has given me remarkable pleasure. But who knows what could happen if it fell into the wrong hands, inexperienced hands like yours Caja.'

Caja looked down at the staff in her hands. She had completely forgotten about it. With her gaze broken, her thoughts began to clear. 'No, I will not,' she said with a little more confidence, not daring to look again at the compelling man in front of her.

Menadue chortled, 'ah, a little defiance is always good. Commendable even. We wouldn't want you to give in too easily.' He took a measured step towards her, 'but this staff does truly interest me, you -'

The faint but clearly discernible sound of female voices stopped him. Caja listened in astonishment. It sounded like they were calling her name.

'Caja, Caja,' came the musical voices again, although louder now.

Menadue appeared disconcerted for a moment, his attention focused on finding the origin of the mysterious voices. Then a suspicious look came into his eyes and he muttered under his breath, 'not those meddling women-'

But Caja did not hear the end of his sentence. For at that moment the voices had abruptly risen to a loud, almost unbearable cacophony, screaming her name. All at once, everything disappeared and she found herself whisked into the air, flying through time and space with no awareness of where she was. It was a short journey. She landed with a thump on a bed of soft grass, her limbs entangled although with the staff still gripped tightly in her hand.

It took a moment for Caja to recover her breath.

'What the hell is going on!' she yelled in frustration, smacking the ground next to her. She looked around. She recognized this place. She was back at the Hidden Lake where the naiads lived near Gwydhenn. As she gazed around her in exasperation, the water again broke in front of her, and the same three naiads arose cleanly from the clear, jade waters.

The leader inclined her head towards Caja, 'Caja, we're glad you came.'

Caja pulled a face of barely contained fury, 'glad I came? Glad I came? I don't think I had a choice though, did I?' she shouted.

The two abreast of the leader giggled in mirth. Caja shook her head in frustration.

'Why've you brought me here? What do you want? Jory's in great danger you know. And I must get back to help him. I must! Now!'

'We asked for you to come when we needed you. And you promised.'

Caja heaved a great sigh, 'so you decided you needed me now. Really, this has to be the worst timing. Why...' she mumbled off into silence.

'We thought it was actually quite good timing Caja. That man can be quite dangerous.'

'But you've left Jory there! Why couldn't you bring him here too! And Gorr-' She did not finish his name, but her face fell even further in desolation, and she muttered to herself, 'how could he?'

The naiads studied her in utmost fascination for a few moments evidently riveted by her anguish before one softly broke the silence, 'we warned you of betrayal in your future Caja.'

Caja almost screamed, 'but why did it have to be him. Gorran! Why did it have to be Gorran?' Shocked tears began to leak down her face that she was completely unaware of. Everything had happened so quickly.

Again the silence as the naiads watchfully considered her, 'do not be sad Caja. His path was already set. Even if Menadue had not found him, he would have betrayed you in some other way.'

This did not seem to console Caja, but instead made her even more distraught, her voice becoming at times consumed by involuntary sobs. 'But what now of Jory. Will you help him? Can you send me back? Maybe I can help with the staff? Maybe I can open a gate for us both to go to Cornwall and save him,' she pleaded in desperation.

'No Caja. You cannot go back now. Jory has his own path to follow. You're a loyal friend. Your loyalty has now been proven twice. We are happy for that. We never envisaged that you would turn out like this when your Aunt Flora and that man brought you to see us so many years ago.'

Caja's broken sobs brusquely stopped and she stared in utter amazement at the naiads, unable to speak for several seconds. 'I've been here before? With my Aunt?'

'Well yes, we already told you that last time. Your Aunt brought you to us when you were just a tiny baby. You had funny, scrunched-up feet like a little baby otter.'

'Aunt Flora? Dark hair, crazy clothes?' asked Caja incredulous.

'Yes, she does wear some marvellous clothes your Aunt Flora. We enjoyed her tremendously.'

'What....how did....why did she bring me here?'

'For your birth reading of course. Many of your kind are brought to us as newly-borns for their reading.'

'What...what did you tell her?'

'You'll have to ask your Aunt Flora that,' announced the leader of the naiads curtly. 'Now you have come here to help us upon our calling, and we thank you for that Caja. Which one of these attires do you think make us the most beautiful?'

The three naiads twirled around in front of her, changing in unison their skin like coverings, from a dusty gold, to a seaweed turquoise, to a shimmering opal jade.

'You brought me here to ask me that?' asked Caja incredulously.

'Yes, why wouldn't we? It's a matter of great importance to us. Now answer us, as you promised.'

'The slimy green one,' she answered abruptly.

Despite her sullen tone, this seemed to please them. 'It has been good to see you again Caja,' they murmured together.

And with that they silently sunk down again into the depths of the serene lake. Caja stood up panicked, undecided for a moment, unsure of what she should do. Suddenly and with a great relief, she realized how close she now was to Gwydhenn. Perhaps Ennor or Talwin would be there? Perhaps they could help? She bent in haste to pick up Merlin's staff, which she had laid carefully on the ground, and as she did so it began to glow again with the swirling patterns. She stared at it in fascination as the world began to spin gently, and then faster and faster.

She once again found herself floating through time and space, the shimmering of distant stars and rushing of wind assailing her senses, and before she knew it she had once again lost consciousness.

*

Ennor and Talwin had ridden hard to reach Lands End in the Hundred of Penwith at the southern tip of Kernow, and had not received the cordial welcome they hoped for. The Penwiths and Quintralls had known each other for years, and had always maintained a friendly if somewhat fractious relationship.

Old Man Penwith, as he was known, was in a foul mood when they arrived. He greeted them at the Castle gates with a frown and an exclamation of, 'come to harangue me even further have you Quintralls! I thought I would have some peace in my old age but no one seems to respect the old anymore!'

He turned and beckoned them to follow him inside without another word. Penwith Castle, perched as it was at the extreme end of Kernow was wracked by merciless sea winds and relentless storms from across the Mor Bretannek, and the whole Castle had a salty and weather-beaten feel to it. Nobleman Penwith led them hesitantly to his sitting room, holding his hand up to stop them speaking before he had settled himself comfortably into his armchair beside a roaring fire.

'Now you may speak friends Ennor and Talwin Quintrall. I believe I know why you're here. I have had that troublesome Helena here to speak to me. She pestered me so much with talk of this and that, I almost had her chased out of the castle by my hunting dogs.' A wry smile flittered across the old man's face at the evidently enticing thought.

'Abel, we're here to gather your support. Kernow is facing the most perilous threat, and it's vital that you support us to defeat this menace,' explained Talwin seriously.

'Yes, yes. I've heard all this talk of dark threats, and some old crony of yours causing problems. But I've heard many threats of this sort before in my lifetime and they never came to anything. And down here in our southern enclave we've witnessed no evidence of dark creatures or the Ereburic.'

'I can vouch for this-' started Ennor but he was interrupted by the old man. 'Wait! I want Oliver here to hear this. Oliver! Oliver! Roger, can you bring Oliver here. As quickly as possible!' He gestured to Roger, his manservant who had entered the room upon his calls. Within moments Penwith's son appeared, a handsome and agile looking middle-aged man with an open and pleasant countenance.

'Oliver, it's good to see you again,' greeted Ennor warmly. Oliver responded to Talwin and Ennor with the same affection.

'Come, sit down Oliver. We have the most crucial matters to discuss,' said Old Man Penwith with mock seriousness.

'Yes Father,' replied Oliver sitting down in the chair closest to his parent.

'Now, Ennor, carry on about these dark creatures that are prowling the land,' encouraged Penwith with a mischievous glint in his eye.

Ennor, with grave composure, gave Penwith a faintly wry look and then carried on with his account of the dangers that threatened them. He talked of the attacks on the villages in the North, the appearance of wolves and hobgoblins, and his sincere belief that it all heralded a great threat from the wizard Menadue who had become immensely powerful in the Ereburic Magic.

'What is worse, we believe John Kilmar has joined Menadue and will use his influence to persuade his neighbours.'

Penwith actually started at this, a look of shock on his face, 'I knew his father well. He was always a terrible tyrant to those he ruled over but I never believed his offspring would go this far. If it's true, it is the most tremendous betrayal of Kernow.' The old man stopped to muse on this for a few moments, his expression at last more sombre.

'You can be assured that the Penwiths will never join with anyone that uses the Ereburic, not in a million years. But I still do not see the need for haste. I don't believe there is much we can do from here, and my knights are such a depleted force that I need to keep them here with me at all times.'

'Your support in the Assembly and Order would be of the greatest help Penwith. There will be a meeting called to discuss this issue soon. Can you come to Truro, to show your support for this critical cause?' enquired Ennor more urgently now.

Penwith shook his head in annoyance and a stubborn stiffness came over him. 'No, no there's no need for that. I can't travel to Truro when there is no real need. And anyway I can't bear that Salisbury or Kilmar, or really that Blake for that matter. I'm sorry but I can't help you.'

Talwin threw a pleading look at Oliver. 'Perhaps your son can come in your place?'

'Absolutely not,' blurted out Penwith, 'he's needed here with me. There's no chance of him gallivanting off to Truro. We've more important matters to attend here. Is that not so Oliver?'

Oliver replied with an impenetrable look, 'yes, Father. Of course, there's much we must attend to here.'

The rest of the meeting did not go any better. The old man became more and more bothered by Ennor and Talwin's entreaties and eventually cut off the conversation altogether, unwilling to talk on the matter anymore. Oliver remained resolutely on his father's side at all times.

Their talk turned to other matters with Oliver joining in the conversation and Old Man Penwith falling silent.

'There are rumours I hear Ennor and Talwin,' commented Oliver at one point. 'Of a strange girl who's been residing with you. I met recently with Natan Palina who spoke of her.'

Ennor spoke cautiously, 'Yes, we've had our great nephew and his friend, Caja staying with us. They're helping us with certain small matters.'

Oliver nodded agreeably at them, 'my friend tells me she is most unusual looking!'

'Ah yes, she could be seen as unusual. She does not come from Kernow, but from Albion,' explained Talwin.

Oliver seemed satisfied with this answer and they all moved to the stately dining room for dinner, where they were served a meal of rabbit stew and vegetables by the downtrodden Roger. Old Man Penwith launched into a long, ambling tale of a fox hunt he had recently been on, recounting with inordinate satisfaction the way he had outwitted the cunning creature.

Ennor and Talwin did not stay the night. It seemed unlikely that they would change the old man's mind in the morning, and they thought it important they now reach Truro to help Caja and Jory in their quest. Not a mile out from

Penwith Castle however, they were stopped in their tracks by the sounds of galloping hooves headed in their direction. A look of practiced understanding passed between them, and they both readied themselves.

After a couple of seconds of tense silence, Talwin breathed a sigh of relief as Oliver Penwith emerged from the shadows of the trees, panting on his horse.

'I'm glad I caught you Ennor and Talwin. I thought I might have missed you. I didn't realize you would leave so soon.'

Ennor lowered his staff. 'Oliver. We didn't see much worth in staying longer with your father. We've more urgent matters to attend in Truro.'

Oliver grimaced, 'I understand. The old man is getting more and more cantankerous and mistrusting in his old age. I'm sorry I couldn't support you more during your discussions. You don't want to witness his fury if I disagree with him in the presence of others. And it's vital that I maintain his trust. I'll try to persuade him of the severity of the threat in private. I've spoken to Natan and Helena about it and understand fully the gravity of the situation.' He paused for a moment. 'There's something else urgent I must talk to you about though. It's about the girl, the GateKeeper, Caja.'

They both looked at him startled.

'How do you know about Caja being a GateKeeper?' asked Talwin with surprise.

'Ah so she is a GateKeeper. Natan told me of her, her name and her uniqueness. I must ask you. Who are her parents? Or should I say, who were her parents? In Cornwall?' he asked urgently.

'And you know of Cornwall?' exclaimed Talwin now looking astonished.

'Yes, yes. Ben and I knew it well,' answered Oliver hurriedly. 'But what of Caja?'

'Caja lives in the small Gatehouse Cottage in Trethewyn with her Aunt Flora. Her parents are sadly dead. Her mother was Flora's sister, Tarlia I believe. Are you talking of Ben

Templeton?'

At Talwin's answer Oliver dropped his head into his hands and became utterly still.

'Oliver, what is it?' asked Talwin alarmed by his reaction.

Oliver lifted his head slightly and replied in a heavy voice burdened with sadness, 'yes I mean Ben Templeton. You know Ben was my best friend. Ben didn't die in a duel as his mother has always asserted. It's a long story but the crux is this. We became friends with Tomas Goodwill, the GateKeeper when we left the Academy and with his help started making forays into Cornwall. For fun you know. We were young after all. A GateKeeper from the other side who Tomas knew would help us back. Her name was Tarlia. Ben fell in love with her, and well, …he married her.'

There was not much that could leave Ennor speechless but this did.

Talwin was reeling in shock, 'Ben left Kernow to live in Cornwall!'

'Ivy was in despair. She couldn't believe her son would do something like that to her. Leave her for a completely different world. She totally disowned him and claimed he was dead. She fell out with her husband, Tristan, over the whole incident although he always stood by her.'

'How did no one ever find out? This is incredible!' exclaimed Ennor.

'But there's more,' continued Oliver, 'Ben and Tarlia had a child in Cornwall and they named her Caja. When I heard you had a girl called Caja staying with you, the same age, it just seemed too much of a coincidence! I thought she'd died along with her parents but she can't have. It seems she's been living with Tarlia's sister, Flora all these years.'

'But that would mean-'

'That Caja is from both worlds, yes. And there's a good chance she's a Telluric, as well as a GateKeeper. The Templetons are a very powerful magical family, as you well know.'

'How could we not have known any of this?' said Ennor

shaking his head.

'Have you never told anyone of this Oliver? It's essential we know. Who else knows of this?' urged Talwin.

Oliver shook his head, 'well hardly anyone. Tomas knew obviously but he's gone. He always felt bad about his part in it all. Ben and I of course, and Ivy and Tristan. Ivy didn't want anyone to know. She saw it as a great disgrace upon the family.'

Ennor arose abruptly, 'thank you Oliver. This is indeed important news. I'm not sure what this will mean for Caja, but we must now take our leave.'

'Yes,' agreed Talwin, 'it's now even more imperative that we reach Caja. We press onto Truro now Ennor, as fast as we can ride.'

CHAPTER NINE

Caja looked around her. She was lying on her back by the solitary gate in the grounds of the ruined Kilmar Castle with Merlin's staff beside her. She thumped the ground hard in frustration. What was she doing back here now in Cornwall? Was this the naiads doing again? She had to find Ennor and Talwin and let them know that Jory had been captured. They had to go and rescue him. Would Menadue hurt Jory? What if he…if he…? No, she could not even think of the possibility. Those damn naiads!

She rolled over and standing up, confidently strode back through the now open gate with the staff clenched in her hand. She closed her eyes tightly and took a deep breath readying herself for the spinning to begin, but felt nothing.

Opening her eyes she found herself back on the other side of the gate and still in the same abandoned grounds. She stamped her foot once more in annoyance. And walked back through again, and then determinedly again but to no avail. She found herself always in the same place, in the grounds of the ruined Kilmar Castle and still firmly ensconced in her own world.

She stopped suddenly, aware that she might look quite odd if anyone happened to be watching, marching back and forth through a random archway with a large stick in her hand. She had to make a plan. This was getting her nowhere. At least she could go and reassure her Aunt Flora now. And suddenly it dawned on her; if what the naiads had said was true Aunt Flora knew all about Kernow, and could possibly even help her return. With this idea set resolutely in her mind she turned and dashed back towards the GateHouse Cottage with the large staff awkwardly clasped to her side, knocking into her knees with every step she took.

Luckily it took her only moments to get there and she burst in through the back door to find Flora, Aggie and Luke sitting by the cosy fire sipping piping hot cups of tea. She stopped for a moment in confusion. She had completely forgotten about Aggie and Luke. Quickly she leant the staff against the wall nearest her. They all turned around looks of relief upon their faces mingled with signs of vague annoyance.

Aggie yelled out first. 'Caja, there you are! We've been waiting for you for over an hour! Really that wasn't very funny. What were you trying to do? Play a game of hide and seek without telling any one else?'

'We were beginning to think that we might have to start seriously worrying about you,' added Luke slowly with a smile, 'we were pondering all variety of search and rescue scenarios.'

Caja stared at them for a moment, unsure of what to say, still tightly focused on returning to Kernow and rescuing Jory.

Flora smiled at her warmly, 'well you did have all of us worried for a moment there Caja. Luke and Aggie told me how you disappeared so suddenly after opening that strange gateway. I told them you were probably up to one of your pranks. You're well known for them.' She stared at Caja, pressing her to speak with a knowing glint in her eyes.

Caja grinned at them all, trying to hide her feelings of panic, 'yes, s...sorry about that guys. It probably wasn't that funny was it? I'm known for my um...terrible pranks. And that was a really terrible one... I actually ended up getting pretty lost in part of the grounds. I didn't mean to be away for so long. Although how long did you say I've been gone?'

'Over an hour now,' replied Aggie.

'Well, it certainly did seem longer than that,' responded Caja with a slightly hysterical laugh collapsing into one of the nearby chairs totally limp. 'Luke, Aggie I don't mean to be completely rude, but I think I'm going to have to rest for awhile. I really don't feel well at all. Do you mind…' her sentence drifted off as she leant back exhausted.

'Oh, no problem Caja, no problem at all, you actually look quite ill,' responded Aggie hastily standing up, all annoyance evaporating. 'Luke and I should be getting home anyway.'

Luke noted with an expression of concern on his face, 'Caja my dear, you do look quite under the weather. You have gone quite ashen. We will leave you to recuperate with your delightful Aunt, who I'm certain will be able to help you recover.'

At this Luke threw a beaming smile at Aunt Flora who smiled back slightly uncertainly. They made their goodbyes and were soon gone leaving Caja alone with Flora to her palpable relief.

'Oh Aunt Flora,' she exclaimed as they heard the garden gate clang shut. 'I've had the most crazy, unbelievable experience. You have to help me! But, you know about it don't you? You…you know about Kernow?'

Flora made no movement for several seconds, and then nodded her head solemnly. She took a slow breath exhaling jaggedly, 'yes Caja. I do know of this Kernow. I realised as soon as Aggie and Luke told me you'd disappeared that that must have been where you'd gone.'

She spoke quietly with a peculiar air of sadness. At this admission, a flood of words poured out of Caja. How she had found herself in this marvellous other world, her meeting with Jory, Ennor and Talwin, and more recently the capture of Jory. There was so much to tell it all began to become quite jumbled up with Caja jumping back and forth, and adding in bits of random explanation.

'Hush, hush Caja. Slow down. You're not making any sense. I do understand... I knew my sister and your father were involved in this world you talk of, as was our mother before her. I myself, was never involved as I'm not a GateKeeper like poor Tarlia, or you dear Caja. And they didn't want to drag me into it all as it can be quite dangerous, or that's what they told me.' Her Aunt gazed at her dejectedly.

'Wow, my mother and father went to Kernow too?' exclaimed Caja oblivious to her Aunt's worried look, 'my mother must have introduced him to it all! Wow! Did they talk of it much? Did they go there often?'

'I don't really know Caja. They never talked to me about it, and I never asked them. I was always quite content enough with this world. I'm sorry, but sadly there's not much I can do to help you.'

'But you went there? The naiads told me you went there. With me? To Kernow?'

Flora nodded her head again slowly, 'yes, yes I did indeed. I took you when you were just a little baby, barely out of the womb.' Her voice lifted a little, 'this nice old man turned up completely out of the blue. Timothy, no....wait....it's in my head somewhere. I just need to locate it...Toby, no, Tomas. That was it, Tomas!'

'Tomas?' Caja pondered this for a moment. 'I wonder if that was Tomas Goodwill? The friend Ennor and Talwin spoke of? It must've been. He was a GateKeeper too. But what did the naiads say to you Auntie? Did they tell you my future?'

'Why I've no idea. The naiads didn't tell me. They told you Caja. They whispered in your tiny ear and your little face lit up like a Christmas tree. It was magical to behold.' An enchanted look at the memory blossomed across Flora's face.

'But they said...' Caja shook her head in exasperation at the naiads inexplicably confusing ways. She stared intently at her Aunt again, 'but surely you can help me open the gate again? You must have gone through it with Tomas.'

'Yes I did, but he did all the work. We went through the

gate just like you. But I can't even remember what he did. It was such a long time ago Caja.'

'Really? You can't remember anything that might help me return?' cried Caja despairingly.

Flora paused for a moment, casting her memory back, 'no. Nope, nothing. Sorry darling,' she sighed heavily, 'I did try once myself, to go through the gate again, a few days after I'd returned from my trip with Tomas, but nothing happened.' Her face took on an unusually serious and sombre look, 'but really Caja, do you think you ought to go back? Ben always warned me that it could be quite dangerous to try and cross the bridge to get there. And with all the things you've told me about Kernow and especially this Menadue character. Are you sure you should go back?'

'Oh Auntie. I have to go back. I can't leave Jory with Menadue without trying to help somehow,' Caja blurted out, an agonised look on her face.

Flora gazed searchingly at Caja, a despairing look in her eyes, as if trying to search for something, anything that could make her change Caja's mind. Eventually she sighed again deeply, a sadly resigned veneer descending over her, 'your mother did warn me that this may happen. I just didn't realize it would happen so soon. You're still so young. If only you were a little older and more experienced, and if only there was a way I could help. But I've always known this other world is not for me. It was the same with Tarlia and Ben.'

Caja noticing Flora's dejection rushed to soothe her, 'Auntie, I'll be safe you know. I'll be with Ennor and Talwin, and no harm can come to me when I'm with them. They're great Wizards you know. Some of the best that Kernow has ever seen!'

Flora smiled weakly at Caja's enthusiasm, 'they do sound very impressive Caja. You must promise to stay with them at all times then. And tell me before you make any more attempts to return. I must know when you are planning to go.'

'Of course Auntie Flora. Thank you for understanding. I

must return to help Jory. I must go and try again now!'

Flora shook her head firmly. 'Caja, I will agree to you returning but not now. Look at you. You're totally exhausted. You must rest first. Anyway from what you tell me, this Menadue will have done what he wanted with Jory by now. There's nothing lost by resting for some time, and recovering your energy before returning.'

Caja looked ready to argue, but finding that she had barely any strength to even do that, decided that perhaps her Auntie did have a point. She wearily walked to the door picking up the staff that she had left there.

'Don't ask,' she said quietly, before Flora could ask her anything about it. Flora appeared quite content not to enquire any further. As she turned to go upstairs to her tiny bedroom she turned back again to her Aunt, 'Auntie, tell me one thing, how did you know about the piskies and the scarf?'

'Piskies? Why piskies are old Cornish folklore Caja. All old Cornish folk know about the piskies,' replied her Aunt with her familiar enigmatic smile emerging once again.

*

Ennor and Talwin rode hard to reach Truro by late the next morning. Oliver's revelation had changed everything although they were unsure how in so many ways. Caja's potential magical abilities meant she was a much more powerful individual than they had thought, and undoubtedly of great use in the fight against Menadue. They had never heard of anyone who had been born of the two worlds, and they were keen to find out exactly what it meant.

Upon arriving at Blake Manor sweating and once again sorely fatigued, they came upon a great flurry of activity within the household. Noblewoman Blake rushed out of the Manor before they had even dismounted, relief mixed with some reluctance upon her face.

'Ennor, Talwin. How good it is to see you! Hicca was just in the middle of trying to summon a firebird to send an urgent message to you but now we don't have to, thankfully. We weren't having any luck! I've grave, grave news about Jory and Caja I'm afraid… And Gorran.'

'Gorran?' exclaimed Ennor surprised, 'he has been here?'

'Well yes,' said Helena dryly, 'we thought he was sent by you. It explains things better I suppose. Come in, come in. I've much to tell you.'

As they hurried in behind her, she yelled in an imperious tone, 'Bolton!....Bolton! I need you now.'

Bolton appeared almost instantly from behind one of the large statues in the hallway right in front of her.

Helena jumped startled. 'Ah there you are,' she said brusquely, 'Come with us. You must tell Ennor and Talwin Quintrall about what you saw.'

She hastily led them all into the drawing room, Bolton sidling languidly behind.

'Noblewoman Blake. It's essential that we talk to Caja as soon as possible. Is she here?' enquired Talwin urgently.

Noblewoman shook her head wearily, 'I'm sorry, she's not here; it's what I must tell you. Now sit down whilst I explain it to you.'

Ennor sank into one of the comfortable armchairs whilst Talwin remained standing. 'Did they arrive safely though? Jory and Caja? Are they alright? Oh Ennor we shouldn't have sent them alone,' she said turning to Ennor with a tone of great dismay.

Helena hastened to reassure her, 'they arrived safely Talwin. I can assure you of that. Yesterday evening, all fine and well, although quite dishevelled. It has…it has been under my protection that they have come to harm,' her eyes fell to the floor in self-reproach.

'Come to harm!' exclaimed Ennor. Seeing Helena's look of devastation he added in a calmer tone, 'you must tell us immediately what has happened so that we can take action.'

'Yes, yes of course. It appears…it appears that Jory has been taken by Menadue and…'

'What! Menadue was here!? In this house?' exclaimed

Talwin, a look of frank horror upon her face.

'And Caja, what of Caja?' urged Ennor.

Helena seemed to shrink further into herself, 'Caja was not taken by Menadue but has ...disappeared. We don't know where. We've searched everywhere believe me... Let me start from the beginning. They arrived as you informed me to search for this Legacy. They were looking in my grandfather's study. I never thought for a moment they could come to harm in there! But it appears they found some secret underground passage that I was entirely unaware of. Entirely! It was Bolton who saw it all. Bolton, tell them what you saw.' She sank wearily into her upright chair grateful to leave the rest of the story to Bolton.

Bolton cleared his throat grandly, and leant forward in his chair, clearly happy to have an audience. It was a rather lengthy story with Helena interrupting regularly to speed up the somewhat meandering tale. He started with a frown, 'it was that boy you know. Always seemed suspicious to me. Was just a little too sure of himself. There was something...not...quite...right about him. He-'

'You mean Jory?' questioned Talwin with a look of disappointed resignation.

'No, not that one. He was alright. T'was the other one. Gorran,' countered Bolton shaking his head.

Talwin's head jerked back in surprise. 'Gorran,' she muttered. Ennor remained mute although his eyes had turned even more stern, waiting for the tale to unfold.

'You know I knew a boy just like him once, angry with the world this boy was. Geoffrey, was that his name? It was something like that. Geoff. Or maybe Giordan. Or...'

'Yes, yes, Bolton. Please do try and stick to the story. Tell Ennor and Talwin what it was you saw this morning,' interrupted Helena with a coaxing expression.

'Certainly Milady. Certainly...' A frown of fierce concentration and purpose came upon his face. 'So it was I found myself up early this morning, so early the sun had not yet risen, waiting for these young ones downstairs in the hallway. I'd followed them before and knew where they were going. And as I felt that one was up to no good, I thought I'd wait and check they didn't get into any trouble. They didn't see me as they crept downstairs. I often find young ones don't tend to see me. They snuck off into the drawing room, and I followed them all the way to Old Man Bentley's Study.' He paused for a moment nodding his head as if to affirm his own story.

They all nodded solemnly in agreement with encouraging expressions.

'The day before, I'd also followed them to the study and gone in after them to talk to them you see. Imagine what a shock it was for me to find that they weren't there! Plain disappeared! But I have good eyesight I do. My mother always did say I had good eyesight. I saw it even in that darkened room! An open trapdoor in the floor. A hole with steps leading down! I was pretty surprised I can tell you that. Been working in the Blake Manor nigh on forty years and I never knew of no hole in Old Man Blake's study. There's a hidden door between two of the bedrooms upstairs. Nobleman Blake used to use that one quite a lot.' His voice lowered to a conspiratorial whisper, 'for the ladies you see. He was quite partial to the ladies was Old Man Blake. There was one redhead in particular-'

'Yes, thank you Bolton. They don't need to know about my grandfather's indiscretions. Can we please go back to this morning's events,' interrupted Helena with a hint of exasperation. Again the thoughtful look and deep frown. 'So this morning when they returned to the study, I decided to actually follow them down through the trapdoor. I climbed down the stairs and into a dark passageway. I could barely see my hand. But I went nonetheless, as I knew they could be up to no good now. Perhaps I should have gone and alerted Noblewoman Blake, but then I might have missed it all! And that could have made matters worse!' He looked to Helena for confirmation.

'Yes Bolton, you did the right thing,' she affirmed,

nodding her head in exaggerated approval.

'So after following the dark passageway for some time, it gave me quite the creeps I can tell you that, I heard voices and so I made sure I was quiet. So that they wouldn't hear me you see. Voices and gushing water I heard. Then suddenly I came out into an open space and so I hid in a small crevice to the side. The three young ones were quite close by, over on the other side of the river in a smaller cavern full of a whole jumble of things. Although, they probably wouldn't have noticed me anyway. You see, young ones don't tend to-'

'Notice you, yes you had mentioned that,' interrupted Ennor, 'but what were they doing? What was in this cavern?'

'Well, they were all focused on a rather dusty looking staff. It was all old and filthy, held onto the wall by something. Then the girl grabbed it and it turned into the most wondrous object!' Bolton's eyes shone at the memory, and then turned darker as he recounted the next part of his tale, 'but that Gorran was up to no good. Fiddling with that cross around his neck, whilst they were all preoccupied, doing something sneaky. And before I knew it, He had appeared.'

'He?' asked Talwin.

'The one they talk of. The one Noblewoman Blake has warned me of. If it wasn't for her great knowledge and insight I wouldn't have had a clue. But I knew straight away who he was.' His voice turned to a deep whisper, 'It was him… M…Menadue.'

Bolton proceeded to tell them about the ensuing conversation between Menadue and the young ones, with great flourishes and elaborate detail. His voice took on a tone of bewilderment as he explained the mysterious voices and Caja's sudden disappearance. Ennor questioned Bolton intently on this, and sighed deeply upon hearing the details of the strange disembodied female voices. 'They do seem to pop up at the most unexpected times,' he muttered to Talwin, 'although we must be thankful that they saved Caja from falling into the hands of Menadue'.

She nodded gravely in agreement.

Bolton continued with his tale in a strident tone, 'once Caja had disappeared, Menadue became very angry. I was quivering in my corner, I can tell you that. He turned his anger upon poor Jory. There was nothing I could do. One minute he was fine, although being pinned against the wall didn't look too comfortable, and the next moment he was writhing on the floor. He looked like he was in a great deal of pain.' Bolton winced at the thought, 'and then, fortunately really, he quite quickly lost consciousness. There was really nothing I could do to help him. . .' Bolton paused lost in thought at the poor boy's pain and his own powerlessness.

'We understand Bolton. You were very brave to stay there at all. Really, there was nothing you could have done,' said Helena soothingly. Bolton perked up somewhat at his mistress' words.

'I think he would have killed poor Jory, his rage was so great,' carried on Bolton, 'but the other boy stopped him. Mentioned something about his worth, particularly as the girl and Jory had become such good friends,' he added with a grimace. He stared off into the distance.

'And what then?' prompted Talwin.

'And then they disappeared. That was it. And I hurried out of that horrible cavern as fast as I could.'

'How did they leave? How did they disappear? Did they use anything?' asked Ennor.

'Menadue used the cross that Gorran was holding and they both vanished taking Jory with them.'

Ennor nodded once, a glimpse of understanding on his face, 'I thought as much. Did he say anything before he left? Did they give any clue as to where they were going?'

Bolton considered this question for a moment, staring fixedly up at the roof. 'Well, they didn't say much to each other after Menadue's reprisal on Jory. I must say Gorran did look somewhat unsettled by all that. Menadue did say one thing to Gorran before they left though.'

'Yes,' urged Talwin, 'what was it?'

'He said,' Bolton brow's furrowed and his voice dropped

almost two octaves into his husky imitation of Menadue, 'there is a chance the girl is back in her world now with her mother. It's your turn Gorran to help me once again. I can't yet risk it. It will give you an opportunity to redeem yourself from this mess. He didn't really say anything else.'

Ennor shot a meaningful look at Talwin who imperceptibly nodded.

'Well, thank you for your help Bolton. Noblewoman Helena, we must be off straight away. Back to West Wivel, to see some naiads. We must find out where Caja is! She is our only hope,' announced Ennor.

'Although you must tell us if you hear anything, anything at all about Menadue or Jory,' added Talwin urgently.

'Yes, yes of course. I will have your horses readied straight away. They have been fed and had some rest. Again, I'm sorry that this has happened under my roof,' replied Helena, her penitent words continuing as they hurried out of the room.

*

Caja had lugged herself upstairs and into her bed and had slept soundly until first light. With the first chirruping of the birds she had pulled some clean clothes on, and gone back outside to try the gate again, completely forgetting Aunt Flora's insistence that she let her know first. Once again, she had tried every conceivable method she could think of to open the gate. In the middle of a strange chant she was singing, in an imitation of something she had heard Talwin once recite, Aunt Flora emerged, and in a rare show of anger dragged her back inside for breakfast.

'I told you to tell me first before you tried opening that darn gate again!'

'I know, I know. I wasn't thinking. I'm sorry Auntie,' beseeched Caja stumbling over her feet as her Aunt pulled her inside by the corner of her elbow.

'You must promise me you will not try again without first

telling me. You must promise.'

Caja readily agreed, 'I promise Auntie. I do. I promise I won't try again without telling you first.'

Looking somewhat appeased, Flora plonked Caja in a kitchen chair, and served her some steaming tea and buttery toast.

'Now, you will be going to school today Caja. It's only your second day and I'm not letting all this otherworldly nonsense get in the way of your schooling!'

'Oh Auntie,' groaned Caja, 'you can't be serious.' But she could tell from her firm tone that there was no chance of persuading her otherwise. And besides, she was having such little luck with opening the gate that it might be a good idea to distract herself for the day at school, and then start afresh in the afternoon once she returned.

She set off to school later that morning virtually oblivious to the hurtling bus, and usual near-misses with other traffic. She could scarcely believe that her first day in Year Nine had been only the day before, it now seemed so long ago. Well, she had spent over a week in Kernow in between so she guessed it wasn't that strange that yesterday didn't feel like yesterday because it wasn't. She felt her head beginning to spin and decided to stop trying to understand the time differences between Kernow and Cornwall. To her huge relief, Aggie was waiting for her at the school gates.

'Hola Caja! How are you feeling? Recovered after yesterday? That was a fun afternoon we spent in Kilmar Castle, until you went all weird on us,' she said although with a friendly smile.

'I know Aggie. I'm sorry again. I don't know what I was thinking. I thought it would be funny, and then I got so lost…gormless me,' she replied apologetically. Luke joined them as they were walking in the front door, jumping playfully onto Aggie's back. She lunged forward hesitantly for a few steps holding his weight before collapsing melodramatically onto the floor and rolling onto her back in feigned exhaustion with Luke trapped beneath her.

'I…I can't breath,' gasped Luke laughing. Aggie appeared unable to get up, floundering around waving her arms and legs in the air at the same time squashing Luke even more.

'Students! Really what do you think you are doing!' came a stern voice from the entry hall. Aggie leapt up energetically, an injured look upon her face.

'Ah Miss Murray. Tripped! Fell! Must have been something in the doorway. Landed on this poor fellow here,' she exclaimed extending her arm to Luke to help pull him up. Caja was trying her hardest not to laugh.

'You mustn't blame her Miss Murray. She was born with no coordination skills whatsoever,' responded Luke seriously. Leaning in conspiratorially to the slightly startled teacher, he added, 'it will undoubtedly blight her life in so many ways. We should give her all the support we can. You should see her trying to tie her shoelaces.' He began to swing his arms back and forth like an ape attempting to do something far beyond its capabilities.

Miss Murray raised an eyebrow in wry amusement, 'don't you have somewhere to be Mr Rainer? The same goes for all three of you, you don't have much time before class starts.'

In the classroom Jennifer joined them, and Aggie began to tell her about their adventures the day before. Jennifer did not seem too interested, 'I don't really know why you want to climb all over some old rotten ruins anyway. I'm glad I wasn't there. Sounds pretty boring to me not to mention grubby. No offence Caja,' she added pulling an apologetic face at her.

'Hmm, maybe it's not for everyone,' responded Aggie munching on some gum she had found in the dregs of her schoolbag, 'but I love that sort of exploring.'

'You don't think you're all a bit old for exploring?' queried Jennifer with an expression of derision.

'Nope, never going to be too old for exploring,' responded Caja cheerfully, 'don't you think Luke?'

'I concur Caja. One can never be too old for adventure!' he replied enthusiastically throwing his arms wide in an expression of exploratory triumph.

The rest of the day had passed quickly and Caja had returned home eager to try and open the gate again. But much to her mounting frustration, she'd had no luck. And before she knew it, she was back at school again, and the days began to speed pass with Kernow becoming more and more like a dream. She slipped back easily into her school days hanging out with Aggie and Luke, and more and more with Jennifer, who was proving to be a great addition to the group with her quick fire wit, and ability to mimic anyone. Then she had a bad day.

Since the first day, Caja had managed to avoid any more confrontations with the three new girls of the year, Patricia and her cronies, as they were now known. But somehow on this particular day, she was one of the last to leave the locker rooms, getting ready for her bus ride home. Before she knew it, all three of them had surrounded her, standing threateningly close. Only a few other students were around and they hightailed it, much to Caja's annoyance, as soon as they saw what was going down.

'We've been wanting to talk to you, Cathy,' said the skinny one.

'My name's Caja.'

'Whatever,' responded the leader Patricia, 'you know we think you've been avoiding us. Have you been avoiding us?'

'Um yes. You're not exactly approachable you know,' said Caja confidently although a little shakily. Where was Aggie when she needed her?

'Think you're better than us don't you? Just because you managed to get your fancy scarf back. Think there's something special about you don't you?'

Caja pondered this for a moment. Being able to open a gate into a whole different world was quite special really. Although it seemed that this ability had disappeared for the time being. She was brought out of her reverie by a sharp kick to the shin.

'Hey!' she yelled out. She had no one to help her. A few

well-aimed kicks and punches had her curled up in a ball in the corner. They were careful though; they hit her nowhere where they would leave obvious marks. Whilst one stood watch, the other two emptied out her bag, taking what they wanted, and ripping up some of her work that was due for the next day. They left her on the floor, anger roaring through her.

*

Despite the memory of Kernow beginning to fade, Caja still tried, almost every day, to open the gateway in the Kilmar Castle ruins. At first she tried with the staff, but after no luck with this she tried without it, using all sorts of words, phrases, expressions and actions. She tried pushing the door as before and falling through the other side; she tried saying special words as she went through; she tried concentrating with all her might on Kernow and all the people she knew there. She even tried hopping through on one leg. Eventually she decided to persuade Luke and Aggie to re-enact their roles for her, which left them totally baffled, but even this did not work.

'So remind me, why are we pushing open a door that goes nowhere, and then pretending to fall to the ground again?' enquired Luke after Caja had made them all shove open the gate for the fourth time.

'Oh Luke. I can't really explain. I'm sorry. You just have to trust me. Do you think I'm completely mad?' moaned Caja.

'Well, yes. Certainly a little Caja. It seems like something has come a little loose ever since that first afternoon we explored the ruins, some part of your brain or something.'

Aggie nodded her head in agreement, 'it's true Caja. Tis true. You have been a little bit weird.'

Caja sighed, 'I know. I know. But you're going to think me even crazier if I tell you….So I think it's better I don't.'

'Well, why don't you try us?' asked Aggie with an encouraging grin.

'Yes, why not? We already think you're bonkers so what harm can it do?' added Luke with what he hoped was a persuasive and understanding expression, but what turned out to be more of a beaming leer.

Caja looked from one to the other considering.

Aggie sensing her wavering added, 'you know you can trust us.'

And Caja felt like she could. Even though she had only known Luke and Aggie for just over a year, they were definitely the best friends she had ever had.

She took a deep exaggerated inhalation, 'well ok, here goes then.' And she launched into her story, starting with falling through the gate with Aggie and Luke, and continuing on to her experiences in Kernow. They both stared at her with increasingly bewildered looks, at times glancing at each other in confirmation that they were both hearing the same thing. At the end of her rambling spiel there was a moment's silence.

And then Luke piped up, 'well I'm sorry Caja. I must confess that you were right and I was in fact, on this very rare occurrence, wrong. I do now think you are crazier than before, and I fear our friendship will never be the same.'

Caja's look of hopefulness plummeted into one of crestfallen disappointment.

Aggie gave Luke a warning stare, 'oh Caja, it's not that we don't believe what you're saying. It's just that it's all a little hard to take in. Isn't it Luke?'

'Um…yes?' responded Luke hesitantly, 'just a little hard to take in. That's it. It's all just a little…' he grappled around for a word that did not sound too offensive, 'off the wall.'

'Yes, I know, I know it must all sound totally crazy,' said Caja despondently, 'I wouldn't believe me if I was you. And there's no way I can prove it to you. But please just believe for now that I am not totally crazy.'

'Don't worry Caja, we wouldn't hang out with you if we thought you were totally crazy,' replied Aggie earnestly.

Luke nodded in agreement, 'yes I must admit you've

shown numerous moments of actual sanity so I would agree that you can't be entirely off your rocker.'

Aggie shot him another reproving look, 'what are you going to do now though Caja? What about this poor Jorry? Is there anything more we can do to…um…help?' asked Aggie with another earnest but rather cautious look.

Caja thought for a moment, 'well, actually there is something you can help me with. I promised Talwin and Ennor that I would hide Merlin's staff somewhere safe. But I can't think of anywhere. Everywhere seems so obvious and I didn't want to hide it in the cottage because that would be the first place someone would look. Do you guys know of anywhere?'

Luke studied her intently for a moment, 'you know Caja. I think I know just the place.'

*

Jory had been puzzling over it for days. It had kept him distracted from the predicament he had found himself in. Who was this strange, gangly boy imprisoned in the dank cell with him? Whilst Jory was kept captive by only a single, feeble chain embedded in the wall, and shackled to his ankle giving him a certain amount of movement; the other boy, who if anything was younger, was heavily wrapped in glowing bonds, his arms stretched taut above him, his feet barely touching the floor. It looked an unbearable position. His shirt was ripped in places revealing deep-red, inflamed wounds that seemed to cover his entire chest. Jory could not understand how he could withstand it. The boy had been silent for the first two days, and Jory had wondered if he was even alive. But when he stared carefully, he was certain he could detect the very gentle movement of incredibly slow rhythmic breathing in his chest.

Jory had not been in a much better state after the beating that Menadue had given him. He had inflicted a pain upon Jory that had taken over all of his senses, until he was unaware of anything except the intensity of his suffering. Luckily he had lost consciousness, only regaining it again once he had been imprisoned in the cell. He had lain entirely still for a day, drifting in and out of sleep. At times he was sure he had awoken to see the other boy gazing at him with a glaring intensity, but he had fallen quickly back into a deep sleep again, with dreams of home mixed with nightmarish scenes of torture. To his surprise, on the second day he had awoken for the first time quite alert, to find that although still painful, the red and purple welts across his body were healing remarkably fast.

His attentions had begun to wander back to the boy in the cell with him, and also to Caja. He was bewildered by what had happened to her, but at the same time deeply relieved that she had escaped Menadue's clutches. Then on the third day, after two days of silence the boy had suddenly spoken.

'Who are you? I…I'm sorry to find you here with me,' he rasped, his voice a thin gurgle.

Jory started from the shallow slumber he had been resting in, 'Oh! You're awake! I'm Jory. Who are you?' Having not spoken for days his voice was croaky and alien to him.

The other boy let out a shaky sigh from the depths of his throat, and then his head sank slowly back to his chest. Jory waited in anticipation.

'Hello!' Can you hear me? What's your name? 'I'm Jory!' he repeated once again desperate for some response. But the boy had disappeared back into a death-like sleep, and would not awaken again in spite of Jory's increasingly desperate protests.

He had spent the rest of that day, and the next, undertaking different exercises to cope with his imprisonment. Ennor had begun to explain to him the power of the mind and he understood the dangerous consequences if he was to lose hope and fall into despair. To avoid this, he divided his day into different occupations, starting with a variety of physical exercises that relieved the ache of his captivity, and kept his muscles from falling into disuse. Then he would focus upon the lessons that Ennor and Talwin had taught him, trying to remember everything they had told him, and practicing all the spells he had learnt. He had quickly discovered that in the cell, his spells had less than a tenth of their normal power. Talwin had explained to him that because of the Telluric Magic's connection to the earth, his abilities would weaken in areas where the connection was not strong. He guessed that within this cold cell in a residence of Menadue's, the connection would be very weak.

Every day, at different times, a faceless jailer would pass in a meagre ration of food and some water through the narrow slot in the bottom of the door. With some straining Jory could just reach this sustenance. It helped enormously in keeping up his strength. Initially he struggled to swallow the watery soup with unidentified floating objects but now he gobbled it down without a thought to the taste. The boy ate and drank nothing.

He was in the midst of one of his stretching exercises, quietly flexing his ankles down and up in a bouncing motion on the fourth day, when once again the boy spoke.

'I…I am sorry. I d…don't think I answered your question. I am W…Willam.' He sounded stronger than before; his voice no longer just a whisper but with some strength of tone.

Jory glanced up, startled once again by the sudden noise but glad to hear a friendly voice. 'Willam…Willam. Hi, I'm Jory. How long have you been in here?' he whispered. He squinted up at Willam's face, which was clearly visible again after days of lolling forward. Willam was young, maybe a year or two younger than Jory, with ivory wan skin, wide-set blue eyes giving him the appearance of innocence, and fair hair with hints of ginger. He was even thinner than Jory.

Willam looked at Jory thinking for a moment, 'I am not sure n…now… What m…month are we in? I think maybe two months.'

Jory looked askance; how could he have survived this torture for two months?

'Why…why are you in here?' Jory asked.

The boy smiled faintly and spoke slowly. 'Menadue does not care much for any of my family. He believes I have knowledge that he requires, hence the methods of persuasion. Would you mind?' Willam nodded towards the filthy jar of water that Jory had next to him.

'Why yes, of course….You haven't eaten or drank anything since I've been in here. You must be so thirsty.'

With difficulty, Jory rose with the jar and staggered towards Willam, who was able to jut his head forward to where Jory could reach with the jar. It was a taxing process and took much effort from both of them. Afterwards, Jory collapsed on the floor panting heavily. Willam had his eyes closed, savouring the few sips he had managed. He gave a great sigh of gratification, 'that…was…most satisfying…thank you…Jory.'

'You are most welcome. But Willam…how are you able to survive without water for so long?'

Willam, looking considerably revived from the small amount of water grinned, 'I'm able to slow my heart-rate down so that my body is in a state of hibernation that needs little nourishment. It's a useful tool.'

Jory nodded admiringly.

'So my friend Jory, how…how come you find yourself in this l…lovely place?'

'We were…well…my friend and I were…well…looking for something and…well I guess Menadue wanted it,' replied Jory, looking sheepish at his weak explanation.

Willam smiled, 'I understand Jory. You don't yet know me. It's a good idea not to trust anyone here.'

Their talk soon turned to more innocent topics, in particular their lives and families. Willam explained how he had spent his very young years in Kernow, but had most recently been living in Breten Vian with his parents. Jory explained how he lived on the farm outside Trethewyn with his Uncle and Aunt.

Willam paused for a moment staring at Jory intently. 'I see

you have some ability…with the Telluric?'

Jory nodded slowly, 'yes, yes I do. Although I've only recently started to learn to use it though.'

'I thought as much. I too, have the ability. But there's not much I can do in this position,' said Willam indicating the glowing bonds that he was so tightly wrapped in. 'But together, perhaps there is something we can do…'

*

'Where did my dad come from Auntie Flora? I don't think you ever told me.' Caja was sitting in the garden with her Auntie, exhausted after another series of strenuous but futile attempts to open the gateway. It had been over a week now since Caja had returned from Kernow, and the agony of not knowing what had happened to Jory coupled with her late nights was beginning to tell. She spent almost every minute when she was not in school either trying to open the gate, or studying old books in the library to try and find any clues on how to open the gate. She had wandered all over the grounds of Kilmar Castle, and had not found anything to help.

The constant harassment from the bullies at school was not helping either. She had to be on constant alert, although Aggie, Luke and Jennifer were all trying to help her as much as they could. Her skin was becoming waxen and pale, and there was a constant tight, pinched look around her mouth. Her Aunt was beginning to worry about her, and had resorted to treating her like a little child.

'Sheffield I think darling. Or Leeds, somewhere up that way. From up North dear. He had a strange accent. I guess one of those Northern ones. I must admit I've never been good at accents. It's funny that I can't remember,' Flora replied musingly.

'Do you think Mum and Dad visited Kernow often? Did they never talk to you about it at all?'

'So rarely Caja. Your mother and father were a very private couple. And I didn't really like to pry. They lived on the other side of the village in the cottage the Leuwins now live in next to that odd couple, the Modleys, who they seemed to be good friends with. Although come to think of it, they did seem especially fond of walking in the Kilmar ruins. I often came across them there.'

Caja looked at her in exasperation. 'And you didn't think that perhaps they were up to something?'

'Well I didn't know until after they were….well later, after you were born, that the gateway was there. I always knew Tarlia was a GateKeeper. Grew up knowing it. But like I said, I didn't get involved. I've always found this world more than enough for me.'

'What were they like? My Mum and Dad?' She had asked this question many times before but this time she felt more of a need to know, like somehow it might help her return to Kernow, a secret they shared together. Caja's uptight expression calmed somewhat as she listened to Aunt Flora talk about her father and mother, their love of Cornwall and its rugged beaches and wide moors.

'You are quite like your father you know Caja. He was always terribly impatient too. Although when you first came to stay with me as a little newborn baby you looked more like your mother. You were premature you know, so tiny.' Caja nodded, she had heard this story many times before.

'Over a month early! You were a surprise. A wonderful surprise.' Flora smiled lovingly at her. There was the creaking sound of the gate opening and Caja jumped up happily.

'At last! They're here.' She had been trying to set a time for days for Luke and Aggie to come and show her Luke's special hiding place for the staff. Their plans had been constantly delayed however, as one thing after another had stopped them all meeting up. Caja, who had kept the staff in her wardrobe for the time being had worried constantly about it.

She hurried over to greet them, and to her surprise found not just Luke and Aggie, but also Jennifer walking towards her. Although she had become quite good friends with her over the last week she had only told Aggie and Luke about

Kernow and was not sure she wanted to reveal her secret to anyone else. But then Caja caught a glimpse of Jennifer's miserable face. Aggie had hinted many times that she did not have a very happy home life, and it was obviously beginning to take its toll. Caja instantly felt a strong sympathy for her.

Jennifer was the first to come over and give Caja a hug. 'Caj, how are you? You look great!' she gushed grinning in a rather strained manner.

'Thanks Jen, all good here. So are you coming with us?' Caja responded glancing at Luke and Aggie.

Jennifer grimaced, 'I hope you don't mind. I know it's a bit annoying of me gate-crashing like this but my parents are arguing again and I just need a break from it all.'

'That's all right isn't it Caja?' asked Aggie uncertainly.

'Yeah sure, not a problem. But remember Jen that this has to be kept a secret. Really it might seem silly but it's really important to me yeah?'

'Of course Caj. Anything important to you is important to me. I don't really understand what it is we're actually doing, but I'm just happy to help you where I can. After all, that's what friends are for,' Jennifer responded with a sincere smile.

'Thanks Jen, it does mean a lot to me.'

'Right comrades. Follow me! To the sea!' declared Luke, giving them all an exaggerated conspiratorial wink, and leading the way out of the gate, down the road towards the local beach.

Trethewyn Beach was a small, relatively unused beach, as the waves were no good for surfing, and the way down was too steep and rocky for most. Only locals, and sometimes teenagers looking for some risky adventure, came to this beach.

Caja had fetched the staff from where it had been perched behind the front door of the kitchen and was clambering down awkwardly with the long stick until Luke, noticing her difficulties politely offered to take it from her. Jennifer had stared in some interest at the staff, and Caja had given her a companionable grin, which she returned with warmth.

As expected there was no one on the beach, and Luke led them right to the southern end. Here he guided them over some large slippery rocks with the sea washing at them only metres away, occasionally spraying them with icy, salt-laden droplets. The going began to get harder, as the rocks thinned out, sandwiching them between the steep cliffs to their left, and the increasingly deep and rough sea to their right. Eventually they were all left standing on two small wet rocks, the waves crashing to their right, soaking them to the skin with sea-water now lapping over their feet.

'Where to now?' spluttered Caja in puzzlement, trying vainly to scrape the wet hair out of her eyes.

'This is the difficult bit,' acknowledged Luke, an uncommon look of concentration upon his face. He glanced at his watch. 'We should now be at low tide, so this is the best time for it. We can't wait any longer. We must jump over to there,' he said indicating to a small ledge jutting out from the cliff, over a metre in front of them with a deep trench of ocean between.

'What!' the three girls exclaimed in disbelief at almost the same time.

'You can't expect us to jump to there!'

'The water's freezing! We're going to fall in!'

'Don't worry, don't worry. It's not as hard as it looks. I've done it loads of times,' muttered Luke ignoring the rest of their entreaties, as he readied himself.

'He's finally gone the whole gazoozle. Barmy as!' whispered Aggie to Caja and Jennifer.

'Now Caja, take the staff. We can use it to help us across. I'll jump first now,' said Luke passing the staff to Caja, and without any further hesitation, he made a tremendous leap, swinging his arms forward and landing easily on the ledge on the other side. There was a little wobble as one of his feet slipped on the wet rock, but he quickly righted himself and turned around casually.

'Wow! Luk..ay! …. I didn't think you had an athletic bone in your body! You should be in the long jump team!' cried

Aggie in surprise.

'That was pretty impressive,' added Caja.

Jennifer was just gaping in surprise. None of them had ever seen Luke engage in anything more energetic than a fast saunter, and even then with such a swagger that he didn't tend to actually cover much ground.

Emboldened by Luke's success, Aggie decided to go next and made the leap, but only just. If Luke hadn't caught her on the other side she would have definitely fallen into the foaming water. Caja also made it across ok, but Jennifer was not so lucky. She faltered at the last minute, missing the ledge completely, and fell with a small shriek into the freezing ocean. She disappeared under for a second, and then emerged abruptly gasping at the cold, her eyes stark open in shock. Luke quickly took command and knelt down with Aggie and Caja holding onto him securely behind. He leant forward with the staff extended to Jennifer so that she could grab it and haul herself in. He knew he had to get her in fast, before a big wave dragged her out into the wild ocean and he worked efficiently and quickly. As soon as she was near he grasped hold of her and with surprising strength pulled her out of the freezing water and onto the rock beside him. Without hesitation, he pulled off her wet jumper, and wrapped her up in his dry jacket.

'Caja, you carry on around there,' he said pointing behind Caja, 'we need to move quickly now.'

Caja dithered, taken aback by Luke's sudden authority and unexpected capabilities.

'C'mon Caja. We need to get Jen warm,' he urged.

She turned around quickly. She had been too focused on Jennifer's plight to notice before, but the ledge extended further back than she had initially thought. She edged along it, as the others followed cautiously behind her and then paused in surprise. A dark opening had materialised in the cliff beside her, with the ledge widening and continuing right into it. The opening was small, only a few inches higher than her head, and the inside was lost in a blank darkness.

'Here Caja, take this,' came Luke's voice from behind as he handed her a torch, 'we'll follow you in.' She hesitantly continued on, a little slower now, the torch lighting up a small tunnel in front of her. Soon they were all moving forward inside the tunnel, with Caja leading and Luke bringing up the rear. As the sound of the waves receded, the air around them began to feel warmer and a little drier. They did not walk for long however, as suddenly the tunnel opened out into a large cave.

'Wow again Luke, this is really something!' commented Aggie entering the cave behind Caja. 'You really are proving to be quite full of surprises.'

Jennifer made some similarly appreciative noises before Luke entered, his expression of seriousness now gone, replaced with grinning pride.

'How on earth did you ever find this place?' Jennifer asked staring around her in admiration. The cave was quite large, with sides that sloped upwards gently and a roof that gave them ample room to stand.

'Well, there were these kids that used to bully me in primary school. You remember them Aggie?' explained Luke.

'Yeah, the Bosworth brothers and their friends. I remember them. They used to give you a real hard time,' she replied sympathetically.

'Well, they found me on the beach one day. And chased me. And I ended up finding this cave. They never did work out where I'd gone. They were quite flummoxed. It was a good day,' he added nodding with a grin of remembrance. 'What do you think Caja? Is this a good place for the staff?'

She replied enthusiastically, 'wow, Luke. This is perfect!'

'So!' said Luke brightly, 'tour time.' There wasn't much to the tour but Luke was evidently excited to show them. Caja stared curiously around her as Luke led them around the empty cave. There was something about this cave that reminded her of Owlers' Cave. She couldn't put her finger on why however, as it certainly looked quite different. After a few "oo's" and "ahh's" at certain features that Luke pointed out, they found a perfect spot to hide the staff behind a boulder perched on a ledge, and then realising that Jennifer was beginning to shiver violently, started back for home.

They all managed to cross the gap successfully this time, with Luke standing firm, prepared for anyone who needed help. They had hurried swiftly back to the GateHouse Cottage where Aunt Flora had fussed inordinately over Jennifer, insisting she sit by the fire, and lending her some of Caja's clothes to go home in. The sun was beginning to set as her friends finally departed with Caja madly waving them goodbye. She was so grateful for their help. As she wandered back into the cottage, the usual feelings of frustration that were now so familiar began to rise again, as they often did towards the end of the day. It signified another day lost without being able to help Jory, another day not knowing what could have possibly happened to him.

'Aunt Flora?'

Flora knew instinctively where Caja wanted to go. 'Yes Caja. Have one more go, but I want you back home within the half-hour, before it's completely dark.'

This time she sat in front of the lonely archway for some minutes just staring and thinking, her composure calm, her breathing regular and even. Think, Caja, think. She asked herself the same questions over and over again. What was she doing wrong? What was she doing when she last went through? What exactly was she doing? They were all pushing, the three of them together, with Luke in the middle, and it had been around this time in the afternoon, and she was laughing because Aggie had something down her shirt…wait there… laughing!

She was laughing the last time she fell through. Maybe that was it! Excited now but still not wanting to get her hopes up too much, she arose and walked carefully to the archway. She needed to laugh, and sincerely. What would make her laugh? She remembered something Luke had done that morning, and without even thinking began to laugh. Still laughing she stepped through the gate, not even focused on what she was doing but immersed in the memory of Luke's antics.

Again the whirring, the darkness and the bright glistening stars of faint colourful hues. Her laughing stopped as the swirling intensified, making her giddy and disorientated. She landed once again with a bump although this time she managed to stay on her feet. She laughed again out loud in a tremendous release of pent up emotions. She was in a forest, a forest of giant trees. Without even looking around she knew where she was. The air felt slightly different, a purer consistency with a stark freshness to it, and the light, the light was so clear and young. She knew she was finally back.

CHAPTER TEN

Jory had been discussing with Willam their plans for escape. It was now his sixth day of captivity and he was feeling stronger by the day. Although Willam still spent much of his time in deep sleep, he was awake for short periods of time during which they would chat earnestly. The small morsels of food and sips of water that Jory managed to give to him seemed to be having an extraordinarily reinvigorating effect.

'Unfortunately my magic is really limited down here so I'm unable to do much at all,' Jory was explaining, 'I've tried breaking these chains, but can't even break these pathetic ankle bonds. So if we can't escape, we must get somebody to help us. I've considered the jailer, but he won't respond to any attempts of contact I've made. But perhaps we can get a message out, to my Aunt Talwin and Uncle Ennor. They-'

Willam, who had been resting momentarily whilst listening to Jory's talk, perked up at this, his eyes suddenly wide open, 'you're related to Ennor and Talwin Quintrall?'

'You've heard of them too?' Jory asked surprised, 'why they're better known than I thought! They're my Great Aunt and Uncle.'

Willam looked exceedingly excited, 'of course I've heard of them. Their prowess as Wizards is well-known in the

Telluric world. This is great news Jory. This will most certainly help with my plan. If we could get a message to them do you think they would come Jory? Would they?' he asked fervently, 'there are not many who can actually help us but perhaps they can.'

'Why yes, of course they would,' replied Jory cautiously, 'but how are we to get a message to them?'

'It's something I've been trying to do for some time,' said Willam lowering his voice to a whisper, 'these bonds are stopping me from connecting with the Telluric. They are made using an exceptionally strong magic that I can't break but I've had some luck with loosening them. See there.' He indicated downwards to his foot. 'See the bond is slipping?'

Jory looked to where Willam was indicating. The bond was indeed looser around his left foot.

'If you can help me loosen this just a little more I may be able to connect enough with the Telluric to call a firebird.'

Jory eagerly began to follow Willam's directions. With much twisting and straining he was able to get himself into a position where he could help work on the bonds on Willam's foot. This involved him lying on his back with his arms stretched awkwardly above him. Upon touching the strangely pulsing bonds, Jory found that they felt hard as steel, almost as if they were melded into place.

'Now I know it seems like they might never move. But I believe that with a sensitive and focused touch, and a little bit of magic, you will be able to move them, even though it may be just a little,' Willam explained.

Jory commenced his efforts upon the small area that Willam had already loosened. At first he found it impossible to make any change to the bonds. His efforts resulted in not one millimetre of movement.

'You need to be less firm. A gentle touch but strong, with total focus. You must try and think of nothing but the bond, and at the same time bring some of your own connection with the Telluric to it,' explained Willam patiently.

It took some time, and necessitated a couple of food

breaks, but eventually Jory saw a tiny but discernible movement in the bond.

'Yes! Well done Jory. I felt that! That's it! Now you need only allow a little more and it should loosen enough for me to send a message.'

After another hour and a half of strenuous efforts on Jory's behalf, Willam claimed there was enough space for him to try. First he drank a couple of sips of water. Then he closed his eyes, and disappeared within himself, his breathing slowing down to barely one breath a minute. Jory waited agonisingly for almost an hour. The minutes ticked past torturously slowly.

Finally, a tiny smile appeared on Willam's face, and he opened his eyelids weakly. 'He's outside,' he whispered, 'I've given him the message. That is the best I can do. All we can do now is wait and see. It has exhausted me though, I must rest for some time.' And with that he shut his eyes and immediately fell into an exhausted sleep.

Jory stared at him for a moment, willing him to wake up, but quickly realising that this would not happen, reluctantly began his stretching exercises once again.

Willam slept for some hours. 'Has anything happened?' he asked suddenly out of the blue.

'Willam, you're awake!' Jory's shoulders dropped, 'no, nothing has happened. I'm sure they will have got your message though. It will just take some time for them to reach us!'

'You're right Jory,' replied Willam reassuringly, 'I'm sure that-' He stopped and lifted his head listening intently. 'He is coming,' he whispered.

Jory immediately knew who he was talking about. Although he had been imprisoned for six days now, he had not seen Menadue since that fateful morning in Owlers' Cave, and from his experience there, he was not looking forward to seeing him again.

All his senses became focused upon the prison door, his

ears straining to hear the measured footsteps now growing in sound. His heart began to pound as the door swung open and Menadue stood framed in the dark doorway.

He gazed at them with a look of malicious pleasure upon his face, 'boys, boys. Have we become well acquainted? I think we have, haven't we? All this chattering, all this bonding. Even I didn't think you would get on quite so well.'

His eyes glittered dangerously, and his pointed tongue darted out of his mouth once, to lick his drawn top lip. Neither of the boys said anything, Willam gazing defiantly into Menadue's face, Jory looking downwards, barely glancing at his captor.

'You have played your parts marvellously well. Well done, well done. Entirely as planned! So much easier than forcing it out of you. All the groaning and moaning can be quite tiring.'

Jory glanced quickly at Willam worried, what was he talking about?

'But now we have the ones I really want coming I don't believe I need you anymore. Played your parts too well hey boys? Willam this will be a pleasure,' he sighed with a look of deep content, 'Jory,' he appeared to be mulling it over, his head moving from side to side, 'I think we'll keep you for awhile longer. A bit of screaming to entice them in further certainly won't go amiss. I must admit I am enjoying the theatrics!' With this, Menadue let out a deeply, unsettling laugh.

Willam's eyes narrowed, 'you think you will win Menadue but you will not. You're blind to so much. You will-'

'Enough!' yelled Menadue abruptly, livid with rage, 'you have gone too far boy!' And without any further warning, vivid dark lines began to appear all over Willam's body as if an invisible scalpel was slicing him open. Menadue's attention was upon him, his eyes radiating a monstrous light. Dreadful sounds of intense pain began to emerge from deep within Willam as the lines began to multiply, appearing all over his body, and even upon his tormented face. Jory looked on in helpless horror, watching as Menadue gleefully began torturing Willam to death.

*

It took Ennor and Talwin, astride Elderson and Pasco, the rest of the day, with barely any stops to complete their journey to Gwydhenn. It was well into the night before they trotted wearily into their glade. They had decided against using magic to lessen the strain of the journey as they were almost certain there would be a time ahead when they would need all the magical strength they possessed. Talwin had used some of her healing magic however to nourish the horses and give them extra energy, as without it they would never have made the arduous trip in one go. She took some time attending to them, stabling them and feeding them, giving wholehearted thanks for their extraordinary efforts before turning to join Ennor. The giant graceful oaken welcomed his tenants home with a tremendous shaking of his branches, causing a light shower of leaves. They both smiled as Ennor called out his greetings, before entering inside and slumping exhausted into their well-used armchairs.

After several minutes of silence Ennor spoke up, 'we must go and see those troublesome lake naiads as soon as possible, and find out what they have done with Caja.'

'Yes Ennor, we must. But first we must rest. There's no point in trying to make our way there tonight. We will sleep now, and go there at first light tomorrow morning.' Ennor grunted in agreement.

The next morning, they arrived at the hidden lake just as the sun was beginning to glisten above the canopy of the trees. Like Caja and Jory before them, they settled themselves on the smooth rock beside the calm waters, and waited patiently. They had to wait some time, before eventually only the lead naiad emerged, cleanly arising from the silken waters of the lake in front of them.

'Ennor, Talwin. It has been some time. Welcome,' greeted the green-eyed naiad.

Talwin eyed her sombrely, 'greetings Ula, we hope you and your sisters have been well.'

Ula smiled enigmatically, 'why yes, we have indeed Talwin. Although we are being disturbed more frequently by all these happenings on land. Does he still grow in power?'

Talwin remained unperturbed, 'yes Menadue does. Ennor and I have been endeavouring to unite the Nobles in our fight to resist him. Is there anything your kind can do to help?'

Ula laughed out loud, as if even the idea was preposterous. 'Oh Talwin…you know we do not involve ourselves in your land-dwellers affairs…well not upon command anyway.' Her eyebrows raised confrontationally. 'But we do what we can….here and there…'

Ennor spoke for the first time. 'That brings us to why we have come to visit you today Ula. We believe you know the whereabouts of the GateKeeper from the outside realm. Her name is Caja.'

Ula regarded them teasingly, 'Caja…Caja. Yes, that name does ring a bell. Oh yes, she came to see us, with that impudent boy!'

'Yes, but we believe you've seen her more recently than that?' asked Talwin.

The naiad raised her eyes to the sky thoughtfully, 'Caja…Caja,' she mused. 'I do remember her. She had such lovely hair. Now have I seen her recently?'

'Ula, we know you have,' said Talwin coaxingly, 'we need to know where she is. It really is of the utmost importance. It would help us greatly.'

'Um, no,' the naiad said abruptly, 'I can't remember seeing her recently. Must have slipped my mind.' She began to giggle childishly.

Ennor's face darkened and he rose from the rock, suddenly taller than before, his shadow dwarfing the tiny naiad. 'Ula, I have never used my magic against you or your kind before but you are trying my patience sorely. Where is Caja?' he commanded in a forceful tone.

Ula's laughing stopped instantly, and her eyes turned sombre, 'well Ennor. It is intriguing to see another side to you. I quite…like it…

Caja was beholden to us for our great favour in releasing that brazen boy. So, we decided we would call in our favour, at a time when he appeared. It was very generous on our behalf, to take her away from that vexing man.'

'So you brought her here?' asked Talwin.

'Yes, yes. She was of great help to us, and then we let her go, as promised.'

'And did she have a staff with her?'

'A staff? Yes she did. She arrived with it. What of it? It looked quite ordinary.'

Ennor ignored her question, 'and then what did you do with her? Where did she go?' he demanded.

'Oh we didn't do anything with her. She did that all by herself. She grabbed the staff, and then whoooosh she was gone, another gate open, back to her own world. We were quite startled. We haven't seen that gate opened in a long time, and it didn't look like she was trying to open it. '

'So she has gone back to her world,' sighed Talwin, 'that's good. She will be safe.' She glanced at Ennor, 'let us hope she will be safe, and that she has hidden the staff well.'

Ula was suddenly interested by this; a sly look came across her face. 'So you have found out about her heritage?' she enquired innocently.

'Yes, what do you know of it?' asked Ennor firmly.

'Exciting isn't it?' she laughed playfully, 'as a GateKeeper with roots from both worlds she will be able to open the doors to the bridge in either world! We have never seen someone with quite the same, special heritage before.' She lowered her voice conspiratorially. 'She could become quite handy couldn't she?' she added raising her eyebrow innocuously.

'Yes,' replied Ennor suspiciously, 'she could. Now is there anything more you can tell us? I trust we will not find that you've missed anything out?' Ennor glared at her ominously.

'Oh you *are* so serious,' she laughed, 'but no, that's all. Do come and see us again soon. We do find our human visitors so entertaining.' And with that she sunk gracefully under the water again, her laughing eyes the last thing to disappear.

'What now Talwin?' asked Ennor, as they swiftly made their way back to Gywdhenn.

'Now we wait. And we carry on as before. We must continue to search for Menadue's hide out. At least we know Caja is safe for now. And hopefully she will remember to hide the staff as we asked,' replied Talwin.

'I'm sure she will. I fear there's not much we'll be able to do for Jory though. All this time we've been searching, and we're no closer to finding out where Menadue is hiding. Let's hope he has reason to keep him alive,' Ennor responded.

Talwin sighed sadly, 'yes we must hope that. As bad as it sounds I hope he plans to use him as a bargaining tool, which will hopefully give us time to save him. Poor Jory,' she muttered again despondently. 'You know that cross that Bolton described? The one Gorran had? I'm sure I've seen it somewhere before.'

'Yes, that might be a good place to start. You look into that. See if you can find out anything about it. I will send messages to our allies, to see if any of them can help us.'

They set to work with a renewed sense of urgency, continuing the research they had been working on for quite some time now. Talwin had collected books from the Kernow Library and from all over the country, and she now started out in earnest, particularly keen to see what she could find out about Gorran's cross. She knew she had seen or read something about the cross. It was now a matter of finding out where…and quickly.

It was a frustrating few days for Ennor and Talwin but as the shadows were beginning to lengthen late one afternoon she exclaimed out to Ennor. 'Ennor! Here it is. I think I've found it. It's not quite where I was expecting.'

Ennor, who had been outside preparing to send another

message to Noblewoman Blake via the stone menhir that stood as if on guard outside Gwydhenn, hurried inside,

'See here. It's another roaming key. Gorran has had a roaming key all this time.'

Ennor fell into deep thought for a moment. 'Then it's as we thought?'

'Yes,' affirmed Talwin, 'Gorran must also be a GateKeeper, the GateKeeper from Kembra. It's the only explanation for why Menadue would find him useful. He's certainly not a Telluric. But a GateKeeper for Menadue could prove very valuable.'

'Yes, very valuable indeed. Do you remember what he said to Gorran in the cave? "I cannot yet risk it." I believe Menadue can't cross the Nexus Bridge between the worlds. I believe it may harm him in some way. Therefore he needs Gorran. You know what this means Talwin?' said Ennor with a deep concerned frown.

Talwin sighed heavily, 'yes. It means Caja is not as safe as we thought. If Menadue has some underling he can send over there. We will-.'

Ennor glanced over at her sudden silence in concern, 'what is it Talwin?'

'There is a firebird outside! Quick, it looks like it has a message!'

They both hurried outside to where the giant, cherry-red flaming bird was patiently waiting.

Talwin cautiously placed her hand upon the bird's enormous golden beak. 'It's from someone I've never felt before,' she said curiously, 'someone with quite powerful abilities. He has...wait...He's with Jory. He's letting us know where they are. I can feel the location. It's in Trigg. By Minerva!'

'What Talwin?' questioned Ennor. He rarely heard her use the names of the gods, and her usually gentle eyes were steely.

'It's Kilmar. Jory is being held in the dungeons at Kilmar Castle by Menadue. All this time, and he was there! Come, we must set off straight away. That John Kilmar is going to get

what's coming to him!'
They both burst into action, eager to get away as soon as possible, their thoughts firmly focused on the journey ahead.
'Hello Gywdhenn,' came a voice from outside.
'Caja!' Talwin exclaimed as Caja entered grinning through the low door. 'You're back!' She held open her arms and Caja ran over to her where she received a tightly squeezed hug. 'It's so good to see you safe Caja. We were so worried about you.'
'Indeed it is,' joined in Ennor patting her rather awkwardly on the back.
Caja was overjoyed to see them again, 'oh Talwin, Ennor it's such a relief to see you. I've been trying so hard to come back. For days and days. After the first week I thought I might've gone mad. You wouldn't believe how hard it's been!'
'But it's only been six days since you left Caja.'
'Six days, really! Wow, this could get really, really confusing,' said Caja rolling her eyes.
'Caja, tell us one thing first. Is the staff safe? Did you hide it somewhere secure that no one else knows of?' demanded Ennor.
'Yes, yes it's safe. In fact, I found somewhere very, very safe where no one will ever think to look! But what of Jory? Have you found him? Is he safe? What's happened to him?' she asked urgently, a look of anguish rushing into her eyes.
'I'm sorry Caja. He was taken by Menadue and we've not been able to find him yet. Although-'
Talwin's concerned explanation was interrupted by a sorrowful outburst from Caja, 'but he could be dead!'
Talwin rubbed her arm soothingly, 'we know he's not dead Caja. We received a message just a few minutes ago. We now know where he's being held captive.'
The words penetrated Caja's consciousness slowly. She heaved a slow sigh of relief, 'oh thank god. Where is he? We must leave now! We must! Let's get the horses ready now!'
'We will be leaving very soon Caja. He's being held at Kilmar Castle. But first we have some extremely important

news that we must tell you. It may come as a bit of a shock. Please, sit down.'

Caja reluctantly took a seat on the edge of one of the hard-backed kitchen chairs, pulsing her foot up and down impatiently.

Ennor and Talwin gazed at her, waiting for her to stop fidgeting. It took some time.

Talwin began. 'Caja, we've just returned from the Penwiths at Lands End where we found out some… well some quite extraordinary news from Oliver Penwith. It concerns you and your family.'

At this mention of her family, Caja leant forward keenly interested her foot arrested in mid-air. 'Me?' she said puzzled, 'and my family?'

'Yes Caja, it's about your father. He…he's not from your land as you thought. He is, well was in fact from here, from Kernow.'

Caja gazed at them dumbfounded, 'what? What do you mean?'

'Your father, Ben was from here, from Kernow. His name was Ben Templeton. And you have already met his mother, Ivy Templeton.'

'WHAT!' yelled Caja, 'that old witch is my grandmother!'

'Caja!' said Ennor sternly, 'she's not all that bad. She may come across as harsh but she has had a hard life.'

'But my father's name was Delaney, not Templeton. It can't be the same Ben.'

Talwin grabbed hold of Caja's limp hand, 'Caja. It was careless of us not to make the connection. Ivy's maiden name is Delaney. Ben decided to take her maiden name when he went to your world.'

Caja felt disjointed, her mind a foggy muddle. How could this be?

'But…but why would he…what…what does this mean?' she stuttered. 'So that's why Noblewoman Templeton kept staring at me!' she exclaimed to herself.

Talwin carried on holding her hand, trying to calm her

agitation, 'Caja, it means you have inherited genes from both of our worlds. Your father's family are a powerful Telluric family in Kernow. Your mother's family a GateKeeper family for countless generations in your world. We believe this means you'll have the unique ability to open gates easily in both worlds without any need for roaming keys.'

Caja looked up, 'But how did my father come to be in Cornwall? How did he get there?'

'It appears your father, Ben, made many ventures into your world with his best friend Oliver Penwith, and the help of Tomas Goodwill,' explained Talwin.

'Although why Tomas didn't think it important to tell us this information I will never understand,' added Ennor solemnly.

'With your father and mother's heritage, it's very possible that you can connect to the Telluric too, that you possess magical abilities Caja,' added Talwin.

Caja was in too much shock to respond. She thought her father was from somewhere in Northern England and now this! Her foot started tapping again incessantly.

'Caja?' queried Talwin concerned.

'I...I just can't quite believe this. I mean, I thought my father was from Sheffield! I just never even thought...well why would you? Wait...did you just say as well as being a GateKeeper I might be able to use magic too?'

'Yes Caja. With your father's family heritage, it's certainly possible. Although we've never heard of a GateKeeper being a Telluric too before. There's usually no connection.'

A glow of delight gradually unfurled across Caja's face. 'Magical! I might be magical! Let's try now! What should I do? How does it work? You have *got* to show me!' She began to wave her hands around theatrically in her attempt at magical gestures.

'Calm down Caja. We can certainly test you. But tell us first, have you had any clues that you might be magical? It's unusual not to have had any indication by your age.'

Caja mused on Talwin's question for a moment before a

light of understanding flickered in her eyes. 'Why yes Talwin! I have! Once in the woods when I thought I heard the trees calling my name. And I had this odd feeling once, a feeling of premonition and I think I saw Menadue's face, way before I ever met him!' She quickly described to them her strange experiences. As she talked, Ennor and Talwin grinned and nodded knowingly at each other.

'It provides compelling evidence Caja. I think it also explains why you were able to turn away from the vorgon,' replied Talwin nodding, 'that did confuse me. I've never heard of one so young doing it before, even with Ennor's help. It will be interesting to find where your strengths lie. Although it does seem you may have something of the Seer about you, which could come in very handy.'

'Because of the weak link to the earth in your own land, your Telluric abilities were probably barely detectable there,' continued Ennor. 'Talwin is right. It seems likely that you possess some intriguing foretelling abilities, those of the Seer. Here, in Kernow, we believe your magic will start manifesting more and your powers will grow stronger,' added Ennor.

Talwin stood up and opening one of the cabinets fetched a candle, bringing it over and setting it upon the table, 'now Caja focus. We must do a test before we leave. This will conclusively prove for us your abilities.'

She lit the candle with some matches from the centre of the table. 'Now, look at the candle, at the flame and try to empty your mind. Concentrate fully on the flame. Once your mind is empty you'll feel something there at the edge of your consciousness. That's the Telluric. You need to try and connect with it. To touch it with your own mind.'

Caja settled down properly on the chair, and concentrated fully for twenty seconds without saying anything. Then her head whipped round to Ennor and Talwin, 'I can't feel it! I knew it! I'm not magical. There's nothing there!'

Ennor responded reassuringly, 'Caja, you have to focus for much longer than that. You have to rid yourself of your desire to do or think about anything else and understand that this is the most important thing you need to do right now.'

Talwin continued on, 'understand Caja, the Telluric has always been there. So it's like detecting a background noise that you have heard all your life, and can suddenly hear.'

'But what's it feel like?' asked Caja impatiently.

'It's indescribable Caja. We can only show you the path towards it. You must empty your mind, and you will be naturally attracted to it. It's connecting with the earth itself which we are all a part of. Use the candle to focus your mind. It'll help you to stop the thinking. We will help you.'

Caja turned back to gaze at the candle, and Talwin and Ennor sat close by, using their own Telluric connection to remove all sounds of distractions, and aid Caja's concentration.

It was a good few minutes this time before she turned back again. 'I felt it! I felt something. I did! I'm sure!'

Ennor smiled, 'good Caja, good. Now see if you can connect again, and then try to put the candle out with your mind, just will it.'

Caja concentrated fiercely on the dancing flame. It gambolled around with no rhythm, at times steady with little movement, at other times jumping wildly. At first, her mind once again jumped around as much as the flame, but with Ennor and Talwin's comforting support beside her, she gradually felt her mind stop its chattering, and she was just gazing at the flame in serenity, willing it to go out. The warmth of the colours was oddly absorbing. She felt completely at peace and at one with all the world around her. Behind her, Talwin smiled as he felt her connect so softly with the Telluric Magic. The flame gently died out.

Caja's head shot up suddenly, 'was that me! Did I really do that?' she asked excitedly.

'Yes Caja, you did indeed. You connected with the earth's deepest energy,' replied Ennor.

'Yes! I felt that too. The same connection I felt before with the vorgon. Oh wait til Jory hears about this. And Gorr-' Caja pulled in a sharp breath. 'Oh Ennor, Talwin, do you know about Gorran?'

Talwin nodded her head sadly, 'yes Caja, we do know. Bolton followed you down to Owlers' Cave. It was how we knew the naiads had taken you.'

'I just can't believe he did it. Why would he do such a thing?' she asked in anguish.

'There are many reasons why people do things Caja. We don't know what sort of life he has had. But it seems that it was one that pushed him towards the Dark.' Talwin paused and then added. 'You must know that Gorran is also a GateKeeper Caja. And we believe he has a roaming key.'

Caja stared at Ennor in amazement, 'Gorran a GateKeeper too?'

'Yes. And his betrayal has explained some other issues that were puzzling us,' continued Ennor. 'We've found out from the Villants, Jory's Uncle and Aunt, that it was he who alerted Menadue to your arrival here. We think he may have been watching you for some time, possibly even in your world. He called in at the farm just after you and Jory left. It's how the wolves found you so quickly.'

Caja let out a long groan of misery, 'that too! How could he?' she muttered abjectly.

'We're sorry for his betrayal, Caja. We'll be more careful with who we choose to aid us from now on. But we must prepare to leave now, to rescue Jory.'

Caja jumped up startled. 'Yes of course! How long will it take us to get there! We must leave straight away.'

Talwin glanced swiftly at Ennor before hesitantly replying, 'Caja, you'll not be able to come with us. It's far too dangerous for you. Especially now. We can't risk you being harmed.'

Caja struggled to contain her frustration. 'NO! I have to come! I have to help find Jory. How can I stay here waiting when I know he's in danger. I must come!'

'Caja, we do understand. But think. How are you going to help? You've only just learnt of your magic and you can't use it yet in any meaningful way. What will you be able to do to help?'

'I…I…I can be the lookout or something. I don't know,' she replied, 'anything. I just need to come with you!'

Ennor's face took on an unyielding expression. 'Caja, you do realize that you'll almost certainly get in our way? Menadue is one of the greatest and most dangerous Wizards to have ever lived. And he wants you. You being with us will just hold us back!'

A look of reluctant acceptance stole across Caja's face. She sighed unhappily, 'OK, OK, I get it. I'll be a pain, get in the way. What am I meant to do whilst you're gone though?'

Talwin answered, 'you can stay here Caja. Gwydhenn will look after you. And you can start your Telluric tuition. There are many books you must read to get even the most basic idea about how magic works.'

Caja glanced upwards at the great monolithic tree serenely swathing the home of Ennor and Talwin. 'Well I guess that won't be so bad. How long will you be gone?'

'It will take us at least four hours on the horses to get there. And to do it that quickly we must first help the horses with magic. We'll start straight away,' responded Ennor.

'Oh so long,' moaned Caja. As Talwin and Ennor hurried over to the stables, she flopped down outside in the glade, disheartened by her inability to help with Jory's rescue. The soft grass was warm and yielding beneath her. The extraordinary news that Ennor and Talwin had given her began to distract her from her frustration. To think her father came from this strange land! And even stranger, that she was in fact magical. She began to realize that her whole life had changed irreversibly in that instant they had told her. Kernow was now indelibly interwoven into her life, her heritage and new abilities a part of the beautiful landscape around her. The possibilities began to stream through her mind; would she be able to do magic in her world? Would she need to leave her world now? Would she need to be trained at Ambrosius like Jory?

Oh Jory, her thoughts flew back to him, and the imminent

trip ahead to rescue him. She gazed at the wispy clouds fleeing past high above her in the vast, azure sky. She so hoped he was unharmed. She felt somehow that it was her fault that he had got messed up in all of this. She stared hard at the clouds lost in her guilt and worries. And as she stared a peculiar thing began to happen. The clouds began to take on shapes, the distinct forms of recognizable creatures. She smiled; she had often played at creating objects out of the clouds, although this was undoubtedly the best she had ever managed. As she continued to stare, her amusement began to turn to bewilderment. Three of the clouds were now in the distinct form of…dragons. And they were moving towards her, fast, in fact very fast. Within a few moments, the three dragon-shaped clouds had taken on definite colours and were barely a mile away.

'Uh….Ennor….Talwin… can you come out here please?' she shouted nervously sitting up onto her elbows as the clouds rapidly hastened towards her.

Talwin emerged from Gwydhenn preoccupied with preparations for their journey. 'Yes Caja, what is it?'

'Look,' whispered Caja mesmerised by the giant cloud dragons that were by now only half a mile away. Their shapes were instantly recognizable, and their colours were no longer just the pale white of clouds but soft hues of emerald, plum, and grey. The three dragons were huge, at least three times the size of an elephant, with droopy, gangling bellies, and flapping wings that seemed too small to hold them up. Their extended snouts did not quite cover their many rows of teeth, and were topped by unblinking eyes that appeared incongruously gentle compared to the rest of them. Their tiny feet which had been tucked into their underbellies were now unfurling like the landing gear of an aircraft. It was clear they were heading straight for them and intending to land close by.

Talwin saw them immediately and stopped in her tracks. 'Ennor, I think you should come here too!' she called with enough urgency in her voice to bring him running from the stable.

It was the first time Caja had ever seen Ennor disconcerted. His expression was one of awe.

'Well I never,' he murmured, 'cloud dragons. They've not been seen for centuries. This is just marvellous!'

'They're n…not…dangerous, are they?' stumbled Caja taken aback by the enormity of the vast creatures.

'No, no not at all,' answered Ennor, 'they're gentle creatures. They're recorded in our histories as appearing to those in times of great need.'

One of the dragons slipped gracefully into the glade. The other two remained hovering just above, unable to fit into the small glade as well. Up close, Caja could see that they were made of an ethereal substance that shifted and flowed in colour and shape.

'Greetings,' uttered the alighted one in a deep sonorous voice, 'we have come to offer our aid in your hour of need.'

Ennor bowed deeply. 'Welcome, we are honoured by your presence and humbled by your offer.'

'We could not sit by and watch when all is threatened by such a one. We have come to take the three of you to Trethewyn, to Kilmar Castle. We are ready to leave.'

'That is most generous. But only I and Talwin will be going on this trip,' replied Ennor.

The lead dragon smiled softly, 'no, all three of you must go. You will not be able to do what you need without Caja.'

Caja gave a whoop of glee. 'Yep, I'm a coming!'

Ennor smiley wanly, 'it appears that is the case Caja.'

'We will leave right away,' rumbled the dragon, 'we have no time to waste.'

The three of them took only moments to prepare and were astride the dragons in no time, rapidly ascending high into the sky above Gwydhenn's glade.

'Hold on now,' instructed the lead dragon, as they swooped off, gliding cleanly through the clear sky.

With her tangle of auburn hair streaming behind her, Caja gazed at the view far below her in awe. Although nervous, the sensation of flying so freely was like nothing she had ever felt before, and left her thrilled. The humble villages, and wild moors of Kernow flowed quickly past, and barely thirty minutes had passed before they caught their first glimpse of the towers of Kilmar Castle, now only a few miles in the distance.

CHAPTER ELEVEN

Jory felt that this was the cruellest torture possible, worse than any pain that Menadue could have inflicted upon him. He watched in unbearable agony as his new-found friend was viciously tortured. It was obvious that Menadue meant to kill him, and he was enjoying the process immensely, a look of savage pleasure upon his face. Willam's whole body was contorted in extreme torment, his legs and arms splayed at unnatural angles, his face distorted beyond recognition in suffering. The black lines were deepening all over him.

Jory fought with all his strength against his bonds, refusing to give in, gouging his ankles deeply against the shackles until blood was pouring from his wounds. Even though he could reach Menadue within the limits of his chains, he appeared to have an invisible shield around him that Jory could not break through. After straining with all his power he realised that he would never be able to break free of his bonds. He took a deep breath and focused intently, searching frantically for the earth connection which would allow him to use his Telluric Magic. As soon as he touched upon it, he started to draw from it, the enormous strength of his emotions allowing him to draw more powerfully than he had ever done before. With a shout he loosened his power, his arm stretched out taut, a blinding white light soaring from his hand straight towards

Menadue's back.

Menadue grunted in surprise and turned, a look of mild discomfort upon his face. He slowly raised his hand spreading his fingers wide and Jory's light abruptly stopped. 'Not bad. Not bad,' he said grinning with a vague look of admiration on his face. 'Ennor and Talwin have been teaching you well I see.' He twisted his hand around gently until his palm was facing up, his middle finger pointed towards Jory. 'Enough though,' he said calmly and pushed his hand a millimetre forward. Jory felt nothing as he instantaneously lost consciousness, sliding to the floor in a slumped huddle. Menadue turned back to Willam who was leaning forward, gasping heavily.

'Willam, apologies for the interruption. Now where was I?' he asked merrily, stretching his arms upwards above his head as if limbering up for a marathon.

'Let's get back to where we were.' Before he could start once again however, he froze, focused upon something Willam could neither hear nor see.

'What? Already? How could that be possible?' Menadue shook his head, an expression of unease upon his face. 'Willam never fear, I will return.'

*

Ennor, Talwin and Caja disembarked from the cloud dragons a few paces away from the forbidding entrance gate of Kilmar Castle. It had quickly turned into a tempestuous day, the sky a ragged grey with blustery winds harassing the trees and frenziedly making their way in through any gaps they could find in the castle walls. Aside from the rackety wind nothing else could be heard however, no song of birds, not a hint of human activity. As Caja nervously glanced around her, she noticed that a dank, cold mist was beginning to creep towards them from the forest.

Talwin frowned in consternation, 'there is definitely something amiss here.'

'Stay close Caja,' said Ennor pulling her towards him protectively. It seemed ill-advised to bring her this close to danger but the cloud dragons had commanded it, and he was not about to defy their great wisdom.

The three of them approached the gate quietly, acutely aware of any noise they made in the gusty stillness. The two-storied gate had been left lightly ajar. As Ennor heaved the gate open further, a shrieking crow flapped off with a great din of cackles and dreary gabbles. Caja moved closer towards the comforting presence of Ennor, her face creased with tension. There appeared to be no one around at all. The outer courtyard of the castle was devoid of any sign of life, no people milling about or horses tied to the wooden railings. Just the wind rustling stray pieces of straw across the barren yard with tentacles of the crawling mist beginning to appear. The main door to the castle had been left open, as if coaxing them to enter.

Ennor, gripping onto his staff tightly, led them through it and into the spacious entrance hallway beyond. Again the same emptiness, although the silence was more overwhelming here, with the wind deadened by the thick castle walls.

'Hmmm. I don't like this one bit,' said Ennor his eyes scanning around suspiciously.

'Where to now?' whispered Caja nervously.

'Jory is in one of the basement dungeons. We know the layout of the castle quite well. Ennor and I have visited the dungeons a number of times,' replied Talwin with distaste, quietly now taking the lead, and advancing towards some shadowy stairs that Caja had not noticed before.

As they descended the steep, wide stairs the light began to fade and Talwin lit a sturdy torch from her pack. The stairs led down to a narrow corridor with a rough, stone-slab floor.

'Follow me carefully, there are a few dungeons along this corridor,' whispered Talwin quietly. She led the way, holding the torch out in front of her although its scanty light only revealed a limited part of the gloomy tunnel around them. They crept along quietly, Talwin in front with Ennor following, and Caja close behind. Talwin abruptly stopped for a moment holding the torch up to a grate in the door of a cell to the left of them. She peered cautiously inside for a moment, and then shaking her head, resumed walking.

Caja followed attentively, picking her feet up with care in order not to trip over any of the uneven slabs. There was an uncomfortably damp silence down here with only the occasional sound of muffled dripping to break the stillness. As Caja's ears became attuned to the quietness however, she became aware of another noise, seemingly from behind her, the rhythmic sound of something that sounded like breathing. Her whole body immediately stiffened, her senses searching for the sound. Yes there it was again, the unmistakeable sound of a ragged, uneven breath.

Before Caja could open her mouth to alert the Quintralls, Ennor had swung around, his staff held in front of him with Talwin, seemingly simultaneously, by his side. He grabbed Caja and pulled her in to him as the most tremendous clamour filled the tunnel around them. Without looking, Caja knew what had made that sound, she had heard it before. It was the sound of the vorgon's screech, greatly amplified in this small space. And not just the sound of one vorgon.

Caja shrunk into Ennor's grip, terrified but unable to stop her compulsion to glance at them. Her heart tightened even further with fear. Not five metres away from them were three vorgons, now illuminated by the torches they held aloft, their hypnotic vulture eyes awash with glee at the sight of their prey. Before they could turn their gaze upon her, she turned away, keenly aware of the peril. The shriek of the vorgons rebounded off the tunnel walls and was now joined by their soft raspy purring of excitement. Without hesitation the vorgons lunged towards them, their bony wings reaching out in front of them, their glaring eyes fixed like beams upon Ennor and Talwin. With one arm Ennor violently shoved Caja behind him, almost knocking her off her feet as he did so.

As the tumultuous roar of the attacking vorgons filled the

tunnel to an almost unbearable level, Talwin and Ennor stepped forward as one, their eyes avoiding the vorgons' direct gaze. Ennor held his staff outstretched, while Talwin had her hands held low in front of her, palms pointed to the ground. Caja recoiled as she felt the power of their connection to the Telluric Magic swell through her. The intensity of it saturated the air around her and left her breathless as the magic poured out with the combined strength of the two Wizards. The vorgons seemed to feel it too. They hesitated in their advance, and Talwin taking advantage, instantly raised her hands upwards. A wave of visible energy bounded from her, growing in ferocity every millimetre, until it reached the vorgons slamming into them with such force that they were ricocheted backwards in a blast that shook the whole tunnel. It was instantly quiet, and now hard to see as the tunnel was filled with a fine dust.

'Stay there Caja,' Ennor urged through gritted teeth, stepping forward carefully to assess the situation.

Caja certainly had no plans of going anywhere, and remained tensely crouched in the narrow corridor. But this seemed to once again be beyond her control, as she felt the slab beneath her feet abruptly slide away, leaving her momentarily standing on thin air. Before she knew it Caja was falling, falling fast before slamming onto what appeared to be a slippery chute, and then sliding even faster downwards, with darkness all around her. It was all too quick for her to even make a sound. Within seconds she had come to the end of the chute, experiencing several milliseconds of back-pedaling flight before landing upon the hard slabs of another stone floor.

'YeeeeOUCH!,' she exclaimed in pain. 'What the? What the…?' She squeezed her eyes tight in frustration and with clenched hands shook them manically in front of her face. 'What the…? What the…?' she muttered again loudly, still waving her tensed arms around in ever bigger swings. This seemed to relieve her however, and after a few minutes she stopped, sighing into a slump. She opened her eyes and looked around her. It was lighter than before, but apart from that, the tunnel looked eerily similar to the one she had so recently been in.

'Was this your doing again naiads?' she accused the emptiness around her, at the same time picking herself delicately off the floor. There appeared to be only one way to go. Directly behind her was an impenetrable stonewall, ahead, the tunnel led on towards some form of light.

'Well, only one thing to do I guess,' she muttered starting off cautiously down the corridor.

As she approached the light she realised it was coming from the bottom of some stairs. She hesitated a second before gingerly starting down them. There was the sound of slow dribbling water and something else. It sounded like someone was talking to himself, over and over again, the same sentence muttered quietly. Taking a deep breath for confidence, Caja stepped carefully down, unwilling to touch the walls, which seemed to be coated in a slimy substance. At the bottom, she could just make out a grim-looking door with heavy, metal studs that was slightly ajar revealing a shadowy light from within. Caja hesitantly took hold of the rough edge of the door and pushed it further open.

'Jory!' she gasped in joy.

Inside the cell, Jory was sitting in front of the prone figure of a young boy hanging awkwardly from metal rings embedded in the wall, his body wrapped by glowing bonds and his head slumped forward. The parts of his body that she could see were covered in hideous dark wounds. Caja recoiled in horror, and then paused, her eyes inexplicably drawn towards the strange figure. Although she could not see his face, there was something intensely familiar about him; she felt a great urge to step forward and...well...hug him.

Tearing away her gaze and resisting this peculiar desire, she turned towards Jory who was pointing at the boy whilst mouthing words rapidly, a look of harsh concentration on his face. He turned around, fear evident on his face at her step, which sharply turned to relief upon seeing Caja, but then quickly returned back to distress. 'Oh Caja! Why are you here? You mustn't be here! Really you mustn't. You're in great danger!' he exclaimed desperately jumping up.

Caja held back, unsure of how to respond, and then rushed forward to give Jory a clumsy hug. He was even skinnier than before, and his cheeks had sunk into hollows giving him a haunted look. 'Jory. Really, it's all ok. I'm here with Talwin and Ennor. We're here to help. We're going to get you out of here!'

Jory was shaking his head, his face screwed up with worry, 'but he knows. He knows everything. It's all part of his plan. A trap! You must get out of here, as soon as possible!'

Caja shook her head firmly, 'we can't leave here without you Jory. I'm not going anywhere!' She stared at the wounded figure in front of her, 'but who is he? We can help him too….I think.'

'Really Caja, you must believe me. It's not safe for you here. He…' his voice dropped off, his stare focused unstintingly on a spot behind Caja's right shoulder.

'I do so love it when everyone comes to me rather than having to chase them around endlessly all over the place,' hissed Menadue from behind with a cheerless chuckle.

Caja's whole body tensed as she turned around slowly to face him.

He greeted Caja with a sardonic grin, and a casually raised eyebrow. 'GateKeeper, we meet again.'

He appeared unfeasibly tall, towering over them from his haughty stance just inside the doorway, his pale, angular face luminous in the dull light. With his gaze upon her, Caja could not look away, could barely think. His sheer presence was intensely gripping; immense power stemming from him in an invisible field that drew those within his vicinity ever closer into him, despite the loathsome feeling that accompanied it.

Jory, standing behind Caja, was motionless, also locked into Menadue's dark gaze.

Menadue grinned at them both revealing his pallid gums, 'now, where were we? I was in the middle of killing young

Willam here when you, my dear little GateKeeper, arrived.' A thoughtful expression appeared on his face. 'How did you get here so quickly Caja? I didn't expect you for at least another few hours.'

Caja found herself answering him without even thinking. 'I...we came on the cloud dragons,' she responded weakly.

Menadue's eyebrows shot up in surprise and his smile melted away, 'cloud dragons, hmmm...that does not bode well.' He gazed into the distance for a couple of seconds considering this new information. The lacklustre grin arose again on his face, 'although they should be quite fascinating to destroy. I've never tried before and I do like a good challenge. I don't get many nowadays, you're all so easy to defeat.' He sighed sorrowfully at this evidently disappointing state of affairs.

'I...I'...,' started Caja, but with some effort stopped herself, realizing that she was about to apologise for her adversarial shortcomings. She must gain control of herself.

Menadue carried on, clearly enjoying himself, 'so now that you've arrived I think it's time we got everyone together.' At this he whipped his arm around forcefully, a black mist draping out in a low arc completely blanketing Caja, Jory and Willam. There was a clamouring noise, and Caja once again lost sense of where she was as everything closed in around her, the walls of the cell rapidly diminishing away. She shut her eyes tightly to stop herself from falling over.

'Here we are then!' came Menadue's deep voice cheerily.

Startled, Caja opened her eyes to find that they were all now in a large throne room, Willam still bound tightly to the wall by his strange bonds, Jory kneeling still shackled and dazed on the floor. Menadue was seated in a gnarled throne, a smile of contentment on his face, one leg crossed over the other with his foot tapping the air merrily. The room had a high ceiling that extended the entire height of the castle whilst the walls were hidden in shadows.

Caja was pervaded with an overwhelming sense of betrayal as she noticed Gorran standing woodenly next to Menadue.

She shook her head from side to side, a grim look in her eyes as her anger overcame her. 'You,' she said disdainfully at the boy who had once been her friend. 'I hope He is treating you well.'

Gorran's face took on a grimace of unbridled rage. 'You don't understand Caja. None of you do. I grew up in a world where magic was everywhere, and those with it had all, whilst the rest of us without, we had nothing,' he spat out bitterly. 'I've always been this close to it, but am constantly denied its privileges and advantages. It's an unfair world Caja, and I've found a way to make it fairer,' he continued a faint smile appearing on his face.

Menadue clapped his hands together, the noise echoing over and over. 'Enough chitter chatter! So here we are, here we are. Like one big, unhappy family!'

There was silence as he looked around at them all expectantly in vicious delight. 'I have been looking forward to this!' Stopping his gaze upon Caja, a look of hunger stole over his face. 'Caja it is you though that I've been most looking forward to meeting. A GateKeeper from the other world is…well…such an unusual guest. And as I have not yet been able to visit you, I hope you can tell me more about your land. But first things first. I know you have the Legacy of that old troublemaker Merlin. I would like it. Can you tell me where it is…please?' he added with a teasing grin.

Caja felt an almighty struggle within herself as she fought against the urge to tell Menadue everything he desired. 'I…I will never…tell you,' she gasped out.

A slow mocking smile spread over Menadue's face, 'really?' he paused a glint in his eyes and then gently shook his head, 'don't you worry yourself over it my dear Caja, because well I haven't been entirely honest with you. I…' He paused and swung his arm out to the side as a long object flew swiftly from out of the shadows landing neatly in his hand. 'I…well, I already have it.' He shrugged his shoulders in feigned apology.

Caja heard Jory's groan as he recognised the staff they had

found in Owlers' cave. 'But...how...how could you?' she stammered bewildered.

Menadue rolled his eyes with a bemused and languid look. 'Oh I'm pretty good at getting what I want...and persuading others to help me.'

At this he glanced to the side as another figure slipped out from the shadows and stood close beside Gorran. Caja's face drained of all colour. She could only mouth the words 'Jennifer' as no actual sound would come out. Gorran took hold of Jennifer's hand and gave her an intimate smile. Jennifer returned his smile uncertainly, looking warily all around her. She caught sight of Caja and a look of hateful pleasure flittered across her face.

'Well, you certainly do look surprised, Caja,' she snarled in a voice unlike anything Caja had ever heard. 'Never expected to see me here too did you? Thought you were the only special one didn't you?'

Shocked, Caja could only mumble a few words, 'Jennifer? What...what? How?' How could this have happened?

Menadue let out a bark of glee. 'Betrayed!' he exclaimed indicating Gorran, 'and then betrayed again!' looking at Jennifer. 'Isn't the world you live in a nasty place? I wouldn't trust anyone if I were you.....' He chuckled darkly, ' it's a lesson that everyone must learn if they wish to scramble ahead of the lowly pack of moaning scum you humans generally are.'

Jory, still shackled mysteriously to thin air, spoke up quietly, 'there are people you can trust in our world. There are. And they will always triumph in the end.'

Menadue glanced to the side and let out an elaborate, elongated sigh, a look of deep boredom upon his face. 'Yes, yes. You people always come out with the same sanctimonious drivel even though you know it to be false. How's life treated you Jory Hobart? Did you have a very happy childhood with your oh-so dedicated parents?'

Jory looked down at the floor, unable to bear Menadue's relish at his distress.

Menadue threw up his hands in a flourish, 'but enough with all this delightful discussion. Let's get down to the nitty-gritty shall we. Caja, you're probably now wondering what it is I want from you. Now that I have the staff why do I need you? It's a good point!' With his penetrating stare once again trained upon her, Caja found it impossible to look away. Jennifer and Gorran were also watching him avidly, a look of devotion upon their faces.

'I am intrigued by your world, and your ability as a GateKeeper. One skill I have not managed to master…not yet at least. I need to know more about your world. You can help me. I have much to do and-' He was interrupted by a spluttering cough.

Menadue glanced over to where the sound had come from. 'Yes, Willam. Did you say something?' he asked politely.

Willam, who had regained consciousness, raised his head, a slight smile evident despite his pained features. 'W…what is all this for Menadue? You know you will only be defeated by the Twofold Power in the end.'

Menadue shook his head in frustration as if a fly were bothering him. 'Well Willam, I think you'll find you don't know everything. I worked it all out before any feeble intelligences such as yours. I destroyed the Twofold Power many, many years ago before it could even manifest itself.'

Jory looked startled and then confused as he heard a chuckle coming from Willam. All eyes turned back to Willam who was grinning softly, his eyes calm and impassive despite the restraints, with strength and wisdom far beyond his years springing from his entire being. 'Merlin was such a complex character. He did enjoy being cryptic. There is so much none of you have comprehended from the Prophecy.'

Menadue looked up towards the roof with the exaggerated air of someone suffering unbelievable foolishness. 'Ok Willam,' he enunciated slowly, 'tell us then. What is it that you know so well that we are all allegedly so unaware of?'

'Aided by my Legacy, released and protected by the

Otherworldly Gatekeeper. The Twofold Power is the sole hope. The Twofold Power cannot be dead as the Twofold Power is also the Otherworldly GateKeeper. They are one and the same.'

All eyes turned to Caja. She looked at them with a raised eyebrow perplexed, 'what?'

'Caja, don't you know what Willam is saying. He's saying you are the Twofold Power that must defeat the Dark,' said Jory feebly, with a look of astonishment.

'But that is not possible!' roared Menadue his composure gone, 'I killed Ben and Tarlia Delaney before their baby was born. This wretched, pea-brained girl cannot be their daughter. She is the daughter of that mad Flora woman!'

Caja stumbled, her knees almost giving way, pale and panting. 'You killed my parents? You? But why?'

Willam spoke up, 'it's true and I'm sorry for your loss Caja. He wanted to kill the Twofold Power before it was even born, well before you were even born. What he couldn't have known was that you would be born early and therefore didn't die alongside your parents as he planned.'

'Me!' gasped Caja dumbstruck, and then it all came flooding back to her. Herself as a baby, in the arms of her Aunt. An older man striding beside them. The feeling of dizziness as they went through the gate. The unearthly voice of the naiad whispering in her ear, 'Caja, you are the one. The one the prophecy speaks of. A GateKeeper and the Twofold Power who will destroy the evil. Take care little one. You have a gruelling task ahead.' She had found the voices beautiful, mesmerising, and they had made her gurgle with merriment.

Without realising it, Caja had slumped to the floor. 'It is me,' she muttered, 'I am the...the...'

Menadue let out a great bellow of intense rage and flung his hand forward holding the staff. A radiant green light encased in swirling black shot out of the staff and headed straight for Caja. Jory yelled, a cry of despair, attempting to leap forward and intercept the beam but managed to move only an inch before he was thrown back by the constraints of his shackles. Caja shrank back, her arms in front of her face to shield herself from the light racing towards her. She let out a stark cry as the dark light touched her on her outstretched arm, but just as quickly the swirling light faded and abruptly vanished. She looked towards Menadue bewildered. It was as if he had been hit by an incredible unseen force, his stomach extended outwards, his back unnaturally arched as he unwillingly slid prone from his throne. His body was wracked by shudders forcing his back up even higher, his eyes blank, staring stricken at an unseen object above him.

Caja gaped at him in morbid fascination before being knocked out of her captivation by Willam's voice. 'Caja, Caja. You must come and help me. You must release me from my bonds!' he yelled. She looked over at Willam startled. What could she do?

'Caja, you must help me,' he repeated intensely. 'Quick, there is not much time.'

Her eyebrows lowered in confusion, she raced over to where Willam was secured. 'But Willam what can I do? How can I undo these bonds?' she gasped, her eyes searching frantically for a way to untie the glowing cords that held Willam steadfastly to the wall.

Willam held her gaze firmly. 'Just untie them Caja. You can do it.'

Caja bent to Willam's ankles, and then began to pick apart the knots in the thick cords. They came undone easily, slipping apart like slithery eels. She moved quickly to his hands. As the last cord fell to the floor, Caja felt struck by an invisible surge rushing through her body. She gasped out in shock. Willam had collapsed to the floor on his hands and knees panting, and appeared to have been hit by the same intense impact. He stayed there for several seconds but then warily arose to his feet.

Whilst Gorran was occupied in aiding Menadue back to a sitting position, Willam barked out a command directed towards Jory, and his shackles fell away instantaneously.

'No!' roared Menadue who was now sitting, although greatly weakened, in his throne, his spasms over. 'No! You children cannot outdo me!' he yelled gathering in strength by the second.

'Perhaps the children cannot outdo you alone, but with our assistance I'm sure they can,' came a quiet voice from the shadows. Talwin stepped out, a determined look on her face, followed closely by a formidable looking Ennor.

Menadue closed his eyes for a split second before turning to face them. 'Old friends!' he said brightly, 'how nice of you to come. S...so,' he stuttered briefly, exhibiting a rare display of weakness. 'So the vorgons didn't keep you occupied for too long? I should have come myself!' he exclaimed with wrathful vigour.

Ennor grunted, 'indeed you should have Menadue.' He gave him a good look over. 'It appears the Ereburic is beginning to weaken you. Perhaps it's time you came with us...and faced the Order.'

'Never!' roared Menadue, and with a colossal heave from deep within himself that seemed to spread in a giant wave from his feet to the crown of his head, he spread his arms wide, a look of disciplined intensity on his face. Menadue, Gorran and Jennifer abruptly disappeared.

Ennor nodded his head slowly, his eyebrow raised in an expression of undisguised admiration. Turning to Talwin he exclaimed, 'he's stronger than we thought Talwin. I've never seen anyone able to transport three people at once like that.'

Talwin gave vent to her frustration, stamping her foot hard upon the ground. 'Oh to have come so close! He was weakened Ennor. We could have had him!'

'Yes, I know,' sighed Ennor, 'but we could not have predicted how strong he has become.'

'We must not underestimate him again. It seems we're always two steps behind!' she exclaimed exasperated.

From behind them came a prolonged groan. Caja was propped up against the wall, eyes staring off into space, anguish and sadness etched all over her face.

'Caja, what is it?' asked Talwin worried.

Jory replied as Caja just continued to stare into space. 'Willam just told us that she is the Twofold Power, and that Menadue killed her parents thinking he had also killed her.'

Talwin nodded slowly and turning to Ennor murmured quietly, 'as we thought.'

She walked over and sitting beside Caja gently took her small slightly quivering hand in her own strong one. Caja stared at her blankly.

Regarding her with great empathy Talwin said softly, 'I understand Caja. Today has been the hardest on you.'

Caja's eyes filled with tears. 'He killed my parents. Because of me. That's why they're dead. And I'm meant to be some great power or something. Everything's changed and it's all so different, and I feel so scared, and so lost. And I just want to go home now. I want everything to go back to normal. And for all this to just be a bad dream.' At this she started sobbing fiercely.

Talwin, taking Caja in her arms, responded tenderly, 'I understand Caja. It's a great burden for someone as young as you. But we're all here for you. You will have someone with you every step of the way, guiding you and supporting you.'

Ennor agreeing vigorously added, 'we will always be here for you Caja. You will never be alone.'

'Come now Caja,' said Talwin soothingly. 'Let's find the cloud dragons and return to Gwydhenn. Jory looks like he needs a week of feeding up and this poor boy urgently needs some healing.' Turning to Willam she asked, 'what is your name young man?'

Willam smiled broadly in response although with a gasp of pain as he did so. 'My name is Willam Renlim. I have heard much about you Talwin Quintrall.'

'Ah Willam, Tomas spoke often of you,' declared Ennor. 'I'm sure there is lots you have to tell us. How you ended up in a place like this caught up with Menadue to start with? But first we must deal with those injuries. The cloud dragons will have us back to Gwydhenn in no time.'

With that the five of them made their way out of Kilmar Castle, which was now almost completely hidden in the thick eerie mist, and on to the waiting dragons outside the castle walls.

CHAPTER TWELVE

Ennor rode the dusky, purple leader of the cloud dragons with Caja grasping on steadily behind. Meanwhile, Talwin was perched on the jade-green dragon holding up a pain-ridden Willam. Jory was whooping in delight on the grey dragon with enormous, heavy-lidded topaz eyes, several hundred metres behind them all. He was instructing Lagas, as his dragon was called, to swoop higgledy-piggledy through the clouds, and career speedily towards earth before soaring steeply upwards at the very last moment.

'Whoah this is fun!' he yelled after a particularly daring mid-air stop. Talwin chuckled at Jory's antics, happy to have some distraction after the gruelling events of the past few days. The dragons had been waiting patiently outside the Castle for them to return, almost concealed by the sea-mist. The lead dragon assured them calmly that he had felt Menadue's departure, and that they were out of danger for now. They had all climbed gratefully onto the dragons spiny yet supple backs, and had lunged off into the sky, grateful to be away from Kilmar Castle and the gloomy atmosphere that seemed to cling to their skin.

As they attained more and more distance from Kilmar, their hearts gradually lightened, and they were able to enjoy the splendour of the scenery below them. Soaring over the darkening, sweeping middle moors of Kernow, they caught glimpses every now and again of small villages with occasional startled upturned faces gazing in awe skywards.

'We're almost home!' thundered Ennor turning his head to check they were all safely behind. He looked startled for a moment as he realised Jory was not there, but then spied him a good distance below guiding his dragon into upside-down loop the loops accompanied by hilarious hoots of exultation. Ennor raised his eyebrow in exasperation, as Talwin continued to grin.

As one, the dragons dipped their wings, and glided gently downwards towards the shadows of Falkelly Forest, the warmth of the wind increasing as they descended towards earth. Caja felt an intense burst of relief and happiness as she spotted the familiar trees of Gwydhenn's glade. The dragons were obliged to land separately in the tiny glade with one stopping to disembark its passengers before taking off and allowing the next dragon to do the same.

'Thank you,' said Ennor gravely, 'your aid has been indispensable, and we offer you our humble gratitude.'

Caja and Jory enthusiastically added their thanks, whilst Willam muttered something unintelligible, his eyes shut and unable to stand without Talwin's support.

'We do it for Kernow,' rumbled the lead plum dragon, 'but there is still much that needs to be done. Yours is not an easy task ahead. We hope that your efforts are favoured under the stars, and by the natural order of the earth. We will return again to help when we can.' And with that the dragons moved off as one, the enormous flapping of their wings creating a great rush of air that shook the entire glade, leading to a light rain of leaves and small twigs that spattered down all over them.

Ennor moved to help Talwin support Willam, and with both their assistance he made it inside. Gwydhenn offered his usual welcoming shake, and Caja patted him warmly on one of the enormous branches that dipped to greet her as she approached the entrance of the cottage. Talwin set to work immediately healing Willam who was lolling listlessly on one of the chairs.

The rest took their seats gratefully whilst Ennor warmed up some Rosentea. After a couple of sips of the soothing brew, the questions began flooding out.

Jory turned almost immediately to Caja, 'where did you disappear to in Owlers' Cave Caja? One minute you were there, and then there were those strange voices, and then you were gone!'

Caja rolled her eyes, 'it was those naiads. They called me back to them. Something I promised them when I got you out of that little fix in the lake.'

Jory looked at her in interest, 'me? Was that why they let me go that time? What did you promise them Caja?'

'Oh just to come when they called. Not that they gave me a choice anyway. But then after I helped them I picked up the staff, and then that was it, before I knew it I was back in Cornwall. Why did that happen?' she said turning to Talwin and Ennor.

Ennor answered, 'it's to do with your powers Caja. As a GateKeeper from both worlds you will have powers that no one has ever had before. There is much we need to learn.'

Jory's face lit up and he asked eagerly, 'so what does this all mean? Caja is the Twofold Power? How can she be from both worlds?'

'Caja's father was from Kernow, Jory. He was Ben Templeton, Ivy's son,' responded Ennor.

Jory started in shock, almost sliding off the narrow kitchen chair he was eagerly perched on. He looked at Caja in alarm, 'what? You're related to that old bag!'

Caja nodded her head solemnly, her eyebrows raised in shared horror whilst Ennor let out an amused sigh, 'she isn't all that bad Jory. She had a tough time when both her husband and son died.' He glanced at Caja and with an encouraging wink adding, 'she'll warm up I promise. Especially when she finds out who you are.'

'Well that does make sense now. Why she was so

interested in you and all staring weird-eyed at you,' exclaimed Jory musingly. 'Hey, maybe you'll be able to spend some cosy weekends at Templeton Castle now, just you, Granny Ivy and the lovely Reena,' he added with a smirk on his face.

Caja did not respond to Jory's jibes. The impact of the revelations were really beginning to sink in now that they were all home and safe. She had a grandmother now? And what of her father? Why did he go to Cornwall? And what of all this Twofold Power talk? She was not sure she even believed in all that power nonsense. She certainly did not feel powerful. And Jennifer's betrayal on top of Gorran's. There was so much to think about, she sunk further into her chair in despondency, overwhelmed by her conflicting thoughts.

Jory carried on cheerfully, oblivious to Caja's increasing distress, 'and what of the staff? I thought you had it Caja? How in the bejeebies did Menadue end up with it?'

Caja looked up dejectedly. 'It was my fault,' she admitted sorrowfully, 'it must have been Jennifer. She knew where it was hidden. I just didn't have…well…the foggiest idea…that Jennifer might be tied up in all this. Otherwise I would never have told her about the staff. I still can't believe she's here, in Kernow, and with Gorran.'

Jory blinked violently again in shock. 'Whaaat? so that girl with Gorran was your friend? And she's from your world, Cornwale?'

'Yes, she's from Cornwall,' responded Caja rather aggressively, adding as an afterthought, 'the lying cow.'

Jory noticing her distress for the first time replied more sensitively, 'so she was your friend. I'm sorry Caja. I didn't realise. That can't be easy.'

She looked up at his gentle tone and smiled sadly at him.

His curiosity was hard to contain however and turning to Ennor he continued impatiently, 'but what now Ennor? Is everything lost? Now that Menadue has Merlin's Legacy?'

'He doesn't,' whispered Willam hoarsely from across the room before Ennor could reply. All faces turned to him with expressions of shared incomprehension.

'What do you mean, Willam?' asked Ennor calmly, 'we saw him with it at Kilmar Castle. There is no doubt in my mind that he was holding Merlin's staff.'

Willam grinned faintly, 'he was holding Merlin's staff, but not Merlin's Legacy. He doesn't have Merlin's Legacy. You do.'

Again, the baffled looks.

'Whaaat?' exclaimed Jory again, 'we have Merlin's Legacy?'

Willam beamed at them all, 'of course you do. Because the staff is not Merlin's Legacy, I am.'

There was a moment of fierce silence as everyone took this in and then a simultaneous outpouring of questions.

Ennor's authoritative voice eventually arose above the torrent, 'quiet everyone. Let Willam explain. Willam, please.'

Willam who was looking somewhat better after Talwin's administrations, took some time to carefully pull himself up into a sitting position, to the increasing impatience of Jory and Caja, before commencing.

'I am Merlin's Legacy. Merlin's staff has well…always been just that….Merlin's staff. I think he wanted to make it appear to be the Legacy to set people off on the wrong track. I'm his Legacy as I'm his great-great-great-great-great-great,' he paused and looked up in thought for a moment counting silently on his fingers, 'great grandson. And I'm here to tutor Caja in her powers. That is my role. That is the role of the Legacy.'

The silence in reaction to this astonishing news was broken by Talwin. 'Oh we have been stupid,' she said, a giant smile beginning to spread across her face, 'but oh this is great, great news, isn't it Ennor?'

'It most certainly is,' responded Ennor heartily.

Even Caja had perked up at the news. In spite of Jennifer's betrayal, they had not in fact lost the Legacy? Could this be true?

Jory appeared to be thinking hard. 'But how come Caja was able to release the staff? Wasn't that part of the Prophecy?' he enquired puzzled.

'Any one magical could've released the staff,' explained Willam, 'you could've if you had tried Jory. Only Gorran wouldn't have been able to as he's not a Telluric. Caja was the only one who was able to release me from my bonds.'

Talwin considered Willam appraisingly, 'hmmm...we knew Merlin had kin, but we believed them all dead and gone, not long after his own disappearance.'

Willam's smile dimmed a little at this. 'After Merlin's disappearance the anger against him grew and grew, and many of my kin were killed. My family ancestors, the last of Merlin's line eventually went into hiding and have not come out since.'

'Did Tomas know about all this?' asked Talwin.

'Yes,' answered Willam simply. 'We talked much of these things when I lived with him. My Telluric abilities came on so young so my parents sent me to be tutored by him. Although I still hope to spend a year or two at Ambrosius,' he added wistfully.

Ennor with a hint of subdued frustration spoke up, 'why would Tomas never think to tell us of this? It would have made many things much simpler.' He sighed resignedly, 'he always did have his strange ways.'

Willam replied glancing downwards with a hint of a smile at his memories, 'yes, I never understood Tomas' ways entirely either.'

'So Willam, you are to be Caja's tutor? Ennor and I've been discussing who could take on that role. It has to be a powerful Telluric but we were not sure that we were right for the task,' queried Talwin.

'Yes,' replied Willam. 'Tomas explained it all to me as well as he could. I am the only one able to help her reach her full potential with her powers. It must be one of Merlin's kin.'

Ennor had an intrigued look on his face. 'And tell me young Willam. Does this make you her Dyskador?'

Willam grinned broadly. 'Yes, yes. The Dyski bond was formed when Caja released me from my chains. We are already joined as student and Dyskador.'

'Of course!' cried Ennor, a look of budding hope in his eyes, 'the sign of the union of Dyski! I didn't see it at the time but now it all makes sense.'

Talwin too was looking overjoyed at these words whilst Caja gazed on in confusion.

'What? What are you all talking about? What is this Dysidoor?' asked Jory eager to join in the excitement.

Talwin turned to explain, 'when someone is born with a unique potential, as you are.' She gave a gentle look to Caja who seemed to shrink into herself a little further. 'There is often only one tutor who is perfectly matched to help them reach their highest potential. This tutor and student have a sacred bond that is initiated upon first touch, as Caja's and Willam's was. This Dyski bond creates a special power; whenever they are together they are protected and it is almost impossible to harm either of them.'

'You mean when Caja and Willam are together, even Menadue can't hurt them?' asked Jory in amazement. His eyes were darting from Willam to Caja, as if in an effort to see this special bond.

Talwin answered, 'yes Jory. Even Menadue would find it hard to hurt them. In fact no one has ever found a way to harm those with a Dyski bond without at the same time destroying themselves.'

Ennor said, 'it's great news Willam. We're happy to welcome you. Although I've never known a Dyskador tutor be quite so young.'

'Wow, this all just gets better and better hey?' said Jory with a slightly forced grin and raised eyebrows. 'But what happened to Menadue in that chamber. When he went jerky and weird, and couldn't do magic anymore?'

Ennor answered this time, 'it's the Ereburic Magic he uses. It's a different sort of magic to the Telluric. It's against the laws of the land to practice it. Darker, eviler. It usually kills you before you can get too strong. We've never known anyone practice it for as long as Menadue has. But it's obvious that it's affecting him now.'

Willam nodded in agreement at this, 'it's one advantage we have over him, that we may be able to use against him.'

Jory's grin faded. 'Willam can I ask you one question though? Don't you think it would have been better not to have told Menadue who Caja was? That she was the Twofold Power that he had tried to kill? Why did you feel the urge to reveal it all to him?' asked Jory gazing at Willam with an unusually serious expression.

'I had glimpsed movement by the door and hoped it was Ennor and Talwin. And I wanted to distract him. It was the only thing I could think of that Menadue would actually believe. I knew it would anger him and possibly give us a chance to overpower him. The Ereburic is harder to control when you are not in charge of your emotions, and the mind is unable to focus clearly. And besides, he's a bit of a know-it-all that Menadue and I wanted to let him know he hadn't worked out everything all by himself. Although come to think of it Ennor and Talwin, you didn't show up for a while there so maybe it wasn't you at the door.'

'Willam you are an extraordinary mix of wisdom beyond your years and utter, youthful foolishness,' remarked Ennor.

Willam grinned mischievously, 'that's exactly what Tomas always used to say to me!'

'So what now?' asked Jory.

Caja looking dejected said, 'I must go back to my Aunt in Cornwall and let her know that I'm safe.'

Willam smiled at her, 'and I will go with you Caja. We must stay together now if you are to remain safe. And we can start your training. 'His smile broadened even further, 'and I have always wanted to visit Cornwall! Tomas would never let me.'

Caja returned his smile, happier to know that he would be with her.

Talwin started flapping her arms at them, 'yes that's all good. You'll return with Caja, Willam. But not until tomorrow. It's late now. We have much to discuss before you go, and your Aunt can wait one night, she has waited many more already. At least this time she knows where you are. Willam, you still have some recovering to do, as do you Jory. Now off to bed, the lot of you.'

They all reluctantly pulled themselves up, with Talwin supporting Willam last, and started up the winding staircase.

'Now that I know Gorran is a GateKeeper too, I'm glad that you will be coming with me,' said Caja to Willam who was weakly struggling behind with Talwin.

'Whaaat!' Jory exclaimed from behind them, 'Gorran is a GateKeeper too!'

'Oh Jory, there is so much to catch up on, we'll fill you in tomorrow,' exclaimed Caja in a weary voice as they clambered up the stairs to bed.

*

They all slept in late, their bodies taking the time to replenish themselves from the exertions of the last few days. Although Caja had known Willam barely for a day, they got along like old friends. They found themselves chattering comfortably at breakfast, with Jory silently eating, looking up every now and again with a faint frown.

Ennor and Talwin were busily engaged in their library. There was much still to learn about Caja's powers, and although Willam was to be her Dyskador, he had not demonstrated so far a profound knowledge of exactly what it was he was going to do.

'Um…you know…teach her in….magic….and stuff?' he stuttered unhelpfully when asked by Talwin what tutoring program he had in mind.

'Did Tomas not give you any further instruction than that?' asked Talwin searchingly. 'Did he not tell you the best ways you may tutor her, how best you might eke out her potential?'

Willam thought for a moment. 'No, not really. He just said I would know.' His stare turned to Caja for a moment, 'although…..hmmm. Nothing's springing up on me just yet. I guess I'll just have to fumble my way along hey,' he said laughingly.

Talwin and Ennor gazed at him with concern, and then at the same time marched off to their extensive library to see what else they could find on Dyskador relationships and the Twofold Power.

'I can't believe you are actually related to Merlin,' Caja was saying, staring at Willam with awe.

'Yeah, that is pretty cool I suppose,' said Jory looking up from his avid contemplation of the odd concoction of food Talwin had presented for breakfast.

Willam nodded thoughtfully, 'I remember when my mother first told me. It was pretty awesome. I was about seven years old. But it also made our lives very difficult at times. I grew up mainly in Breten Vian, not in Kernow. My parents decided it was safer there.'

'Where's Breten Vian?' asked Caja.

'It's in Northern France. I know all the names of the countries in your land Caja. Tomas taught me,' replied Willam.

'So, you must be strong in the Telluric Magic then?' asked Jory in a careful, neutral tone.

Willam's expression did not change. 'Yes. Tomas always told me I was one of the strongest he'd ever come across. Menadue told me the same...' At the mention of his name, Willam moved uncomfortably in his chair. His wounds from his time as Menadue's captive were still incredibly raw.

Jory continued with his questioning, 'so where are your parents now? Won't they be worried about you?'

Willam smiled in amusement at this, 'no, no. My parents are old now. They sent me off to live here a few years ago. I send them messages to let them know I am safe now and again, but they know I have great work to do here in Kernow.'

'So does Menadue actually know who you are? Is that why he took you?' enquired Caja interestedly.

'Yes, he knows I'm Merlin's descendant, although he

never guessed my part as Merlin's Legacy. Which is lucky. Otherwise he would have killed me on the spot!' Willam let out an amused chuckle whilst Caja stared at him in bemusement.

They had spent much of the day discussing their different exploits, and filling in gaps. Jory was shocked to hear that Gorran had been in Caja's world. It was clear now that he had been the shadowy figure that Caja had seen in her own world.

'I can't believe he was there. Spying on me,' exclaimed Caja in disgust. 'All that time.'

Jory shook his head in sorrow, 'I'm sorry Caja. I feel bad about all this. He was my friend. I'd known him for three years. We spent loads of time together and I never picked up on anything, not a thing! I didn't have an inkling that he was involved with Menadue!'

'Oh you could never have known Jory. I don't blame you one bit. I was exactly the same with Jennifer. I never guessed! We've got to be more careful from now on!'

Ennor took Caja aside at one point, to teach her the words that would open the gates. 'Now that we know you can open gates in both worlds, we can teach you the GateKeeper sayings that will open the gates,' he explained.

'So I can open any gate now?' asked Caja, 'any gate in either world?'

'That's right Caja, as you are from both worlds, you do not need a roaming key to open them. Unlike other GateKeepers, such as Gorran, you can open gates wherever you are. Gorran will need a roaming key to open a gate in your world. Which unfortunately he has.'

Ennor had made Caja repeat the phrase over and over until she could say it perfectly. 'Igeri ganow, igeri ganow,' she repeated as she wandered around the glade.

Ennor had explained that she had to be completely relaxed when she said them. He had chuckled when she had told him how she had opened the gate in her own world.

'Laughter! I see. An interesting way. I can see how it could work, as the gates open when there is no stress or fear in your mind whatsoever. I think you'll find that these words will make the job easier though.' His tone became more serious. 'Now, we believe Menadue can't cross the Nexus Bridge, so you don't need to worry about him once you're there.'

'But what makes you so certain that he can't? Are you sure?' asked Caja, hoping that she would never have to encounter Menadue again.

Ennor frowned. 'It's something we heard Menadue say to Gorran. Well, something Bolton heard him say. We're not quite sure yet why he can't cross the Bridge to Cornwall but we think it may have something to do with the Ereburic Magic that he practices, and the fits that are attacking him. He's been using Gorran to enter Cornwall for him, so you must be careful. Look out for him.'

They had all spent the rest of the day talking, knowing that they would soon be separated.

Eventually Talwin announced the words they had all been expecting, 'come, it's time for Caja and Willam to leave now. You will both be safer in Cornwall than here. There is a gate not far from here that Caja will be able to open.'

They all walked together, chatting contentedly to the small glade where Caja had found herself upon her second entrance to Kernow.

'This small kelly, or grove is also a gate. Tomas would use this at times when he stayed with us,' explained Talwin.

It was decided that the sooner they left the better, so with only brief goodbyes, Caja recited the words that Ennor had taught her, holding firmly onto Willam's hand and just like that they were gone.

Talwin turned to Ennor, 'I do hope they will be safe.'

'Yes, let us hope so. Thank goodness for the protection of the Dyskador. It does make things so much better.' A smile spread slowly across his face, 'I wonder how long it will take Menadue to work it all out.'

'Probably not long,' said Talwin grimly. She turned to Jory who was stood staring at the spot where Caja and Willam had disappeared, his face glum.

'Come Jory, we have much to do now. We have some more training for you before you can start Ambrosius.'

Jory's face lit up. 'Ambrosius Academy! Of course. When am I to start?'

'You'll start in the New Year, after Winter Solstice. Until then you can stay with us. I'm afraid your Aunt and Uncle will not want you back once they find out about your abilities.'

Jory's face lit up even further. 'No, I guess they won't! Are you going to tell them or should I?' he said, an uncontrollable grin on his face. 'Maybe we can all go?'

*

Caja was now beginning to get quite used to the disorientating sensation of travelling between the worlds, but Willam never having experienced it before lay on the ground gasping, his eyes squeezed tightly shut. Caja stood beside the old gate looking around anxiously.

'Has it finished? Oh tell me it's finished Caja,' he asked desperately.

'Yes Willam. We're here. You can get up now,' responded Caja leaning over to give him a help up. 'It actually knocked me out cold the first time so you're doing quite well!'

'Good to know,' muttered Willam, still looking a ghostly shade of green as he hauled himself up. They were standing once again in the grounds of Kilmar Castle, beside the arched doorway not far away from the Gatehouse Cottage. Willam started peering around intently, keen to see this new land.

Looking slightly disappointed he said, 'well it's not quite as different as I was expecting. Looks pretty similar to Kernow in fact.'

'Don't you worry,' said Caja smiling knowingly. 'You are going to see some really different things soon. Do you realize that is Kilmar Castle over there?'

Willam gaped, 'wow, really? I wish John Kilmar could see

this. He would not be happy!'

'C'mon, follow me, that's my home,' said Caja indicating the cottage. Her spirits surged as they trudged towards the cottage, as they always did upon returning home. Before they had even entered the cottage's back garden the back door had swung open and Flora came running out in a cloud of purple and green, incense and sequins.

'Oh Caja! You are back. Come here! Come here. I've been so worried!' she exclaimed rushing towards her with her arms wide open. Upon reaching a somewhat overwhelmed Caja, she pulled her into an all enveloping hug rocking her from side to side, her head bent towards Caja's hair.

Caja's muffled laughter could barely be heard in the encompassing embrace. Lifting her head up she smiled at her Aunt, 'oh Auntie you needn't have worried. We rescued Jory and we found Willam!'

Releasing Caja, Flora turned to acknowledge the strange boy Caja had arrived with. 'Is this Willam?' she asked. Caja nodded in confirmation. 'Well, welcome, welcome. Are you…are you from Kernow?' she added hesitantly.

'Yes he is!' cried Caja excitedly, 'he is my Dyskador, or we are a Dyskador, or something like that. Which means he is to be my teacher. Because, well…Auntie…I have…I have magical powers!' At this she beamed at her Auntie.

Flora smiled carefully at her, 'yes Caja. I thought there was the possibility of that. Like your father Ben.'

Caja's forehead scrunched up in shock and frustration, 'you knew Auntie. You knew?' she almost yelled.

Flora replied slightly taken aback by Caja's ferocity, 'knew what darling? I knew your father had some rather strange abilities. But that's it. I wondered if it was something he had learnt in Sheffield?'

Caja shook her head at her eccentric Aunt baffled. She could see she would never entirely understand her. They all entered the cottage, with Caja describing the rest of her time in Kernow to Flora. She nodded interestingly at Caja's excited chatter, and did not seem at all fazed when Caja announced that Willam would be living with them for awhile.

'That does seem very sensible. If you are safer with him here, then I am more than happy. I will prepare the spare room straight away. It looks like you could certainly do with some feeding up and a good rest,' she said directing this last comment at an excited but still haggard looking Willam.

The first few hours were exhausting, with Willam bounding around the house, albeit with a pronounced limp and many winces, demanding explanations for everything he had never seen before. The television had fascinated him for a full hour, although he had finally been distracted from it by the sound of Boris' clanking bus coming to a roaring halt outside.

He had raced out before Caja could stop him and shouted out to Boris in a commanding tone, 'good man of Cornwall. What hideous creature do you ride?'

Caja had dragged him back inside waving apologetically in an attempt to mollify Boris who was looking utterly confused, before making Willam promise that he did nothing, absolutely nothing without asking her first. He agreed that this was probably in fact a wise idea. After all, he did not want to stand out too much in this strange new world.

Willam found very quickly that the Telluric Magic of the earth was very faint in this new land, although he could access it lightly at certain points when outside.

'It has faded through misuse,' he said musingly as he wandered around the garden with Caja later that day, gently swaying the bright flowers as he went past with his weakened magic.

*

The next day, Caja had returned to school, approaching her friends at first a little apprehensively, noting as she neared them the anxious and miserable expressions on Aggie and Luke's faces.

'Oh have you heard Caja? It's the most terrible news!'

exclaimed Aggie.

Caja's happy expression plummeted into anguish, 'what is it Aggie? What's happened?'

Her mind immediately began thinking of all the bad things that could have happened. Had Gorran been there again?

Aggie clearly distressed rushed on, 'it's Jennifer. She's disappeared! Her parents think she's run away as half her clothes and stuff are missing.'

Caja's anguish abruptly vanished and she struggled to keep a grim smile from surfacing. 'Oh that is terrible,' she said in a strained tone.

Aggie stopped and looked at her oddly, 'what's up Caja? Do you know something? About where she might have gone?'

Caja gazed at her for a moment, 'look Aggie, I can't tell you where she is. I really don't know. But believe me I do know she is safe. Well, for now.'

Aggie was confused, 'what…what do you mean Caja? Does this have something to do with all that strange stuff you told us about?'

'Yes,' replied Caja simply. 'And I can promise you she's doing nothing that she doesn't want to do.'

They had left it at that for now, and a few days later, once Willam had recovered some more, Caja had taken him along to school too, which he had found all terribly entertaining. The introduction to her friends had gone well. Unsurprisingly Willam and Luke had got on like a house on fire. Flora had managed somehow to enrol Willam in Penrow even though it was near the end of the year. Her Aunt's resourcefulness sometimes certainly did impress her. Needless to say he was hopeless in every class, and completely baffled most of his teachers. His answers were random and generally incomprehensible, and the teachers quickly stopped asking him anything. Caja was quite surprised that they put up with him so well, until Flora had explained to her in confidence that she had described Willam as having certain mental health issues. Willam seemed to be enjoying it all thoroughly though, treating it all as one big game, and was extremely popular with the other students. Although there were still days when the torture that Menadue had inflicted upon him would lead to him waking up weak and in agony. On those days he was unable to get out of bed, and Flora would stay at home and look after him. Gradually over time, the days Willam spent in bed got less and less.

When not in school, Willam began to train Caja, somewhat haphazardly in Telluric Magic. Talwin and Ennor had explained that at this stage Willam could just teach her the basics, which they thought him capable of, just. Fortunately, due to the weakness of the Telluric connection, Willam found there was very little chance that Caja could actually cause any damage. She found her abilities utterly engrossing, and was desperate to find out what her powers might be like in Kernow, where Willam had explained they would be much stronger. Willam insisted they never use their magic outside the cottage and gardens, as it was far too dangerous, and they both kept strictly to this, except for on one occasion.

A few days after Willam had arrived, they had been at school when Caja had been accosted once again by Patricia and her cronies in the locker room. She had completely forgotten about needing to be careful since the arrival of Willam, and cursed herself for her forgetfulness as they rounded upon her once again. They surrounded her menacingly, with Patricia moving in first, cruelly slapping Caja with a loud smack across the cheek. Caja had cried out in pain, raising her hand to her stinging face.

Patricia smirked at her. 'Well Cathy. We've told you before. We don't like it−'

Her sentence was cut short as a whirling dervish entered the room. It was Willam in a state Caja had never seen before, of immense, uncontrollable fury. He appeared taller than ever, and his face was a violent crimson.

'You dare!' he yelled in a low tone, throwing his hand

forward. The three girls all flew backwards slamming into the walls, knocking benches over along the way.

'You dare!' he repeated as they scrambled up, falling over in their haste to exit the room. He had let them leave, yelling after them what he would do to them if he saw them again, and Caja had grinned at him relieved.

'Thanks Willam, they were really beginning to annoy me.'

The three bullies never came near her again.

*

Willam settled in well, and Caja enjoyed having him around immensely, although they both began to miss Kernow. Ennor had been firm with them however. They were not to return to Kernow until they received a message from him. He insisted that they would be much safer in Cornwall.

The weeks seemed to speed up, and Kernow began to seem more and more like a dream for Caja. Without Willam to frequently remind her of the magic of Cornwall's twin world, she would probably have even begun to doubt its existence.

Winter had descended upon the little village of Trethewyn and the rest of Cornwall with a clear determination to be as thoroughly wintery as possible. The days were cold, the nights even colder, and the first flakes of snow arrived earlier than anyone could remember, deluging the land in a gentle white cloak.

Willam had been amazed by his introduction to central heating, 'the whole house is warm! All of it. Everywhere! Outside we have a winter as cold as any I have seen before, yet here inside it's summer! What marvellous magic is this!'

Caja had shown him the radiators dotted around the house, and he had been fascinated by the idea of all those hidden pipelines crisscrossing the country to deliver gas to all the homes. It had delighted him almost as much as electricity.

'You know, even though your land lacks even basic

magical wonders, it really has come up with some remarkable innovations,' he noted admiringly.

Caja, Willam and Flora were sitting inside one particularly bitingly-cold evening the day before Christmas Eve, when there was a faint knocking at the door. Flora turned around in surprise. The knocking was not coming from the front door, but rather from the door to the back garden.
'Who could that be?' she asked looking at Caja wonderingly. Willam had been ignoring them all for hours, fixated as he was on Caja's iPod. He had the earphones in upside down, and was shaking his head spasmodically, out of time to the beat of the music that could faintly be heard. Caja shook her head vaguely worried, as Flora walked over to the window to peer outside, although she could not see much through the lightly falling snow.
'I can't see anyone,' she said, wandering over to the door hesitantly. Willam noticing the movement took his earphones out and looked up questioningly, 'what's up?' He was making every effort to pick up local phrases.
'There's somebody knocking at the door,' whispered Caja standing up, as Flora unlocked the door, opening it cautiously. There was no one there. But upon the ground there was a crinkled brown envelope. She picked it up carefully, all the while looking around bewildered.
'There's definitely no one there,' Flora confirmed, eventually shutting the door behind her and vigilantly locking it again. 'But here Caja, there's a letter for you. It has your name on it.'
Caja took the envelope intrigued, and without any hesitation opened it up eagerly. 'It's from Ennor!', and then her face fell in an expression of horror, 'oh no!'
'What is it Caja?' urged Willam anxiously.
'It's Talwin, she has disappeared.'

J.D. Roberts

ABOUT THE AUTHOR

J.D. Roberts is originally from England, but now lives in Fremantle, in Western Australia with her husband and daughter. Her mother's family are from Cornwall, and she spent all her summers down there as a child, growing to love its magic and beauty.

Printed in Great Britain
by Amazon